DEATH IN THE AIR

❖

The first explosion came as a surprise. Moreira saw one wall of his hut fold away from under the roof as if it were made of cardboard.

He heard screams then, and the firing of many rifles. Another explosion, then another and another, deep crumpling sounds that seemed to shake the earth, and balls of fire inflated like balloons.

He saw people running in every direction as he dragged Mariela by the arm and pulled her into the trees and down to the ground. Covering her and the children as best he could with his own body, he stared through the undergrowth. His neighbors were milling around like ants, running every which way, and the chatter of the automatic rifles grew louder and louder. Screams, shrill and stark, were all but swallowed by the flame and thunder as hut after hut exploded into broken sticks and strips of rusted metal.

"Do something," Mariela whispered. "You have to do something."

He saw the attackers now, men in uniforms firing bursts from their rifles into the ruins, sometimes backing away and throwing grenades into the flames. All over the ground lay shadows, thick, motionless—the bodies of Kumbala's people.

"I have to tell someone," he whispered. "Someone has to know. Someone has to know . . ."

Also by Charlie McDade

RED SPIDER

From
HarperPaperbacks

ATTENTION: ORGANIZATIONS AND CORPORATIONS

Most HarperPaperbacks are available at special quantity discounts for bulk purchases for sales promotions, premiums, or fund-raising. For information, please call or write:
**Special Markets Department, HarperCollins Publishers,
10 East 53rd Street, New York, N.Y. 10022.**
Telephone: (212) 207-7528. Fax: (212) 207-7222.

BLACK MAMBA

Charlie McDade

HarperPaperbacks
A Division of HarperCollinsPublishers

If you purchased this book without a cover, you should be aware that this book is stolen property. It was reported as "unsold and destroyed" to the publisher and neither the author nor the publisher has received any payment for this "stripped book."

This is a work of fiction. The characters, incidents, and dialogues are products of the author's imagination and are not to be construed as real. Any resemblance to actual events or persons, living or dead, is entirely coincidental.

HarperPaperbacks *A Division of* HarperCollins*Publishers*
10 East 53rd Street, New York, N.Y. 10022

Copyright © 1993 by Charlie McDade
All rights reserved. No part of this book may be used or reproduced in any manner whatsoever without written permission of the publisher, except in the case of brief quotations embodied in critical articles and reviews. For information address HarperCollins*Publishers,*
10 East 53rd Street, New York, N.Y. 10022.

Cover illustration by Michael Sabanosh

First printing: February 1993

Printed in the United States of America

HarperPaperbacks and colophon are trademarks of HarperCollins*Publishers*

❖ 10 9 8 7 6 5 4 3 2 1

To My Father

*I love you, Dad.
Better late than never.
Rest in peace.*

And, as always, for MBM and RBM.

PART
ONE

ONE

❖

October 1, 1974

Kumbala was silent. A single light burned in the largest of the forty-odd huts. Rain fell on the rust covered, corrugated steel roofs, its soft splash amplified by the metal and turned into a steady drumming. It was the rainy season, and everyone in Mawindi knew that this was just the beginning—the beginning of the rain, the beginning of a long, oppressive winter, the beginning of one hundred and fifty days of mud and mildew. Although the inhabitants of Kumbala didn't know it, it had been like that for millions of years, and they accepted it because they had no choice, just as they had no choice about much else in their lives.

The single road that led into Kumbala from the south widened just a bit as it passed through, then closed again to a narrow channel through the rainforest, and was slowly becoming a brook, as it did every autumn when the rains came. Even jeeps had their difficulties in the thick, clinging muck that collected on the insides of their wheels, oozed out around the tires like a sculptor's clay, then shaped itself into rounded ridges that broke axles and ankles when the summer came and the unrelenting sun baked the mud to a rocky hardness.

Usually, jeeps were few and far between in Kumbala. People who lived there could go weeks, even months, without seeing one. And if one did happen to pass, the chances were they paid it no mind. They were busy, too busy to turn and peer out through the trees, too busy to lower their machetes, too busy to stop hacking a living from the tangled forest. It was a precarious living at best, and one never knew when one more tree cut for its hard wood, one more bunch of bananas, one more sack of manioc, would make the difference between living and dying.

Death was the one sure thing in the lives of the people of Kumbala, and living was how they passed the time until it came for them. And this rainy night, at the beginning of the long rainy season, would see another kind of rain, as soon as the seven jeeps managed to ooze their way across the border from Zaire and travel the last ten miles to the sleepy village.

Justin Moreira adjusted his lamp, turning the kerosene flame a bit higher. There was so much paperwork, and so little time. Exhausted from a long day logging, he could barely keep his eyes open. His hands, callused from holding the bucking chain saw, rested on either side of the stack of papers, his fingers drumming nervously as he read.

The meeting had probably been a mistake. He knew that now, but it was too late for him to do anything about it. There had been too many people who wanted it, people who were tired of dangling on the end of some invisible filament, like spiders descending from the trees on silk so fine even a determined man couldn't see it. All he could do was flick a hand out and sever the silk. Even then, the spider wouldn't fall. The silk was too sticky, and would attach itself to the man's hand while the tiny arachnid spun faster, its legs curled around the spinneret to help shape the thread that held it aloft.

Moreira felt like such a spider. No matter how hard he looked, he couldn't see what held him up. All he knew was that it was a long fall, that the ground was very hard, and that if the filament broke, he would die.

Ever since the coup in Portugal, things had been

unstable, not just in Kumbala, but in Mawindi itself. Political parties seemed to form out of thin air, changing shape overnight and disappearing by the following afternoon. To Justin Moreira, such changeability meant two things, neither of them good. It meant that people were desperately unhappy, which he understood only too well, being one of them. But it also meant that someone would try to exploit that unhappiness, just as the Portuguese had done. The only difference between those who would fill the vacuum and those who had created it in the first place was the color of their skins.

Moreira was considered a cynic by his neighbors, but he preferred to think of himself as a realist. He had warned them that meeting with a representative of any of the contending parties would immediately earn the suspicion, if not the outright enmity, of all the others. Fledgling movements were jealous of their potential adherents. He knew that from his time in Europe. There seemed to be more energy spent on raiding one another's converts than on addressing the very real problems that affected everyone.

Mawindi, he argued, was no different. But because he had two years of college, they wanted him to represent them, and to contact the Pan-African Movement and ask someone to come speak to them.

The PAM contact had been everything Moreira expected. Reynaldo Carvalho affected military dress, wearing a hodge podge of gray and khaki, all neatly pressed and obviously custom tailored. He had worn sunglasses the way dictators did in cheap movies about Central America, even though it was nearly sundown before he arrived, and not yet sunrise when he'd left.

All during the meeting, the feeble light from the lamps had glittered and flashed from the lenses of the sunglasses. Each time he turned his head, it looked as if he were sending slender scalpels of orange flame in every direction. Carvalho had even carried a swagger stick, which he'd kept tapping against his neatly pressed thighs. It had sounded like a ticking clock—thwack . . . thwack . . . thwack . . . thwack.

But what Reynaldo Carvalho had brought was mostly paper. Leaflets, position papers, broadsides, posters, open letters from Jorge Caulfield, the leader of the PAM, and newspaper clippings which he'd assembled in a cheap pasteboard scrapbook. Surrounded by the people of Kumbala in the tiny room, he had placed the scrapbook on the rickety table with a flourish, and begun to turn the pages.

There were stories from newspapers all over Europe, most of them in languages the attendees couldn't read, something that Carvalho seemed not to realize or, if he did realize, something about which he did not care. The fact was that in all of Kumbala, only Justin Moreira and his wife could even read Portuguese. The stories seemed to have been chosen not so much for their headlines, each of which grandly emblazoned the name of Caulfield, but for their accompanying photographs, the yellowed newsprint and faded ink almost obscuring the presence of Carvalho but not enough that he couldn't be noticed.

Like an athlete past his prime, determined to relive a past that daily grew more distant, Carvalho had turned the pages, jabbing at the photographs. "Mao," he'd said, "a very great man. And here is Fidel. This is Brezhnev. President Ford, the American." And always, Carvalho's sunglasses obscured his eyes.

But it was the eyes that Justin Moreira wanted to see. Only there could you tell what a man was really thinking when he spoke to you. His words meant nothing. It was the fluttering of the eyelids when he lied. The evasive dart of the glance as the truth was shaded. The wide-eyed stare as he manufactured an answer to a question for which he had none.

It had not gone well. The people were disappointed in Carvalho. They seemed unmoved by the slickness of his arguments, words, just words, that seemed to be about some other Kumbala and some other people who lived there. They didn't like him and they didn't trust him. And they didn't care if he knew it.

"They have nothing to do with us, your words," Augustinho Arancha shouted. "The MLF will look out for us. Bandolo understands us. He cares. Go away and let us be. Tell your Senhor Caulfield to mind his own business."

Carvalho had been angry, but he had gone away, leaving behind the mound of papers. The people had asked Justin to read them, and to tell them what they said. He had agreed against his better judgment, knowing that the papers would be full of lies and evasions and manufactured answers. But when a neighbor asked for help, you gave it.

Even when you were exhausted.

Moreira's eyes felt heavy. The lids sagged, and hot needles stabbed into them from behind. He pushed the papers away and got up to look in on his wife and their two children. Mariela was expecting their third child in a month or so, and it had not been an easy pregnancy. She was supposed to stay in bed as much as possible, but since it wasn't at all possible, she went to sleep early and got up a little later than usual.

Now, she lay on her side, her legs tucked up toward her chin. Moreira tiptoed to the side of the bed and knelt down. Reaching out with one hand, he let his fingertips graze her cheek, tucking a few strands of hair out of the way. Her eyelids fluttered and he held his breath, not wanting to wake her.

When the movement stopped, he backed away on his knees a few feet, then straightened. Going back into the other room of the two-room hut, he walked to the door and listened to the rain. It rattled on the roof and poured down in a series of slender cascades from the channels in the corrugated roof. Right in front of the door, the cascades caught the orange light from the lamp and they looked so much like liquid gold, he wanted to throw open the door and cup his hands to catch not a fortune, but just enough to change things, to make Mariela's life better, enough to send his children to school with new shoes on their feet for the first time since they'd been born.

It wasn't gold, but he threw open the door anyway and stepped out into the rain. Walking away from the hut a little way, he listened to the steady drumming of the drops on every tin roof in Kumbala. He could hear something in the distance, almost like the rumble of thunder, but not quite. He leaned toward the sound, trying to identify it, but it was too distant, more like a muttering than a rumble now.

He glanced at the sky, thinking perhaps to see a flash of lightning, but the heavens were bleak and uniformly gray. The rain felt good as it trickled down his collar. Tilting his face up, he closed his burning eyes and let the rain collect in the wells around them. He felt it tickle as it tried to seep through the tightly closed lids, and he squeezed them even tighter, sending little waves out over his cheekbones to dribble into his ears.

Moreira went back inside and groped in the dark for a flashlight. It was old and the batteries were weak, but it was the only portable light he had. Stepping outside again, he wrapped the flashlight in the tail of his shirt and clicked it on. A pale halo of light reflected off the puddles in front of the hut.

Moving toward the road, he started to walk, picking his way around the deeper ruts already full of standing water. The sound was closer now, and he knew it had to be engines, more than one for sure, but how many he couldn't tell. The pitch was too high for it to be trucks. Probably something smaller, he thought. But why more than one?

The missionaries who occasionally visited Kumbala usually came in daylight in their four-wheel drive vans, but they knew better than to try to negotiate the roads during the rainy season, even early. Perhaps it was some emergency, he thought.

Away from the huts, he realized just how weak the flashlight beam was. Orange, it seemed to wax and wane, almost like a candle flame as the exhausted batteries tried to keep the bulb glowing.

In frustration, he shook the flashlight. For a moment, the light flared brightly, then sank back even lower than before, its pale beam little more than a thin orange circle on the muddy water. The trees pressed in around him, in some places interlacing their branches overhead. He looked up, but it was too dark to see. He only knew that he was in one of the leafy tunnels when the rain stopped pelting him steadily, and was replaced by the intermittent drip of water collecting on the canopy until its weight bent the leaves and released the heavy pools.

His feet splashed in an unseen puddle, but that didn't matter now. He was overwhelmed by curiosity. The mutter changed to a rumble, then stopped altogether. Far ahead, he saw a blaze of artificial light. It seemed to disappear in steps. Unconsciously he counted, almost whispering. Headlights, he thought. Seven pairs of headlights.

He heard a voice for an instant, too far and too indistinct to know what was being said. Why did they stop so far from the village, he wondered.

Without thinking, he extinguished the nearly useless light and tucked it into his back pocket. He didn't like being in the forest at night. There were too many things to step on, others to wrap themselves around his neck, and still others that would leap at him from the trees and sink their teeth into his flesh.

He wished now that he had thought to bring his rifle. It was old, but it would have been better than nothing. He could hear the steady splashing of footsteps now, but no more voices, as if the men up ahead wanted to approach Kumbala not just in the dead of night but in perfect silence, as well.

Something was wrong. He turned and started back, his feet slipping on the sopping clay beneath him. He could feel his heart pounding in his chest, as if someone were trapped inside and demanding to be let out.

Moreira slipped and fell, scrambled to his feet, ignoring the thick clay clinging to his pants and coating his hands all the way up past his wrists. The single light in his hut suddenly appeared, and he ran toward it, glad that he had decided not to turn it off. He felt his feet slipping on the slick clay again and again. Out in the open now, where the water was almost a solid sheet, just small hummocks of grass and mud jutting up through the rippling surface, he stumbled to the hut and darted inside.

"Mariela," he whispered. "Wake up." He went to the bed and shook her.

"What is it? What's wrong?"

"I don't know. Something . . . get the children up. Someone is coming."

"Who? Who is coming here? Now?"

He shook his head. "Get them up."

He went back to the outer room and took his rifle down from its rack on the wall. Grabbing a half-empty box of shells from a shelf, he stuck it into his pants and went to the table where he blew out the lamp.

He could hear Mariela fumbling in the darkness, the children jabbering excitedly.

"Come on!" he whispered, his voice seeming too loud in his ears.

Mariela groped toward him, not realizing where he was until her hand closed around one muddy wrist. "What is that on your arm?"

"Never mind. Get the children and get outside." He pushed her almost roughly. There was a dread in him now, a live thing with fang and claw that tore at his entrails. It was more than fear. It was the certainty of stark, blood-freezing terror.

She stumbled through the door and out into the rain, one child in her arms, the other dragged like an empty sack behind her. Moreira followed her out, the rifle in his right hand. She looked at him but could not see his face in the darkness. He sensed where she was and reached for her with his free hand, taking her by the arm and pulling her around behind their hut and toward the edge of the forest.

Mariela stumbled and fell, losing her grip on their son, and turning her body to avoid falling on the smaller girl in her arms. Moreira bent to help her up. The first noise was sudden, a sharp pop high overhead and he looked up to see a white star hanging in the air, very bright, sparks flying in every direction, a band of gray smoke rippling up and past the white thing from which the small star dangled. Except for the smoke, it reminded him of Nativity paintings he had seen in Europe, the bright star marking something important, something extraordinary, significant, above the rude stable. He sensed intuitively that this star, too, marked something important, but there was no time to understand just what.

The first explosion came as more of a surprise. He saw one wall of his hut fold away from under the roof as if it were made of cardboard. There was a ball of orange flame then, and smoke that looked very white under the glare from the slowly descending flare.

He heard screams then, and the firing of many rifles. Another explosion, then another and another, deep crumpling sounds that seemed to shake the earth, and balls of fire inflated like balloons. His own hut was a sheet of flame now, even with the rain continuing to cascade down.

He saw people running in every direction as he dragged Mariela by the arm and pulled her into the trees and down to the ground. Covering her and the children as best he could with his own body, he stared through the undergrowth. His neighbors were milling around like ants, running every which way, and the chatter of the automatic rifles grew louder and louder. Screams, shrill and stark, were all but swallowed by the flame and thunder as hut after hut exploded into broken sticks and strips of rusted metal.

"Do something," Mariela whispered. "You have to do something."

He saw the attackers now, men in uniforms. The center of Kumbala was bright as day, but painted orange and full of wavering shadows as men ran from hut to burning hut, sometimes firing bursts from their rifles into the ruins, sometimes backing away and throwing grenades into the flames. All over the ground lay other shadows, thick, motionless—the bodies of Kumbala's people.

"I have to tell someone," he whispered. "Someone has to know. Someone has to know..."

A figure caught his eye then, far across the corpse-littered center of the village. He recognized the sunglasses even before he saw the swagger stick. Reynaldo Carvalho had come back.

TWO
❖

July 1, 1975

David Ripley stared at the ceiling, the whup . . . whup . . . whup of chopper blades pounding in his skull. Two months, he thought, two fucking months, and still it won't go away. Every night, the sound would slowly creep up on him as soon as his head hit the pillow. It would be far off in the distance at first, almost indistinct, but he knew what it was from the first beat of the blades.

It would come closer, and closer and closer. Soon, he could feel the downdraft whipping sand into his face, see the scraps of paper that never made it into the burn bags loft up and away like so many autumn leaves. He could see people milling around, pressing against the fence far below him, the ones in front squeezed tightly against the wrought iron gates like so much pasta in a colander. The ones behind them raised a fist, sometimes both of them, as if to make up for the crushing immobility of those nearest the fence.

But over it all was that sound, the roaring, as terrible and frightening as the sound of those giant ants in a horror movie he'd seen as a kid. *Them* he thought it was called, and the ants were everywhere, crawling out of the desert, creeping through the storm drains of Los Angeles, their gargantuan mandibles clicking, their massive antennae waving and their eyes, huge and glittering as they bore down on Kenneth Tobey, or whoever the hell it was. Nothing could stop them—not bullets or flamethrowers, not grenades, not even bazookas. Like most such films of the period, it was radiation that had created the monsters, and it was the bomb that had to take them out before they took over.

But radiation was old hat now. Now there were new demons, little ones, men with slanted eyes and alien tongues, their black pajamas like flags of death as they slipped through the dark and silent jungles, or crept through the tunnels of Cu Chi, where poisonous snakes and spiders the size of sofa cushions lay in wait for the unwary and the reckless.

He had been there at the end. Saigon, the roof of the embassy, where the choppers came out of the sky like mutant insects with swollen bellies. And above it all, that sound, the sound of the rotors beating as regular as an athlete's heart. And he couldn't sleep for the terror of it all.

Tonight was no different. It had been two months since he was lifted off the roof, watching people he'd known, worked with, liked and, in some cases even come to admire, staring up, their faces blank as the sky above them as the choppers dwindled away to tiny specks.

It had all been in the eyes—the disappointment, the terror and the sense of betrayal, deeper than any chasm. Why, the lips whispered, the words whipped away by the vortex churned by the huge rotors of the ravenous choppers. He saw those faces, too, as if those left behind had heard the same thunder of the choppers and come running, hoping this time it would be different, that this time there would be a place for them on the last chopper or the one before it or the one before that.

But there never was, and David Ripley knew that no matter how many nights he lay there staring at the ceiling, there never would be. It had come down to triage. Whose skin do we save, and whose do we leave behind to be nailed up on some wall? The decisions hadn't been his to make, but he was haunted by them nonetheless. What it all boiled down to, he knew, was that he felt responsible, partly because that was the kind of man he was but mostly because he knew that somebody ought to feel responsible and that if he didn't no one would.

So tomorrow he would get on a plane, leave behind the cool waters of the Powder River and fly to Washington, DC where, if he could manage to keep his hands from shaking long enough, he would sign the letter of resignation already tucked away in his briefcase. His leave was about to expire, and he had to choose. They had been quite explicit about that. Choose, David, take sides. That casually, as if it were some pick-up basketball game. Well, he had chosen. He was going to leave. And he would hope that maybe, if he could run far enough, and hide his head under enough pillows, the choppers would finally leave him alone.

Maybe.

But he was torn. There was a sense of loss gnawing at his insides, as if he were turning his back not just on his job, but on the idealistic young man he had been not that long ago. How long had it been? That time was so fog bound, seemed so ancient, he might have been excavating a stone-age bog man. But the body was there, perfectly preserved, its skin a little wrinkled, the color darkened a bit from lying so long in the iron-laden water. But there.

He could still see the earnest scholar, spending long hours in the library, buried in mounds of history books others thought moldy. He could feel the grass under his cleats as he slanted off tackle, then cut for the sidelines, a thousand pounds of beef hard on his heels. It was an age of innocence, when steroids were used for medical purposes, when politics seemed honorable, when cigarettes were a quarter a pack. That long, he thought. Not long. Only fifteen years. And how had he aged so much in such a short time, he wondered.

Things had happened, of course. A president, a young man himself, had been slain, his skull blasted, its pieces scattered over the street of a Texas city. A war had crept up out of MacArthur's worst nightmare, a thing from far underground that seemed to feed on uncertainty and arrogance. Another president had overstepped his bounds, had his political pulse taken and been declared terminal. That would do it, he thought, that would put a few wrinkles on the bog man, turn a few hairs gray.

But tomorrow he would fly two-thirds of the way across the continent, scrawl a quavering signature on a one paragraph letter, and ride off into some metaphorical sunset.

Or would he?

Sighing, he sat up, clapping his hands over his ears to shut out the thumping rotors. He started to hum to drown out the sound, then reached for the night light, which seemed to be the only thing that worked, the only thing that could knock those pregnant beetles out of the sky. He walked to the stereo in the living room, a pack of Marlboros in his hand, and turned on the amplifier.

He clicked on the turntable and watched the tone arm stutter its way out over the disc, smoothly lower the stylus into the first groove, and waited for the first stumbling chords of "Brake's Sake" to rattle the speaker cones. Adjusting the volume, making it just a little louder, the way it ought to be, he turned his attention to the idiosyncratic logic of Thelonious Monk. The odd rhythms and odder chords made sense to him now the way they had not and, perhaps, could not have ten years before.

He flopped on the couch, reached overhead for an ashtray, not looking because he knew exactly where it was, and set it on the hardwood floor. Lighting a cigarette, he sucked greedily until his lungs were full of smoke. The rhythm section was getting into it now, the bass walking solidly, Ben Riley using brushes to drive Charlie Rouse into a searing tenor solo less cerebral than usual, more visceral.

Sometimes, he thought, the best thing was not to think at all. Just lie back and let things happen around you. Observe with a reserved if not outrightly jaundiced eye.

He didn't want to quit, but wanted a reason not to, a reason that would convince not just the man he was at the moment, but the man he had been all those years ago to nod, to feel a little stirring, and say, "I think that is something worth doing."

But there were so damned few things *worth* doing. He had seen so much go sour. What he needed was a burst of wide-eyed innocence, something to tempt him to stick his head in the lion's mouth one more time. Maybe if it turned out right, he could spend the rest of his days behind a desk in Langley, worrying about how far his parking place was from his office, worrying about whether he would lose his window, whether he would have one secretary or two, about whether he had a chance to make GS-16 before he called it quits.

But Langley was a world away at the moment. He'd rather hang around with Thelonious a while, let drums pound in his ears instead of Huey rotors. The cigarette was gripped loosely in his fingers, its smoke tickling his nose as it floated toward the light and up through the shade. He didn't like smoking much anymore, did it as much out of habit as anything else. It was only the first rush, that first hit of nicotine, that he needed. He'd ruined more sweaters than he could count, burned enough holes in his furniture that his wife had left him, or at least that was the reason she had given him if a two line scrawl on a napkin constituted a reason, and scarred the floors of the Montana cabin he called home so badly that they had to be redone.

"Brake's Sake" finished and "Nice Work If You Can Get It" picked up where it left off. He noticed the irony for a moment, then brushed it aside, impatiently, almost petulantly. There was no room in his skull for irony at the moment.

By the time the stylus had worked its way in toward the label and lifted off with a pop of static electricity, leaving a small ball of dust behind on the record, he was almost asleep. The cigarette burned his fingers a few seconds later and he sat up with a curse, crushing the butt in the ashtray. He brushed the ashes from his sweatshirt, and got up to pile a stack of records on.

With enough music, he might actually get some sleep before the alarm went off at seven. It would only be five EDT, and he could think about the letter in his briefcase while he ate breakfast. He could think about it as he drove to Miles City to the airport, for the hop to Denver. He could think about it some more while he changed planes, and all the way into Dulles. He could even consider it one more time on the drive to Langley.

Thinking back over the past fifteen years, he realized that consideration had never been his long suit. He had not been considerate of Amy, and she had left him. Before that, he had not been considerate of his father, and it had killed the old man.

It seemed odd, and not a little sad, that now that he was finally able to consider things, there was no one left to lose. His selfishness was a streak he hadn't liked to acknowledge, even when those closest to him, and therefore its most immediate victims, had pointed an accusing finger. It had been easy to turn the accusation around, point his own finger, and charge them with trying to deprive him of his right to be his own man.

Well, now he was his own man. And there was no one to strut for, no one who gave a damn. He was like the last man on earth. He had it all, and there was no one to impress. What good is the Hope Diamond if you have no one to dazzle with it, no one to give it to, no one who envies you?

Yes, he would consider things. He would sign the letter then hand it in. It was time to get on with his life, he would say, and time to hope he could unlearn some of the less valuable lessons of the past fifteen years. He was a clown who could no longer stand the circus. He needed to find a balance, find a way to keep on his feet while he walked the trembling cable back into the real world, an umbrella in one hand, floppy shoes on his nervous feet, all the while teetering like a drunk while someone tried to shake him loose and send him hurtling, netless, into the yawning void that was a million miles deep and just a single misstep away.

Yes, he would consider things. But not now. Now he needed to sleep.

THREE
❖

Ripley turned into the long approach road, thankful to be out of the heavy traffic. He hadn't done much driving the past few months, and what little he had done was confined to the lonely stretches of Montana where passing another car was a little like finding the skeleton of an allosaurus. You knew they were out there, but you hardly ever actually saw one.

The main headquarters of the CIA loomed up ahead of him, its architecture stark and faceless as its employees were supposed to be. Instinctively, he reached for the briefcase on the seat beside him and patted it the way he would a pet that needed reassurance. The letter was inside, still crisp, still neat, and still unsigned.

He had a one o'clock appointment with Jack Devereaux, a man he had never met but about whom he had heard much, most of it good. Devereaux had been nearly a legend in the Agency when Ripley had come aboard. Like Conein and Lansdale, he had been an advocate of covert action early and often. In furtherance of his beliefs, he had received postings that made him the envy of all the young case officers—Indonesia, when Sukarno was riding high, Israel during the Six Day War, Laos in the early sixties. Like a heat-seeking missile, Devereaux had managed to find just about every hot spot on the planet in his twenty-five years of service.

Devereaux had done two tours in Vietnam, one with the Phoenix program, but neither tour had overlapped with Ripley's own two. They had mutual friends scattered all over the globe, and it never failed to turn Ripley's head when someone told him that Devereaux had been taking an interest in his career.

Now they were going to meet for the first time face to face. It was a scenario that David Ripley could not have imagined, even with the aid of any combination of hallucinogens. As the new head of the West Africa division, Devereaux was office bound now, but still anxious to shake a few acorns off the nearest tree. He had asked for Ripley personally, and what he was getting was anything but the wide-eyed, young go-getter that had so impressed him.

Instead, Ripley thought, he will find himself face to face with the burned out shell of that enthusiast. It was no longer easy, if even possible, to believe that covert operations could shape the world in America's likeness. Rather, it seemed to be that the men who planned those delicate maneuvers were more concerned with shaping it to America's liking, and there were a thousand light years between those two suffixes.

He parked in the West lot, and got out of his rented Chevrolet, walked around to the passenger side and leaned in through the open window to retrieve the briefcase. It seemed heavier than it should have been, and he thought for a moment that he had taken the wrong one. Only when he remembered the letter did he realize it was his heart, and not the briefcase, that was so heavy.

He took his time walking to the main entrance, a kid reluctant to face the principal. He stood in front of the glass door for a while, looking up at the anonymous facade, then shrugged. There was no point in delaying any longer.

Ripley went inside, fishing for his wallet. The security men watched him with blank faces. They tried to seem as if they were remote, even robotic, as if this was a procedure in which they had no personal stake, but one which they had mastered. In fact, everyone had heard the stories, about people using fake credentials, about people flashing

Visas or Mastercards and wandering through the halls unchecked and unattended. So much for security.

Opening his wallet, he found his ID, handed it to the taller and more massive of the two security men, watched the guard's hands, where the small plastic card sat like a poker chip in the huge palm. Only when the hand moved toward him and he closed his fingers over the card again did Ripley look up. The man's eyes were just a tad softer than they had been. Apparently, Ripley thought, I've passed muster. He tucked the card back into his wallet, nodded to the guards, and moved into the main lobby, where the seal of the agency, emblazoned with its motto "Ye shall know the truth, and the truth shall set ye free . . ." stared down at everyone who entered, like a single unblinking eye.

Ripley walked to the elevator bank, pressed the soft amber glow of the up button, and turned to look back into the sunlight beyond the entrance.

The elevator hummed as it descended, a soft hiss escaping through the rubber strips between the two doors, which parted with a dull thud. He turned, stepped into the elevator and pressed another button for the third floor. He noticed that the Braille symbols for the various floors were adjacent to each button, and thought how ironic it was that the sightless were expected here. The blind receiving the blind, he thought as the doors bumped closed and the elevator lurched into motion.

When the car stopped, he stepped out onto the gray tile. Wall Street's favorite color, he thought. Everything here seemed designed not to assault the eye, but to bore it, as if the ultimate security lay in being in plain sight but supremely uninteresting.

The walls were painted some off-white color, shell or ivory, whatever the marketing geniuses of Sherwin-Williams thought sounded appealing. The only touch of color was the staggered lattice of doorways in darker, primary colors, regularly alternating, of course.

He found Devereaux at the end of the hall, his door open, his feet on his desk and his thin, nervous hands fiddling with his open collar and the uneven knot of his tie, which was pulled a few inches below the prominent Adam's apple bulging in a muscular neck.

"David Ripley?" Devereaux asked, letting his feet fall to the gray carpet without a sound.

Ripley nodded.

"Close the door," Devereaux said.

Ripley turned to shove the door. Its pneumatic piston whooshed as the heavy door swung shut, hesitating a split second before meeting the jamb with a dull thump.

"Pleasure to meet you," Devereaux said. He leaned forward, extending a hand across his cluttered desk. "Heard a lot about you over the years."

Ripley tried to smile, but his face felt as if it had been laminated and any movement would crack the plastic. He grasped the hand, shook it once then, thinking that seemed too perfunctory, shook it twice more awkwardly before letting go.

"Have a seat, David," Devereaux said. "Want a drink?"

Ripley shrugged.

"Coffee? Tea?"

"No, thanks. Do you have Tab?"

"Can get it, Dave," he said, reaching for the phone. Cradling the receiver in one hand, he pushed the intercom buzzer with his pinkie.

Ripley listened while Devereaux spoke into the phone. "And add some ice," Devereaux said as the receiver was already drifting toward its cradle. Then, leaning back in his chair, he twisted his neck until a sharp crack echoed off the high ceiling. "That's better," he muttered.

The door opened, and a slender brunette entered. Devereaux looked up with a crooked grin. "Thanks, Madge." He reached for the tall tumbler still spitting bubbles over its rim. The ice tinkled against the glass as he took it from her.

Setting the glass on a stack of cables, he said, "Madge, this is David Ripley. David, Madge Carter." The woman smiled and Ripley moved to get up.

"Don't bother," she said, extending a hand. "You'll spoil me. Most of the cowboys around here hardly grunt to acknowledge me."

Ripley shook her hand, noticing the hint of perfume that swirled around him as she leaned forward.

BLACK MAMBA 31

"David's going to head up the Mawindi Task Force, Madge. I imagine you'll be seeing quite a bit of him in the next few months."

"Wait a minute, Mister Devereaux, I . . ."

"It's Jack, Dave, just plain Jack."

He nodded at Madge, who caught the hint. "Welcome aboard, David, and holler if you want any more pop." She closed the door softly behind her.

"Went to school in Boston." Devereaux grinned. "To the rest of the world, it's soda, but to Bostonians, no matter how short the tenure, it's pop."

"What is this Mawindi Task Force?" David said. "I don't know anything about it. In fact, I came here to tender my resignation."

"What? What the fuck are you talking about, resignation. This is the chance of a lifetime, Dave. I mean, whole careers are built on jobs like this one. Don't you . . ."

"That's what they told me about Saigon, Mister Devereaux. And I . . ."

"It's Jack, I said. And forget that shit. Saigon is ancient history. Dead and buried. You ought to know that. Once the plug gets pulled, the light goes out and that's all she wrote. Saigon is over. I'm talking about the future. My future, your future. Hell, the future of the whole damn Company, if it has one once those jackals on the Hill get through gnawing at the carcass."

"I don't know if I can . . ."

Devereaux slapped the desk with the flat of his hand. "Damn it, Dave. I went out on a limb to get you. Had to go all the way to the DDO for this. From what I hear, he talked to the Director before making up his mind. You got a rising star pulling your wagon, Dave. All you got to do is hold on to your hat. Anyhow, don't make up your mind until I have a chance to talk to you about it a little. Just hear me out. Do me that favor, all right?"

Ripley nodded faintly. "All right."

Faint as it was, Deveraux noticed. In fact, Ripley thought, he would have seen the assent even if there hadn't been any.

"You were raised in Africa, that right?"

Ripley nodded. "Zaire. Actually, it was called the Congo, back then. My father was a geological engineer. We lived in Katanga Province when I was a kid. Spent a couple of years in Angola, too."

"Mawindi? Ever been there?"

"Spent a year there. The Portuguese thought they had found the next motherlode of diamonds. They were wrong, but . . . "

"Know the local lingo, do you?"

"Which one? There are a few dozen languages in Central Africa."

"Portuguese, I guess. I don't mean any of that tribal horseshit. Any conversations in Mawindi that matter will be in English or Portuguese."

"I speak Portuguese, yes. And a couple of Bantu dialects, as well."

"That's gravy, Dave. It's Portuguese that counts.

Portugal, Jesus." He snorted. "Damn country, all it's good for is sardines and anchovies. Should be part of Spain, you ask me. There's entirely too many goddamn countries in the world as it is, and we got a whole truckload comin' up the road. Frogs and Brits fucked things up royally, no pun intended. Leave us to clean up the mess."

"What mess is that, Jack?"

Devereaux ignored the question and tossed another of his own across the desk. "What do you know about Mawindi?"

"Only what I read in the papers. Just like Angola. The coup in Portugal threw the whole place into turmoil. Must be a dozen guerrilla groups jockeying for position. Whoever's on top come November gets to run the place as long as the rest of them are good losers. That's about all I know."

"There's more. A whole lot more. It's a goddamn Gordian knot, Dave. And you're just the man to unravel it."

"As I recall, Alexander didn't bother. He used a sword."

"What the hell do you think I'm talking about? That's exactly what we need. Somebody to cut through all the snarls, make some sense out of that rat's nest."

"I don't know." Ripley reached into his pocket for a pack of cigarettes, pulled out a Marlboro and lit it before looking for an ashtray.

Devereaux started to shuffle the papers on his

desk, finally finding what he was looking for under the cables. "Here," he said, sliding a tuna fish can to the edge of the desk. "It's what I use."

Taking a drag on the Marlboro, Ripley used the pause to reach down for his briefcase, balanced it on his knees to open it, and removed the folder with his resignation letter.

"What's that?" Devereaux asked. "That the letter of resignation? Lemme see."

Ripley leaned forward to slide the single sheet across the desk. Devereaux read it through once, humming to himself. Tapping it with a fingernail, he said, "You write well, too. That's good. We're gonna need that in Salazar."

"Did you read the letter, Jack?"

"Of course I did. How the hell would I know it was well written, if I didn't?"

"What do you think?"

Devereaux smiled. "I'll show you." He leaned back behind his chair. Holding the letter delicately between fingertips, he shook it until the sheet of paper rattled, then said, "Watch this."

A moment later, Ripley heard a familiar whirring as the letter was shredded into a hundred strips a sixteenth of an inch wide. Turning back to Ripley, Devereaux leaned forward to catch his weight on his elbows, his fingers steepled under his chin.

"That's what I think, Dave." He got up from his chair. "Come on, there's a lot to do. I got five hundred pounds of crap for you to read."

Ripley sat there for a moment, not knowing whether to laugh or hurl himself on Devereaux. Then, knowing that he would probably regret it, he clicked the briefcase closed, set it on the floor beside his chair and stood up.

"Show me," he said.

FOUR

❖

They gave him a cubbyhole in the corner occupied by the West Africa Division. They also gave him stacks of paper—files, clippings, cables, raw data, white papers, a Presidential finding and six cartons optimistically marked "miscellaneous." Now, all he had to do was plow through it all, break it down and digest it, as if he were some over-sized microbe expected single-handedly to solve the pollution problem.

There was no money in the budget for secretarial help, which told him just how steep was the hill they expected him to climb. He spent the first day trying for chronological order. Some of the documents were undated, others were outdated, but he refused to be intimidated. Madge Carter helped when she could, but Devereaux had her hopping, and the few free moments she had available were spent sitting on the floor, since the budget had room for a single chair which held a stack of files nearly two feet high, and which teetered precariously every time someone opened the door.

To Ripley, it seemed intelligence was not the right noun for the dog-eared midden that threatened to devour him. Late the first afternoon, he had the distinct impression that he would be interred under more and more paper until, fifty years down the road when the building had to be evacuated, someone would open the door to his cubbyhole once more and wonder about the small mound of digits lying atop the mountain of paper like some ju-ju doctor's omen bones.

It was nearly seven-thirty when Madge stuck her head in, holding a glistening tumbler of soda high overhead, shaking it enough to make the ice tinkle. "Thirsty?" she asked.

Ripley nodded. "Yeah. But I'm too damn stupefied to worry about it. How in the hell is anybody supposed to make any sense out of all this garbage?"

Madge snorted. "I asked Jack the same question this morning. You know what he said?"

Ripley shook his head. "No, what?"

"He said you weren't supposed to make sense

out of it. All you had to do was read it. 'No surprises, that's what we want, Madge, no surprises. You tell David not to worry. Just tell him to make sure there are no surprises.'"

"I take it that's a direct quote?"

Madge nodded. "Straight from the horse's ass."

Ripley grinned. "You don't think too highly of him, do you?"

"Jack? Oh, hell, he's fine. A lot better than some I've worked for. But I've been with the Agency for eleven years, and I haven't seen them do it right yet. I sometimes think I won't be allowed to retire until they do. And that, Mister Ripley, means I'll die at my desk. A very gray and withered old crone. It's not a pretty prospect."

"Jack around?"

She shook her head. "He's gone to a reception at the Zairian Embassy. Why, anything important?"

"No. Not really. I haven't even started reading this junk yet. It'll take me another day to get it organized."

"Organized? Is that what you said? Organized? You really don't fit in around here, do you?" He expected her to laugh, but she didn't so much as crack a smile. "I'm done with my own work, but I don't have anything to do tonight, so if you want some help, I guess I can hang around for a couple of hours."

He got up and took the glass of soda from her, and with one foot shoved aside a stack of neatly clipped and stapled magazine articles about everything from Angola to Zaire. She dropped to her knees with a grace that could only have come from much practice, clapped her hands, and said, "What do you want me to do?"

Ripley pointed to the nearest pile of files, rubber banded and stacked like firewood. "Sort them out, I guess. They're field reports from Bob Karp in Salazar. I'm trying to organize them by political party."

"You got it."

Madge slipped off her shoes and tossed them into the one corner of the small office that was free of paper. She worked quickly, but the mass of documents was overwhelming.

Ripley had mounds of his own to sort, and it was nearly midnight before he leaned back, rubbed his eyes with his knuckles, and said, "Christ almighty, there has to be an easier way to go blind."

"Ja," Madge said, affecting a Viennese accent, "but zat also makes hair grow on ze palms."

Ripley cracked up. Shaking his head, he said, "You must be beat, Madge. Can I buy you dinner?"

"Thanks, but I have a rule. Actually, my mother made it for me when I started working here, and I think it's a good one. 'Don't get too close to the spies,' she told me. 'You can't trust them.' But thanks. I think I'll just go home and change. Have to be back here at seven. Jack's an early riser."

"All right. Thanks for all your help tonight." He watched her get up, her dress riding up over her legs as she bent to retrieve her shoes. Barefoot, she padded out into the hall and Ripley realized her legs weren't her only asset. He wondered why she was single. As soon as the thought crossed his mind, he got mad at himself. When he considered things a moment, it dawned on him that a job like hers, working seventy or eighty hours a week for slave wages, probably left her very little time for anything else.

He was suddenly very tired, and thought about sleeping on the floor, but forced himself to get up and lock the office.

Down in the lobby, he stood looking up at the Agency emblem. It sounded so neat, so economical. The only problem was truth was a scarce commodity. He had found lots of opinion, much of it contradictory. He had opened file after file to the whine of a whetstone and the sound of axes being ground. Reports from the field were riddled with obvious inconsistency, ill-disguised envy, calumny, libel, slander and just plain old-fashioned character assassination.

It was difficult enough to tell who did what, let alone why, and Ripley had the feeling that the truth, if there even was such a thing in Mawindi, existed somewhere in the chinks between files, in the spaces between words. It was like ether, out there in the void, scentless, invisible and silent. The truth was what someone didn't say, the thought not voiced, the observation not committed to paper. And all Jack Devereaux was asking him to do was find it and act on it. It was like being given a month to bring back a Yeti. But if he found it, and if he managed to bring it back, how it would set anyone free was something still to be understood.

He was just turning away when Madge stepped out of the elevator. He walked over to meet her. "Wondering about the motto, were you?" she asked.

Ripley nodded.

"That's the Company hobby," she said, laughing. "I do the same thing every day. Lots of us do. It's what we do instead of bowling or softball. It isn't much but at least you don't have to rent shoes and you can play even when it rains."

Ripley walked her out, nodding to the security men, both of whom looked just the least bit sleepy and barely acknowledged his goodnight.

When they were outside, Madge said, "I'm in the East lot. I guess I'll see you in a few hours. Goodnight."

"Night."

It went that way for three days. On the morning of July fourth, despite the holiday, Devereaux was waiting in the small borrowed office. "David," he said, "Morning. How's it going?"

Ripley shrugged. "Who knows?"

"Well, I sure as hell hope you do. You're leaving tomorrow."

"Leaving? Where am I going?"

"Mawindi."

"But I don't..."

Devereaux shook his head impatiently. "Don't argue, David. You're going. It's all arranged. You need some time on the scene. If you're going to run this task force, you have to get a feel for the place."

"I'm not ready, Jack. I just don't know enough."

"What's to know?" He spread his arms to take in the mass of paper surrounding them. "You read this stuff, right?"

"Most of it, yeah, but..."

"Well, there you are, then. It's all here. What else could you possibly need to know?"

"I have a lot of questions."

"I've got some time. Shoot."

Ripley took a deep breath. "Look, as near as I can figure it out, there's three groups that could possibly win this five and dime war. Joshua Bandolo's Mawindi Liberation Front, Jorge Caulfield and his Pan-African Movement and Oscar Nkele's African People's Party. According to COS Salazar, Caulfield's our man. Bandolo's getting help from the Soviets, Nkele's tight with the North Koreans and he's not trustworthy, so Caulfield wins by default."

Devereaux smiled. "See? And you were worried you didn't know enough." Devereaux started to get up.

"Wait a minute, Jack. I said that's what it looks like. But the information is skewed. There's a whole lot on Caulfield. The stuff on the MLF is well documented, but mostly from the popular press. And Nkele's almost a cipher."

"So?"

"So why do we pick Caulfield when we don't know enough about the other two?"

"That was Bob Karp's call. He's COS in Salazar, as you know. He's a good man, and we have to trust his judgment. Besides, you said yourself that Bandolo and Nkele are sleeping with the enemy."

"So's Caulfield. He's been getting arms from the Chinese, and—"

"Can't blame him for that. You want to fight a war, you need guns. What's he supposed to do, take on the rest of them with spears and slingshots? Besides, the Chinese are pulling back. There's a vacuum there, and we're gonna fill it."

"Jack, I don't understand the logic. If it's okay for Caulfield, why isn't it okay for Bandolo and Nkele?"

"I guess you'll find out when you get there, won't you?"

"But..."

Devereaux sighed in exasperation. "Look, David, don't ask me, ask Karp when you get to Salazar. All I know is we got a directive from the 40 Committee. We got a presidential finding authorizing this operation, and they gave us a handful of pocket change to get it done. You know the budget. That's all there is. There just ain't no more money. Right now, Caulfield's got five times the troops Nkele does. If we're going to stop the MLF, we have to use him."

"But this thing is more complicated than that. There's the tribal element, and..."

"I'm not an anthropologist, David. I don't know from tribes. That's not my job."

"Look, Jack. I was raised in Africa. And I can tell you that tribal politics are more important than ideology. Look at Nigeria. That was Ibo against Hausa and Fulani. Look at Uganda. That wasn't just Amin against Obote. It was tribal, too. Idi Amin was a Ganda, and that mattered more than anything else to him. The tribes are where the power bases are. You ignore that fact and it doesn't matter what your intentions are; you fuck up. Period!"

"David, I don't have..."

"Wait, Jack, I'm not finished. This is important. Nkele, Caulfield and Bandolo all have separate constituencies because they come from different tribes. That's point one. Point two is that Nkele's tribal group, the Orobundu, is the largest, far and away. There are nearly five million Orobundu. Caulfield's a Bundu, and there are only two million of them. Bandolo's a Simbundu, and that gives him two million, too. That means if we back Nkele, we back the man with the greatest potential support among the people. That's pretty obvious. Point three is the simplest of all..."

"You're right, David. Point three *is* pretty goddamned simple. Point three is this—Kissinger wants Caulfield. Period. Case closed. You're here because you know more about Africa than I do. Hell, more than anybody in the Division. So tomorrow you go on your fact-finding mission, and you find facts. And those facts will tell you what I'm telling you now. Caulfield's the man."

"How do you know what the facts will tell me when you don't know what the facts are, Jack?"

"I know because our job is not to set policy, it's to implement it. I told you the policy. Now you do your part and everybody's happy."

"And suppose I'm right? What than?"

"Then I guess you can take Kissinger's place, David. What do you want from me, a gold star?"

"No, just assurances that if I'm right, you'll go to the 40 Committee and ask them to reconsider."

"I don't get the 40 Committee on the phone and tell them I got to talk to them, David. I have to go through channels. And those channels are pretty well backed up with shit right now. We're drowning in it here, and I don't know what I'll be able to do."

"Will you at least try?"

Devereaux nodded. "I'll try. But let's cross that bridge before you burn it, all right?"

FIVE

July 5, 1975

David Ripley ran for the plane, his briefcase thumping against his leg. Muttering a silent prayer under his breath, he just managed to reach the gate as the last passenger in line received his boarding pass. The ticket attendant scowled at him as she processed his ticket, rifling through the pages again and again until he was certain some terrible mistake had been made and he would miss the flight.

"You're out of breath," she said, as he stood there panting.

"I'm late," he answered.

Pointedly, she stopped scanning the pages long enough to stare at him. "I know," she said, leaving no doubt she disapproved. Then, stamping the boarding pass with a violence that seemed out of place from so prim and slender a woman, she jammed it into his outstretched hand, and stuffed the ticket booklet back into its envelope. Every click of the stapler sent a stab into his chest until, finally, she was done. He grabbed the envelope and ran for the plane.

The familiar draft of cool air that seemed somehow synthetic and smelled vaguely of medicine swirled around him as he entered the plane. The aisle was still jammed as he worked his way to his seat, the briefcase banging against seat arms and one careless knee before he found his place.

Across the aisle, he saw Ronnny Lang, one of the two communications people Devereaux had assigned to him for the duration of the trip. Ignoring Lang, who glanced at him only once over the top of a *Sports Illustrated*, Ripley dropped into his seat and held the briefcase on his lap.

There would be no chance to use the nine hour flight to Kinshasa to deal with any of the papers in the case. They were too sensitive to risk someone reading over his shoulder. But he was way behind in the paperwork, and there was still too much he didn't know about the operation, dubbed QTHONEY by some wag in the cryptonym assignment section.

But the deeper he drove a shaft into the mountain of paper that predated his assignment to the Mawindi Task Force, the more convinced he had become that he had to read it all. It seemed like every other cable contradicted the one before it. Position papers didn't square with field reports, and genuine information seemed to be almost non-existent. Going over it all again in his mind, he was amazed that he had even considered trying to swallow so much information in so short a time. Well, he thought, I guess I'll know in seventy-two hours.

He had a window seat, and peered out at the luggage handlers as they practiced some obscure Olympic field event by throwing suitcases as far up the loading conveyor as possible, despite the fact that it was motorized and constantly moving.

Ripley found himself wondering whether all the paperwork with Zairian customs people had been taken care of. But he wouldn't bet the farm on it. Bob Karp, the Chief of Station in Salazar, Mawindi's capital, had tried to block Ripley's visit and when that failed, had taken control on the African end. Ripley had seen it all a hundred times before, the COS exercising bureaucratic control in order to maintain hegemony in the field. And Bob Karp, by all indications, had lost nothing of his ability in paper management.

He knew Bob Karp, had served a tour in the Sudan when Karp was COS in Khartoum, and he knew that Karp was a past master of obfuscation, preferring smoke and mirrors to genuine intelligence, because he owned the mirrors and knew how to make smoke. The wonder of it was that it hadn't seemed to hurt Karp's career. On the contrary, it seemed to have helped.

Karp's operational theories were simple—stick your neck out as little as possible, and tell them what they want to hear. Who precisely "they" were would change from operation to operation and sometimes even day to day, but Karp ran no risk at all, since he was a barnacle firmly attached to the ship of state. Part of the ivy-draped old crowd, his father had been a law partner of Bill Donovan's, and served in OSS in Switzerland during World War II under Allen Dulles. When young Bob had come out of Dartmouth in 1959, footloose and aimless, it had taken a single phone call from Thomas Karp to Dulles to land the boy a job.

Bob Karp knew a good thing when it fell in his lap, and he was still on the job, probably still the same spoiled boy he'd always been. "It's my way or the highway," he was known to say, as if secretly under all the Ivy League trappings and the Riviera tan, he were some hardworking cowboy.

Ripley watched New York Harbor fall away under the wings of the 727, and as the plane circled, found himself looking out over the mammoth petroleum facilities along the Jersey shore, their flame-tipped fractioning towers belching feathers of rich, black smoke. The plane banked, and then there was nothing beneath him but clouds and the vast grayness of the Atlantic. Ahead of him lay another vast empty space where he was expected to create something out of nothing, and for a moment he envied Karp his smoke and mirrors.

He fell asleep, dreaming of the five cases of electronic gear in the cargo hold of the 727. They were to be his link to Langley while in the field, which he hoped would not be for more than three days. Part of Ripley was every bit the gunslinger Karp fancied himself to be, and he kept telling himself that he could learn all he needed to know with a whirlwind tour, then he could fly back to the States and, like some resident of Olympus, fashion the future of Mawindi and its ten million inhabitants between sips of lemonade.

He awoke in a sweat, his white-knuckled claws curled around the leatherette of the arm rests. It took him a few seconds to realize where he was, and a few more to remember what had frightened him so. It came to him reluctantly, out of the mists of ruptured sleep. It had been the shipping crates. He had been in a small, windowless room, alone with the cases. There was no door, and the ceiling was high and blank. In his left hand he had a crowbar. Inserting it under the first lid, he had tapped it home with the heel of his hand. The room was suddenly full of the screech of steel on wood as the lid came up and the nails gave way with the sound of rending sheet metal.

Tossing aside the lid, he leaned over the opened

crate, and the lights had gone out. Standing as if paralyzed, the echo of the screaming nails still reverberating in his skull, he heard it then for the first time—the hissing. He knew something was wrong and backed up a step involuntarily just as the lights came on again.

It slithered up and over the yawning lip of the crate, an enormous serpent, its skin shimmering under the solitary bulb like black fire. Its tongue was black, and flicked once, then again as the snake fixed its unblinking eyes on him, the flat, obsidian head wavering slightly as the snake uncoiled out of the crate, reached the floor and started to glide toward him.

He had looked around the room, but there was no furniture, nothing he could climb on but the remaining crates. He had run toward the nearest one, only to find that its lid was gone and another serpent had begun to glide out of it. He knew then that it was a black mamba, that all the crates carried identical cargo, and there was no place for him to hide. And that was when he had screamed.

Now the other passengers were looking at him strangely, all except Ronny Lang, whose apparent disinterest stuck out like a sore thumb. The flight attendant was scurrying toward him. "Are you all right, sir?" she asked.

Ripley waved her away. "Fine, fine, just a bad dream."

"Can I get you anything?"

Ripley shook his head. "No, really, I'm fine."

She looked skeptical, but relieved, and turned away as if afraid he might begin to tell her about his nightmare. He shifted in the seat, suddenly uncomfortable, then realized he had a paperback in his coat pocket that was caught under his hip. Reaching into his jacket he removed the book and opened it, using the briefcase as a table.

It was a study of Angola, Mawindi and Mozambique, Portugal's major African colonies, written by a journalist named Michelle Harkness he'd never heard of. The blurb on the back listed her impressive credentials. A journalism degree from Columbia, two Pulitzer nominations, a Newman Fellowship, and a slew of other prizes, few of which meant a thing to him. He wished there was a photograph, thinking perhaps he could place the face even if the name were unfamiliar.

With a shrug, he opened the book and began to read. They still had six hours in the air, and he thought he might knock off most of the book before landing at Ndjili Airport in Kinshasa. But his exhaustion got the better of him, and he was out again before page fifty.

He was awakened by a hand on his shoulder and instinctively looked at it. Tan, tapered fingers, the nails neatly manicured and painted a tasteful, warm pink. He noticed there was no ring, and no white line against the tan to indicate there had been one recently. Only then did he look up at the flight attendant's face. He realized for the first time how pretty she was, and smiled.

She smiled back, a practiced squeeze of the thirteen critical muscles necessary to keep passengers feeling at home. It vanished as quickly as it had appeared. "Fasten your seat belt, sir," she said, giving him another smile. "We'll be landing in a few minutes."

Ripley glanced up, saw that the seat belt light was on, and nodded. "Sorry," he said. She patted his shoulder and moved on past.

He looked over at Ronny Lang then, who was watching him curiously. Ripley gave him a nod, but said nothing, and turned his attention once more to the paperback. He was too flustered to read, though, and closed the book almost immediately, tucked it away in his pocket, and stared out the window.

He could see the coast of Africa now, a dark gray-green mass, curved like the blade of a scythe, off to the right. As the plane descended, he watched the stippling of whitecaps as they rose and fell, almost able to hear the thunder as they broke, and smell the cool, salty tang of the sea. Beyond, the white masses of breakers against the sand swept away in both directions along the shoreline.

As the plane dropped lower, more details jumped at him. The single narrow white line of a paved highway slicing through heavy rainforest, all but featureless from his altitude, looked misplaced. Clusters of buildings along the shore, mostly long and low, probably warehouses he thought, caught the sun on their corrugated metal roofs, sending shafts of white light slashing in every direction. Off to the south several coastal freighters churned greasy wakes offshore, and to the north, the mouth of the Congo River spewed silt-laden water into the blue-green of the Atlantic.

The plane headed inland, and he watched the thick green canopy below for nearly twenty minutes. From his altitude, it reminded him of micrographs on a microscope slide, or a computer mapping of the ocean floor, all bumps and hollows, full of mystery rather than meaning to the untrained eye. Further inland, he could just make out the tarmac apron and the concrete runways of Ndjili Airport.

An afternoon mist swirled over the forest, concealing the buildings of Kinshasa, ten miles deeper into the continent. The plane banked again as it started to spiral downward. It had been a long time since he'd been to this part of the world, and he felt a hollowness in his stomach. He felt ill-prepared for his mission, too ignorant by half to be in charge of so delicate an operation, and was beginning to feel the familiar beating in the pit of his stomach as the butterflies of doubt left their cocoons once more.

When the plane touched down, he waited for Ronny Lang to get out of his seat, then followed three or four passengers behind him. Up ahead, he saw Rick Brown, the other communications man, sporting a flowered shirt straight out of some Hawaiian nightmare as he made his way toward the exit.

Once outside the plane, he descended the gangway stairs and walked across the hot tarmac. It felt soft under his shoes, and he glanced at the sun for a moment as if only now realizing where he was. Lang and Brown were inside the terminal by the time Ripley followed.

Leaving them to handle the customs paperwork on the comm gear, he walked to the main desk, thankful for the air conditioning, and looked for Karp. Checking at the information desk, he asked for the Salazar COS to be paged, and then scanned the terminal waiting room. There was no sign of Karp, but a short black man in a blue wash and wear business suit was hurrying toward the main desk.

When he got within hailing distance, the man said, "Mister Ripley?"

Ripley nodded.

"Mister Karp asked me to meet you. He has been detained on business. Meeting with President Mobutu, you see." Sticking out his hand, he said, "I'm Amos Cordeiro."

"Detained, you say?" Ripley shook the offered hand absently.

Cordeiro nodded. "Yes, with the president." He wiped a sheen of sweat from his bald head with a damp handkerchief. "I'll take you to the embassy. He wants you to meet the Zairian ambassador this afternoon."

"But I have to wait..."

"Ripley?" Ronny Lang called to him. Ripley turned to see the communications man running toward him.

"What's wrong?"

"What's wrong? I'll tell you what's wrong. These bastards are busting my chops on the gear. They claim there's no paperwork, no manifests, the duties haven't been paid and I don't know what all. I thought you said it was all clear."

"So I was told," Ripley said. "According to Bob Karp, it's all been arranged."

"Well, nobody told the customs honchos anything about it. It's gonna take me a couple of hours. And you can tell that asshole Karp that I . . . shit! Never mind. I'll tell him myself."

"You want me to see what I can do?"

"No, I'll handle it. But let me know where you're gonna be, just in case."

Ripley looked at Cordeiro. "Do you have the telephone number of the American Embassy?"

Cordeiro nodded. He fished a small pad out of his jacket pocket, pulled a pen from his shirt pocket, and scribbled the number, licking the pencil point twice in a gesture Ripley hadn't seen anyone use since his grandfather had died.

Lang snatched at the paper before Cordeiro even had it out of the pad, and stormed off. Ripley apologized for him, but Cordeiro seemed indifferent to that kind of behavior.

"I'll get my bags, Mister Cordeiro, and we can go," he said.

SIX
❖

July 6, 1975

By the time he reached the American Embassy in Salazar where Karp had his office Ripley was boiling. He'd been stood up in Kinshasa, and ever since, he had felt the anger accumulate inside him like magma looking for a way to the surface. All of Karp's apologetic messages had made no difference. Sleeping on the rage hadn't diminished it either. But he swallowed it, determined to make his three days in Mawindi short and, if not exactly sweet, at least fruitful. For that, he needed Karp's cooperation. That he had not yet seen much evidence of it was something he would have to overlook.

The lavish appointments of the embassy did little to calm him down. Instead, they just made him more resentful. Karp was on easy street and he was making the most of it. As far as the outside world was concerned, Karp was an assistant for political affairs. That sort of State Department cover was about as effective as walking around town with CIA emblazoned on your forehead in neon letters. But it was popular with Agency types because it meant they got to graze on the State Department pasture, where the grass was thicker and a hell of a lot sweeter.

When Ripley arrived at the embassy, Karp was still not in, and he was forced to sit in the reception area cooling his heels. Karp's executive assistant, a woman who seemed to have been carved out of some exotic African wood, was busy with paperwork. A carved plaque of black plastic identified her as Marilyn Cisneros.

She offered him coffee, which he declined. "Mister Karp should be here any minute," she informed him, then returned to her work. Ripley realized that the woman must have sensed his annoyance. As she sat with her delicate wrists slightly curved, her hands all but motionless over the IBM Selectric, she kept glancing at him as if she expected him to sprout a second pair of arms or start pulling rabbits out of his jacket pocket. And eating them.

A smorgasbord of magazines was splayed on the gleaming marble top of a coffee table in front of the leather sofa on which Ripley sat. *Time* and *Newsweek* were prominently featured, and a few outdated issues of *Sports Illustrated* featuring football players on their covers were the only concession to popular taste. The rest of the magazines were thick journals bound in the dullest imaginable heavy paper covers—*Foreign Affairs, Geopolitical Review, World Economic Journal* and similar publications sat in neat stacks, like flapjacks for the global strategist. They had all the appeal to the casual visitor that *Gum Irrigation Monthly* might hold for the average dental patient.

Ripley browsed through the latest issue of *Time*, turning the pages and admiring the slickness of the magazine's prose style at the same time he found himself getting angry at its willful disregard for genuine analysis. Apparently, while Ripley had been busting his hump in the Vietnamese highlands, American journalism had entered the era of the one-liner. The presiding genius of the age was no longer Edward R. Murrow; it was Henny Youngman—take my fluff, please. If you can't say anything glib, don't say anything at all.

Ripley was halfway through the pile of *Time* before Bob Karp appeared. He saw Ripley, but ignored him to head straight for Cisneros's desk. He was carrying a squarish package under his right arm. It was wrapped in brown paper, and

Ripley could have sworn it was making noise of some kind. The package seemed to emit a steady crinkling sound as if the paper itself were alive. Cisneros leaned forward to whisper something, and Karp turned to look at Ripley as if aware of his presence for the first time.

His face seemed to decompose into segments, an eggshall fracturing, then the fragments rearranged themselves into a smile. "David Ripley. I didn't realize it was you sitting there." He crossed the open space between desk and coffee table, leaned over with his left hand extended while shifting the package to a slightly more secure position on his right hip. "Pleased to see you again. It's been a long time."

Not so goddamned long that you didn't recognize me, Ripley thought.

Getting to his feet, Ripley grasped the offered hand. "Bob, how've you been?"

Waving expansively, Karp said, "Fine, fine. Anytime you get to have an office like this, and an assistant like Marilyn, you're on top of the world." He laughed, and let Ripley's hand go. Ripley noticed that Marilyn Cisneros wasn't quite as sure of her good fortune as Karp seemed to be of his own. She wrinkled her nose and shook her head slightly, not enough to attract attention, but enough to catch Ripley's eye.

"Come on in," Karp said, leading the way past Cisneros and on into a spacious office beyond her desk. He waited for Ripley to enter, then closed the tall, broad walnut door. Ripley caught the scent of lemon oil wafting from the wood as it swung past.

"Have a seat, David. We have a lot to catch up on." Karp set his package on a massive desk, the same dark and recently oiled walnut as the door. It was neat beyond efficiency, sporting only a pair of interoffice mail trays, one empty, the other stacked with outgoing. Completing the ensemble were a desk set and dark green blotter, fixed in a black leather holder that looked to Ripley like genuine goat skin, its borders gleaming with gilded inlay.

Ripley noticed a large vivarium behind the desk, occupying nearly a third of the rear wall, on the left between the frame of the ceiling-high window and the left corner. It was nearly eight feet across, five feet deep, and five feet high, and sat on a black metal table. Thick foliage and several large stones surrounded a small pool of water tucked in one corner, and a five-foot length of rotted log obliquely bisected the mulch-covered floor.

"Hang on a sec, I have something I have to do," Karp said. "Com'ere and watch this." He ran a hand through his unruly brown curls, and Ripley noticed the faint band of white beneath a newly-trimmed collar line.

Karp snatched at the package, precipitating a sudden flurry of crinkling noises once more. Turning to look over his shoulder, he waved Ripley closer. "Check this out, Davey," he said, dropping to one knee to tap on the glass with his Dartmouth class ring. Ripley knelt beside the COS, more resigned than curious.

"See him, there in the corner?" Karp jabbed a finger against the glass. Ripley looked closer, still not sure what he was looking for. Then a sudden movement, so quick it was over almost before it registered, one he might have imagined, caused him to look even closer. All but hidden in thick greenery, he saw where—shiny black with a slight brownish cast, as if carved from obsidian and polished to high gloss—a snake lay coiled against the log, just its head showing. Its tongue flicked again, and Ripley realized what he had seen a few moments before.

Unwrapping the package, Karp reached inside then stood up, a white rat dangling by its tail from his extended arm. He reached up and over the top of the vivarium, groping for something with his left hand, clicked a latch and lifted a wire mesh door just enough to drop the rodent through. The latch clicked again and Karp returned to his knee.

The rat landed on its feet and immediately ran for a corner. Smoothly, like hot tar oozing, the snake slid out from behind the log, heading toward the rodent which stood on its hind legs, its tiny front paws coiled like baby fists against the white fur of its belly. The snake gathered itself into a tight coil, its head seeming to rest on its body, the tongue darting rapidly now, its yellow-green, lidless eyes fixed and motionless as a pair of glassies at rest. The rat squealed once, then fell silent.

Karp rapped on the glass and the snake, as if in response, rose up and, in one motion, struck, its jaws gaping and its head tilted slightly to the rear. The fangs seemed to catch the light and sparkled a white brilliant enough for a toothpaste commercial. In a split second, they buried themselves in the rodent's side as it tried to run, then the snake withdrew. The rat spun in circles, not chasing its tail so much as trying to run away from it, then fell on its side. Its chest rose and fell convulsively and its feet quivered spastically a few moments.

The snake, satisfied that its toxin had done its work, took the rodent in its jaws and glided behind the log, preferring to have its meal in some privacy.

Karp was smiling. He clapped Ripley on the back. "Ain't that a bitch? Damnedest thing I ever saw. And I never get tired of watching it. I wish I could feed that sucker every day, but a couple times a month is all it needs. Know what that baby is?"

Ripley shook his head.

"That, my friend, is a black mamba, maybe the deadliest damn snake on the whole fucking planet. People talk about bushmasters and cobras and shit, but for my money there ain't nothing can hold a candle to that little fucker. This one's a prize. Blacker than most, from what I understand."

"What the hell are you doing with it in your office?"

Karp laughed. "A reminder. Keeps me on my toes. Indigenous life form, you know? This is what's out there in the grass, waiting for us all. Anonymous and unremarkable, invisible as death itself. You'll be walking along, minding your own business. One false step and *bam!* You're history. I kind of admire the damn things. I'm fascinated by them, maybe even obsessed. A full grown black mamba can put you in a pine box in thirty seconds, Davey. Remember that when you're out there humpin' through the bush, lookin' for facts or whatever the hell else you're supposed to be doing here. And remember, too, that mambas come in all kinds. And all colors."

Ripley was repulsed. He thought back to his dream on the flight, and wondered about the coincidence. He hadn't realized it on the plane, but in one field report Jorge Caulfield had characterized Oscar Nkele as a black mamba. It hadn't meant much at the time, but now . . . For a moment, he thought about mentioning it, but sensed that would be playing to Karp's strength. The serpent was a prop, something Karp used to gain a bit of an edge. He swallowed his gorge and stood up.

Karp dropped into the high-backed leather chair behind his desk, swung around, and put his feet up. "Have a seat, Davey," he said.

Ripley took the chair on the opposite side of the desk. He reached into his pocket for his

Marlboros, lit a cigarette, and leaned over to drop the smoking match into a large green glass ashtray on a smoking stand beside him.

"Where the hell were you yesterday?" he asked.

Karp squeezed his face into another smile. "Sorry about that. Mobutu is a bit of a character. He's our best friend in this part of the continent, and when he says jump, I have to ask 'Who?' By the time I was finished, it was too late to get together with you. That's why I made arrangements for you to come down separately. You'll stay with us again tonight."

"Why weren't the Kinshasa customs people told about Lang's comm gear?"

"They weren't?" It was a question devoid of surprise.

Ripley shook his head. "They weren't."

"Well, hell, I got a lot of irons in the fire, Davey. I thought it had been taken care of. Anyhow, you're here, and Ronny's in the basement where he belongs. Those guys are like fucking millstones, anyhow. I'd just as soon lock 'em in a trailer and throw away the key. Take my word for it, the less you have to do with them, the better. This is a need-to-know business. They tell you that the first day at The Farm, and you hear it the rest of your fucking Company life. It's like a goddamned mantra. Well, I made them words to live by."

"I need to be in constant touch with Jack Devereaux."

"Who says so? You or Jack?"

"Does it matter?"

Karp shook his head. "Not to me. You want to, you can send a cable every time you take a leak. I wouldn't, if I were you, but . . . besides, Devereaux already has all he needs."

"I'm not so sure about that, Bob."

"What's not to be sure about? Hell, I must have sent him five hundred cables in the last ten months."

"One thousand, eleven hundred and seventeen."

Karp laughed. "You stupid fuck. You actually *counted* them? What the hell for?"

"Not me, but somebody did."

"Well, look. The way I see it, you're here to get on-site feel, the kind of shit they call ambiance in the restaurant business. That's more important than facts. How does it *feel*? That's what I always want to know. Does this guy *feel* right to me? We'll go out into the bush, take a look around. You can take some pictures, talk to some people. It won't change anything, but Jack'll feel better. He can tell everybody his man's been there. Then the Hillbillies'll get the fuck out of the way and we can do our jobs."

"Tell me about Jorge Caulfield."

"What do you want to know?"

Ripley shrugged. "I read your reports. I saw the cables. I don't want you to rehash that. Tell me about the man himself. Do you trust him?"

"Sure. Why shouldn't I?"

"I don't know. Maybe, to use your word, he

doesn't *feel* right to me. There's a lot of hot air in his balloon."

"Look, he's got the best background for us. He's pro-West, and he takes orders. What else could we want?"

"How about somebody who can actually lead the country? Since we're not going to be here forever, that would be a help."

Karp leaned back in his chair. "Come on, David, the man with the most guns has the most power. We give Caulfield enough support, he can do the job."

"For how long?"

"As long as we want him to."

"I thought we were supposed to be looking for someone who can put Mawindi back on its feet after the war. I thought we wanted someone with genuine leadership ability, a man who can put a cabinet together, who can hold the pieces of this country together long enough for the bones to knit."

"You saying Caulfield can't do that?"

"I'm saying I don't think he can. I'm saying he doesn't *feel* right."

"Why?"

"Because he's got a long and checkered past. He was in the middle of the trouble in '65. He had control of one province for about two months and more than three thousand people were executed. He's a fucking vampire, Bob. And I know you know that, because it's all in the record. Why should we sweep that under the carpet?"

"He's not like that now. Sure, a few eggs'll get broken along the way, but how else do you expect to make egg salad? You want to hang on to power, you have to consolidate it. Everybody knows that. Hell, that's a notion goes all the way back to Sun Tzu. For all I know, the first Cro-Magnon cracked a few Neanderthal heads as soon as he crossed the Pyrenees, or wherever the hell else he came from. Because he had to. Otherwise, we'd all have a brow ridge you could put your bowling trophies on and we'd walk like chimpanzees. You get rid of the knuckle draggers. That's progress. That's what Mawindi needs, and that's what we want. Caulfield knows that."

"At what cost?"

"How much are you willing to pay?"

"That's not the question, Bob. How much is Mawindi going to have to pay?"

Karp grinned. "Like they say, Davey, if you have to ask, maybe you can't afford it."

SEVEN

July 7, 1975

The jeep rocked over the rutted road, and Karp kept yelling to make himself heard. "I'm telling you, Ripley, Caulfield is our man. No way I'd trust Nkele, no way in hell. And the other bunch are sitting under a pipe from Moscow with their mouths open like baby robins waiting for worms."

Ripley nodded. He'd already heard the same song and dance half a dozen times in less than twenty-four hours. Me thinks he doth protest too much he thought to himself. "That's what I'm here to see, Bob. They call it a fact finding mission because I'm supposed to find facts."

"Look, you can be as smug as you want, David, but I'm telling you, those assholes in the 40 Committee don't have the foggiest idea of what's going on out here. They like to sit in their ivory tower with the windows closed and the air conditioning on, and make plans for all the rest of us. We're the grunts of this war, plain and simple. God forbid they should get their manicured hands a little dirty."

"Don't you mean bloody?" Ripley hollered back as the jeep sank into mud up to its hubs and the driver gunned the engine until it sounded as if it was ready to throw a rod.

"In our business, blood is the only dirt, David. You know that as well as I do. Nothing else counts."

"I don't think this is as cut and dried as you seem to. Caulfield has a pretty spotty reputation. That uprising in '65 got a lot of people killed. I would think it wouldn't be in our best interest to have that kind of thing repeated."

"You're spooked by Vietnam. You're afraid it's gonna be a re-run."

"Don't say spooked. You'll blow my cover."

"I'm serious, Ripley. You think because we didn't kick Charlie's butt we ought to throw in the towel. But you forget that I was there too, longer than you were. It was hairy as all hell, but we didn't win because we weren't allowed to. We didn't lose it, it was taken away from us. And by the same kind of chicken shit bastards we got pulling punches this time around. Hell's bells, man, Kissinger is still calling the shots."

"I rest my case, Bob. You go preaching pie in the sky to Caulfield, he'll go off half-cocked, thinking that if he gets in trouble we go from covert assistance to advisors, and from advisors to air support and eventually, if he fucks up often enough, ground troops to bail him out. But it's not in the cards."

"Maybe not now. Things change, though."

"Not this time around. I told you the budget. You know how much we can get for fourteen million dollars. Hell, the navy's charging us five hundred thousand dollars for the use of one damn ship, one damn time. It's two hundred grand every time we fly a C-130 into Kinshasa. And half of the stuff on board's for Mobutu. Caulfield claims he's got fifty thousand troops. You know how much it costs to outfit that many men, and I'm talking about minimal levels of equipage?"

"I don't want to talk numbers, David. This is not about numbers, it's about politics."

"The hell it is. Politics is the last thing it's about. You tell me Bandolo is getting weapons from Moscow. Well, Caulfield has gotten arms from China and North Korea. So has Oscar Nkele. Where's the politics there? These guys are all getting weapons anyplace they can. It's about money, because money means guns and the one with the most firepower wins. It couldn't be any simpler than that."

"But it is, Ripley. Trust me on this, it is." Karp turned away in annoyance.

Ripley didn't give a shit. He was tired of arguing, tired of Karp's blinkered wisdom, tired of the self-serving logic that made pretzels out of straight lines. He was determined to see for himself, and that's all there was to it. Karp heard what he wanted to hear. He ignored anything that didn't fit into his simplistic analysis. Karp was like a man with a thousand pieces to a jigsaw puzzle throwing all but twelve into the trash, then hacking the corners off the dozen that remained, just to make them fit.

The itinerary called for a stop at Santo Cruzeiro, a small town that Caulfield claimed to have captured after a fierce battle against the overwhelming forces of the Mawindi Liberation Front. Joshua Bandolo had founded the MLF more than twenty years before. Outside of Africa he was best known, if he was known at all, as a poet. The evidence seemed to indicate that this was one poet who knew how to use the sword as well as the pen.

But Bob Karp had taken Caulfield at his word. He had been impressed and sent a flurry of cables in the three days before Ripley had come to Africa. Each was more extravagant than the last, until it sounded as if Jorge Caulfield had presided over Armageddon and now was the last man alive on the continent.

But there was something about the story that

didn't quite make sense. All other sources of independent intelligence, both satellite and SR-71 overflight reconnaissance, as well as feeds from three NATO intelligence sources, suggested that the MLF had fewer than a third as many men in the area as Caulfield claimed to have engaged.

Some of the Blackbird snapshots, close-ups of Santo Cruzeiro that clearly resolved things as small as one meter across, taken during what Caulfield claimed was the height of the four day pitched battle, showed no armor at all in action, while the PAM leader claimed to have turned back a combined tank and APC assault of nearly forty armored vehicles.

It didn't jibe, and Ripley wanted to know why. He hadn't told Karp about the photos because he was starting to suspect that Karp was too committed. He wasn't sure, but he wouldn't be surprised. That was usually the way it happened. You got in bed with someone, and rather than see the wrinkles and the warts, you turned out the lights. It was a hell of a lot easier, and nine times out of ten, nobody bothered to turn them back on, ever.

But Ripley wasn't going to stand by and let something like that happen again. Not if he could help it. That meant not only seeing warts and wrinkles, but taking a magnifying glass to them. Fourteen million dollars wasn't much money in the grand scheme of things, but he'd be damned if he was going to piss it away on a pipe dream.

Karp seemed determined not to speak to him

again, and kept his head turned toward the forest as they rocked and rolled through the endless chain of puddles and mud wallows that passed for a road. Salazar was already well behind them, and ahead was supposed to be territory firmly in Caulfield's control. It was also supposed to be one of his main staging areas, where a significant portion of his fifty thousand soldiers were located.

So far, the only sign of Caulfield's Pan-African Movement was the trio of jeeps dead ahead, each emblazoned with a bumper sticker featuring Caulfield's sunglassed visage. That didn't necessarily mean anything, but intelligence was the art of seeing what wasn't there every bit as clearly as what was, especially when you held purse strings in your hands.

The lead jeep slowed a bit as it crossed a particularly deep wallow, more like a pond, and sent waves of muddy water off into the bush on either side. One by one the jeeps dipped and torqued their way through the muck, the water sloshing onto the running boards, the tires sucking like pneumonia-stricken lungs as they pulled free and spun onto firmer ground.

The heat was terrible, the bugs even worse. Ripley opened a flask of insect repellant, smeared his neck and face, and the exposed portions of his arms. He felt slimy as he tucked the flask away, and noticed how his skin glistened under the oily lotion. It did no good, and he hadn't really expected that it would, but he had long since learned that you use whatever is in your arsenal.

Taking advantage of a lull in the whine and throb of the jeep engines, he leaned toward Karp. "How far to Santo Cruzeiro?" he asked.

Karp held up a hand, his thumb folded across the palm and waggled four fingers.

"Klicks or miles?" Ripley asked.

"Miles." Karp fell silent and turned away.

Ripley examined the bush on either side. It was typical rainforest, the trees towering a hundred feet and more. He couldn't see more than ten or fifteen feet into the undergrowth on either side, and realized that ambushes here would be as easy and, more than likely as common, as in Southeast Asia. But there were so many other things to worry about, he just tagged that one onto the bottom of the mental list.

Further southeast was the region the geographers called the Transition Zone, a belt of steep escarpments where the high plateau of the eastern part of Mawindi abruptly stepped down to the coastal flats. The forest was flush up against sheer rock faces, striped with cascades where the eastern rivers flowed over the rim and fell hundreds of feet to the coastal plain on their way to the Atlantic. Beyond the Transition Zone was a region of grasslands, an extension of the South African veldt, that swept away toward the Cape.

The road started to widen out, and Ripley knew that Santo Cruzeiro was just ahead. The jeeps seemed to hesitate as if the drivers were uncertain whether to proceed or not. Karp stood up and shouted to the lead driver, and the man looked back at him from under the brim of his fatigue cap and waved vaguely, whether to signify that he understood what Karp wanted or to tell him to mind his own business wasn't readily apparent. The jeeps continued to crawl.

Ripley was getting impatient. He wanted to see evidence that Caulfield was what Karp claimed he was. When the bush thinned on either side of the road, revealing a few fields marked out where slash and burn agriculture had been practiced, he stopped worrying about an ambush and started to make mental notes. He fingered the camera slung around his neck, removing the lens cover and pocketing it, then advancing the film. He wanted to be ready to shoot anything that caught his eye.

He could see a few buildings now, mostly cinder block, with metal roofs. The windows stared vacantly, most missing their glass. But it looked more like a ghost town than the scene of fierce combat. The jeeps rolled into a clearing and straggled to a halt one by one. Ripley jumped down, loosening the flap on the holster holding the Browning 9mm automatic on his hip.

The PAM soldiers unlimbered their automatic rifles, mostly AK-47's provided from Agency stores in South Carolina. The CIA had been stockpiling weapons from all over the world, some captured, some obtained on the open market, all supposed to be untraceable, or at least to be free of Agency taint so they could be denied.

Ripley walked toward the nearest of the buildings, looking for some signs of combat. There was a single jeep, upturned, its hulk burned out, and the bare metal already beginning to rust from the high humidity, but there was no way to tell whether it had been destroyed by weapons or simply turned on its side and set afire.

Some of the buildings had bullet pock marks in the cinder block, the dull gray of the blocks showing through where the whitewash had been blasted away. But the bullet marks were few, and hardly evidence of a four-day firefight.

One by one, Ripley entered the buildings through yawning doors and poked around in the gloomy interiors. Santo Cruzeiro, if Karp's cables were to be believed, had been a stronghold of the MLF until Caulfield's assault dislodged them. Ripley wanted evidence, not words, and so far there was none. Concentrating at first on the pock-marked structures, he used a flashlight, looking for anything, a mound of shell casings, abandoned foodstuffs, even a body, anything at all that would prove the place had been defended.

There was nothing.

Outside, sheets of paper were everywhere, littered like snow, the pages all soggy, smeared with mud and pinned to the damp ground or sun-dried and curling, rolling over in the hot wind.

Karp stood in the center of the abandoned village, arms folded across his chest. Ripley walked toward him, debating whether or not to voice his suspicions.

Karp gave Ripley a broad smile. "Told you they tore hell out of this place, didn't I?" he said. "Get any pictures? Washington loves pictures. The more the merrier."

"Looks more like everybody packed up and moved away," Ripley said.

"What's that supposed to mean?"

"It means it doesn't look like there was much of a fight here."

"You see any of Bandolo's men around, Ripley?"

Ripley shook his head. "No. But I don't see any proof they were ever here, either."

"What the hell do you want? You want videotape of the battle, is that it? You want signed affidavits from the dead men, telling you where they died and who killed them?"

"I don't see any evidence that anyone died here. Look at the buildings, Bob. A few bullet holes. No signs of mortars or rockets. No sign of heavy machine gun fire. No shell casings, no holes in the ground from grenades. No blood, no bodies. No ruined vehicles. Where the hell is the wreckage? That's what I don't see—junk. Damn it, Bob, war is the business of making junk out of the other guy's stuff. But there isn't anything like that here. Nothing at all."

Ripley turned his back and gazed around the

deserted village once more, shielding his eyes from the sun with one visoring palm.

Santo Cruzeiro was more like a movie set than anything else. The buildings looked lonely, not devastated. There wasn't even much glass on the ground, nowhere near enough to account for the empty panes. Unless Jorge Caulfield was as much a janitor as he was a military man, there should have been something more than open doors and blindly staring window frames to demonstrate that he had been there.

Ripley was starting to feel uneasy. He walked off into the bush, thinking he might find what he was looking for among the trees. There should be the heavy shell casings of mortar rounds, piles of empty machine-gun shells. In four days, men had to eat. Where was the evidence of food—ration cans, paper wrappers, plastic and cellophane?

What the fuck was going on?

EIGHT

❖

July 8, 1975

Salazar looked like most African capitals. A mix of anonymous modern buildings and ancient architecture, almost a history of structural fashion as it unfolded in the homeland of the colonial powers. The main hotel, the Salazar Continental, once home away from home for vacationing Portuguese elite, now looked forlorn. Since the coup, tourism had virtually stopped. An occasional businessman, sent out from the home office with orders to save what he could and sell what he couldn't, made it a temporary headquarters.

Dignitaries from those countries with Mawindian axes to grind set up shop for two or three weeks, then vanished into the diplomatic smoke that seemed to enwreathe the capital more and more as independence approached. There were spies and fast buck artists, arms merchants and con men, importers and smugglers, but their numbers were small and their business conducted in haste and in the dead of night.

David Ripley checked in with mud still on his boots, but the clerk was used to such breaches of decorum and didn't so much as raise an eyebrow.

"Will you be staying long?" he asked, a pro forma question to which he already knew the answer.

Ripley did nothing to frustrate expectation. "Two or three days," he said. He waited for the bellman to take his bags, then followed him to the elevator. His room was on the seventh floor and after tipping the bellman, he walked to the window and jerked the chain to open the drapes wide. The room smelled vaguely of lemons, and the cool air wafting from the air conditioner was more than welcome.

He looked out over the city, its few tall spires glistening in the late afternoon sun like sword blades fresh from the armorer's forge. They jutted up out of a welter of one and two story buildings that more often than not smacked of Iberia, their cloistered gardens surrounded by tile-topped walls. Beyond the city's center he could see the rows of shanties, separated by narrow alleys where he imagined the stench of sewage and the fetid stink of rotting vegetation mixed in a heady brew.

Further away, he could see the stacks of ocean-going freighters, their masts rust red and gray fingers clawing at the cloudless sky. Plumes of black smoke drifted on the seabreeze, flattening into sheets that frayed then tore into rags as they headed inland.

Free of Karp for the rest of the day, Ripley felt as if a straightjacket had been removed. Staying with Karp the last two nights had been tense. Ripley felt as if he were attending a play he didn't like and wasn't allowed to leave. It seemed almost as if everything he'd seen was being staged for him, as if he were a customer and Karp were desperate for a sale. The more he saw, the more confused he was, and the more convinced he became that there was much more to the murky politics of Mawindi than anyone in Langley could have dreamed. Already he'd been forced to extend his stay by a couple of days, and maybe even longer.

The apparent deception at Santo Cruzeiro was something he couldn't ignore. He couldn't believe that Karp would have stood there pointing to the deserted village with such pride, as if he were pointing out El Alamein or Thermopylae. It had been Karp's manner, a certain glee, almost as if he were a social director, orchestrating an affair for Ripley's benefit. Karp had intended to make a point, Ripley thought, but if one had been made, he didn't have a clue what in the hell it was.

Walking away from the window, he laid down on the bed and propped his head on folded arms. He watched the sky for a while, noticing the streaks on the windows, and an occasional bird soaring on the air currents out over the harbor. He wanted a drink, but was afraid that he wanted it a little too much, and was determined to decompress a bit before wandering down to the hotel bar.

The following day he would get to meet Jorge Caulfield himself, and he wanted to be clearheaded. He couldn't afford to buy snake oil this time around. The Agency already had more than it could use in its apparently bottomless reservoir, and Caulfield, he was sure, would try to sell him a bit more.

He got up and snatched his briefcase from the table near the window, let it slap his thigh as he tugged it from the table, and carried it back to the bed. Lying down again, he turned on one hip, opened the case and grabbed a fistful of papers. It wasn't going to be stimulating reading, but he wanted to know exactly how PAM had been painted for Langley before he met its master in the morning.

He started on the first white paper, and the more he read, the less he recognized. Someone, whether Karp, Caulfield himself, or some anonymous drone buried in the depths of the bureaucracy, had created out of whole cloth a Mawindi he could not believe existed anywhere but on the papers in front of him.

Paper after paper, photocopies of the underlying cables neatly clipped to the cover sheets, droned on, extolling the virtues of Caulfield the man, making him sound more like a saint than a politician, and reaching almost epic hyperbole when describing the military accomplishments of the Pan-African Movement. If Ripley didn't know better, he'd think he was on the eve of meeting Alexander the Great or Napoleon.

It was nearly eight when he felt his eyes beginning to sting from the forced reading. He pushed the mass of papers away, jerked a pad out of the bottom of the briefcase, and quickly filled its first three pages with notes from memory. When he was finished, he had a shopping list—conundrums, questions, puzzles and mysteries—all of which demanded answers before he could begin to tell Langley what was needed.

He took a quick shower, pausing in front of the foggy mirror to stare into his own face with a detachment more appropriate to someone scrutinizing a suspect stranger. His blue eyes were red rimmed, his cheeks and chin grizzled with brownish blond whiskers. Rubbing briskly with the stiff towel, he scraped his skin red, and shook his head. "Who in the hell am I?" he whispered. "Why am I here?"

His body was still sound, still muscular, the veins still prominent on his forearms, a legacy of

Vietnam and all the heavy lifting that had gone into nearly two years of fire-base duty with the Montagnards in the north. He felt strong, maybe stronger than he'd ever felt. But Ripley doubted his own assessment, suspecting that maybe he was kidding himself, trying to cover the uneasiness that kept whispering into his ear every time he turned out the lights.

He thought about shaving, then realized there was no one in Mawindi he wanted to impress. It made no difference what he looked like. He was just going to go down to the hotel restaurant and have a bite to eat. Throwing on some jeans and a short-sleeved white shirt, he slipped his feet into a pair of battered loafers, made sure he had his wallet and keys, then moved out into the hall, looking around the room once before pulling the door closed.

The hall smelled of moth balls, as if the carpet had been stored away in an attic somewhere. At the elevator, he waited impatiently, patting his shirt pocket to make sure he had cigarettes and a lighter.

When the elevator car arrived, he stepped inside, jabbing the button for the first floor impatiently, anxious to get away from the sweet smell of paradichlorobenzene. When he reached the lobby, he checked the directory, chose the less expensive of the two in-house restaurants, and walked to the entrance. The maitre d' scowled at his casual dress, but since he was hardly in a position to turn away patrons, he turned Ripley over to an eager waiter, who waved a grand hand, asking him to choose his table.

Ripley noticed that there would be entertainment. A small bandstand stacked with Fender amps, their standby lights already glowing in the dim light, occupied one corner of the large room. A pair of Gibson guitars, one Les Paul and one ES-335, Ludwig drum kit, a Fender bass and a Fender-Rhodes electric piano appeared to be the only instruments. Turning to the waiter, he asked, "No accordion, right?"

"Senhor?"

"The band . . . nobody plays the accordion in the band, right?"

"Oh, si, si. No accordion."

"Fine, I'll take a table up close, then."

"They are good musicians, Senhor, Americans like you."

He took a seat, ordered a Coke, then scanned the menu. He didn't want much, but the room was not exactly a burger joint, so he opted for broiled fish. As he closed the menu, he looked up to see the waiter coming back with his drink and a striking young woman following behind him.

The waiter handed him the Coke and asked if he were ready to order, but the woman, who had planted herself directly across the table, said, "Not yet, Senhor."

"Very good," he said. "Will you be wanting another menu?"

"No, thank you, I'll just use Mister Ripley's." She flashed him a brilliant smile, then turned its high voltage on Ripley. "That is, if you don't mind, Mister Ripley?"

Ripley shook his head. "No, I don't mind. Especially if you're buying."

"Not hardly. Actually, I was hoping to hit you up for a free meal."

Ripley studied her for several moments. She was tall, maybe five eight. The light overhead gave her honey-colored hair a luster that looked almost natural. "How do you know who I am?" he asked.

She batted her eyelids in mock seduction, at least Ripley assumed it was mock, and caught the gleam in her green eyes. "Bob Karp told me you'd be staying here. He told me you were CIA. He told me what you look like and . . ."

Ripley shook his head in disgust. "Jesus Christ, did he tell you my shoe size, too?"

"Eleven-D? That's just a guess, though. And he didn't tell me you were so good-looking. Or that you didn't know how to shave."

Ripley laughed in spite of himself. "It's a pity he didn't tell me who *you* are."

"Jesus, I'm sorry." She stuck a hand across the table, and Ripley grasped it. "Michelle Harkness." Her full lips parted, the glossy lipstick speckled with gold where the moisture reflected the house lights.

Ripley tilted his head back. "That explains it."

"Explains what?"

"The book. I was wondering how you managed to get access to so much information."

"Luca Brazzi sleeps with the fishes, Mister Ripley. I don't, if that's what you're hinting. I work hard, the way my grandfather taught me." She looked at him then as if taking his measure. After a long silence, she said, "Well?"

"Well what?"

"What every writer wants to know, Mister Ripley. The book, what did you think of it?"

"Very well done. I learned quite a bit. You seem to have access to most of the principals."

She nodded. "Most of them."

"Let me guess. Not Caulfield, right?"

"Was it that obvious?" And when Ripley shook his head, she asked, "Then how did you know?"

"Just a hunch. Tell me about Nkele. He's the big mystery to me."

"Not Caulfield?"

"No, not yet. He's penny candy. A dime a dozen."

"Do I get that meal?"

Ripley nodded. "Hell, uncle's buying. But then you already know that."

"What do you want to know?"

"Everything there is to know."

"We'd better order, then," she said. "I'll have whatever you're having."

Ripley caught the waiter's eye. After ordering the meal, he looked at Michelle. "Wine?"

She shook her head. "Not on the job."

The waiter went away, and Michelle cleared her throat. "Everything, you said?"

"Everything."

"Here goes . . . You stop me if anything needs clarification."

She was still talking when the busboy came to clear away the meal. The band was on stage, and the whine of guitar strings being tuned made it difficult to talk any longer.

"There's a lot more," she said, leaning forward and shouting to be heard over a couple of power chords. One of the two guitarists launched into a couple of Hendrix runs, and the scream of feedback was deafening.

"You know anyplace we can go?"

"That a variation on 'My place or yours?' Mister Ripley?"

"I'm not that crude, Miss Harkness."

"Maybe I am . . ." Her smile was dazzling.

He nodded, considering the lush figure under her blue workshirt and jeans, and tried to imagine the contours with something that was half geometry and half lust.

"Are you . . . ?"

The smile grew even broader. "You bet your ass."

NINE

❖

July 9, 1975

Ripley hadn't gotten much sleep. Michelle lay beside him, a sheet pulled up to her waist, her arms all but buried in the masses of hair that flowed like butterscotch over her sun-bronzed skin. Sometime during the night, Ripley wasn't quite sure when and less sure why, they had decided that Michelle would give up her room at the Salazar Hilton and move in with him. He remembered only that it had seemed like a good idea at the time. He was far less sanguine about it now, but he didn't want to wake her, and sure as hell couldn't leave a note telling her not to bother.

He dressed quickly. Karp was supposed to meet him out in front of the hotel at seven A.M. It was already five minutes past, and he felt just a little like a truant as he hurried to the elevator. Once in the lobby, he spotted Karp immediately, pacing back and forth near the revolving door to the street.

"It's about time, dammit!" The COS was not exactly renowned for his patience. It was easy to see why.

Hitting an opening in the door like a fullback slanting off tackle, Karp bulled his way out into the street. The same jeep, its running boards and fenders still caked with mud, sat at the curb, Amos Cordeiro at the wheel.

Karp vaulted into the front seat and turned as Ripley made it outside. "Come on, David, move your ass, will you?"

Ripley held up a hand, trying to placate the angry man. "Hang on a second, Bob. Let's not get off on the wrong foot. It's too early. I'm only half awake."

"You can sleep when you get back. I don't want to keep Caulfield waiting. We've got a reputation to maintain. How the hell is he supposed to trust us if we can't keep our appointments?"

"For Christ's sake, Bob. Five minutes? If he's that volatile, then maybe he's not the man for us in the first place. The last thing we need is a prima donna."

"Don't you tell me what we need, damn you." Karp was nearly frothing at the mouth, and the vehemence took Ripley aback.

"Bob, that's why I'm here, remember, to see what we need? To see what's what and who's who? Or didn't you read the cable?"

Ripley climbed over the right quarter-panel and was hurled into the seat as Cordeiro popped the clutch hard enough to lay a patch in the street.

Turning to rest one arm on the back of his seat, Karp shouted over the roaring of the engine and the rush of air over the windscreen. "It's an hour to the goddamned airport, and another hour by chopper to our destination. We're already behind schedule, thanks to you. Christ almighty, David, I—"

"Don't you lecture me, dammit. Not you, of all people. What the hell do you mean by telling Michelle Harkness who I am, and what I do, for crying out loud?"

"Don't get your balls in an uproar. Hell, I didn't tell her anything she couldn't find out in fifteen minutes, if she really put her mind to it. Christ, how many white men are coming into Salazar these days? And if they're not Portuguese, what the hell else could they be? Shit, just last week there were three frogs from S-deck here. The week before that, there were two krauts. How long do you think it took anybody who cared to figure out they were from BND? There ain't no secrets in Salazar, Davey. *None.* Besides, I figured you needed to get your ashes hauled. How was she?"

"None of your fucking business."

Karp smiled. "It's your fucking business we're talking about. Not mine."

"So what are you saying? Did you pay her? Is that what you're trying to tell me?"

"Did she get any information out of you?"

"No."

"Too bad. Then I guess I'll *have* to pay her. Unless you're a whole lot better in bed than I hear you are."

Ripley turned away to watch the city fall off to the rear. He was in no mood to trade insults with the COS. And since he couldn't get away with shooting him, he'd just have to bite his tongue.

From a distance, Salazar didn't look quite as desolate. The taller, more modern buildings were the only ones visible now as they headed along the shore road, and without the shanties to temper the impression, the capital didn't look half bad. The shoreline off to the right was a two-hundred yard wide strip of magnificent white sand and a whiter line of pounding surf, the waves foaming and churning as they rushed toward the beach. To the left, forest marched off into the mists swirling down off the escarpments of the Transition Zone.

Ripley noticed more than a few similarities to the northern coast of Vietnam, where the South China Sea spent itself against the picturesque beaches above Da Nang and Cam Ranh Bay. A snapshot on a vacationland billboard wouldn't have seemed out of place. But somehow the notion of a slogan, "Surf Mawindi" or "Mawindi, Africa's Piece of Heaven" didn't seem credible.

Five more minutes, and the road began to peter out. The Avenida Antonio Salazar changed abruptly from four lanes of faultless asphalt to two of potholed concrete, then to gravel within the space of a quarter-mile. The rattle of the gravel against the fenders of the jeep was mind-numbing in its intensity, since Cordeiro hadn't seemed to notice the deterioration of the surface.

Looking out over the ocean, Ripley noticed a small jet, probably a Lear, running parallel to the shore, heading away from him. He pointed to the plane, and Karp followed the extended finger, glanced at the plane, but said nothing.

Ripley nodded, chewing on his lower lip. All right, he thought, if that's how you want it.

It took another fifteen minutes before the road changed to dirt, and now even the hell-driving Cordeiro knew he was beaten. He downshifted the jeep, tapped the brakes three or four times, and let second gear do the work. The whining of the transmission was like the snarl of a hungry leopard. The jeep lurched over the bumpy road, hurling all three men about in their seats, and Ripley was forced to grab the seat back to keep from losing his balance altogether.

Cordeiro turned around to grin at him, gunned the engine a bit, braked, then gunned it again, making the jeep lurch ahead in fits and starts.

"Knock it off, Amos," Karp barked.

Cordeiro gave him a flash of impossibly white teeth, but did as he was told. Glancing at Karp for a second, he shouted to Ripley, "No Disneyland in Mawindi, so this is what we do for amusement."

Karp, however, was not amused.

The road veered to the left now, and they were heading inland. The forest was dense on both sides of the road. Branches rattled against the sides of the jeep, tattooed the windshield and slapped at its passengers with increasing vehemence. It seemed to Ripley that leafy arms were reaching out into the road, trying to pluck him from the back seat.

The clearing seemed to explode, so suddenly did it appear in front of them. A broad swath had been cut in a long narrow field of grass, surrounded on all four sides by tall trees. Ripley didn't need to see the helicopter sitting in the middle of the open field to realize they had reached the first stop. Cordeiro pulled the jeep all the way across the field and parked it under a camouflage net laced with severed branches. Two more jeeps and a light plane sat cheek by jowl, flush against the trunks of trees from which the lower limbs had been lopped.

As Cordeiro killed his engine, Ripley heard the sputtering cough of the Huey, and before he could step out of the jeep, the big Lycoming turboshaft engine had sprung fully to life. Karp was already running toward the chopper. He looked back, waving one arm furiously. His lips moved, but the roar of the chopper drowned out his words.

Karp disappeared into the open door, using a pintle supporting an M-60 mini-gun, and Ripley froze. It was all too familiar to him. The sound of the chopper. The mini-gun. The forest on all sides. He looked at the solid green wall, half expecting to see the figures of Viet Cong darting among the leaves like fish in dark waters. Karp was hanging out of the Huey, still swirling his right arm, urging Ripley to hurry. He glanced at his wrist, then shouted so loudly Ripley could almost make out the words.

Reluctantly, Ripley started moving again, sprinted the last few yards to the Huey and hauled himself aboard. Before he had even reached the bench seat against the chopper wall, the Huey lifted off, tilting its nose down, then slipping sidewise as it climbed. Through the still open door, Ripley could see the ground falling away, and for a moment thought he was going to be sick. This wasn't how it was supposed to be, he thought. Not again. Not this time!

Karp was sitting across from him, and Ripley got to his feet to change seats. Sitting next to the COS he leaned close and shouted, "Where are we going?"

"Porto Grande. It's a way down the coast."

"I thought we were supposed to meet Jorge Caulfield this morning."

"We are. He's already there. And we're still late."

Not quite certain what Karp was worried about, he nodded. For a split second, he framed an apology but bit down on his tongue and swallowed the half-formed words.

They were out over the water now, and Ripley watched the undulating gray of the Atlantic. Little curls of white snapped like whip-ends a thousand feet below, and he imagined that he could almost hear the dull slap of water on water as waves rose and fell, collapsing in on themselves and dying before they were fully formed.

The flight lasted more than an hour, and Karp kept looking at his watch like a man late for his own wedding. His body English was so pronounced as he bobbed back and forth like a davening Chasid, it seemed to drive the chopper forward without the need of the Lycoming.

The pilot banked suddenly, and Ripley grabbed onto a length of cargo netting nailed against the wooden sheathing to keep his seat. Leaning toward the door, he could see a small village, its bleached buildings running in a narrow strip along the beach. Several jeeps were visible, and he could see several dozen men arranged in rank and file along the sand, just out of reach of the waves. The sand beneath them was smooth and beige where the receding tide had troweled it into a trackless plane. The gouges made by the men's shoes led back toward the nearest row of buildings.

The pilot dropped the Huey almost straight down now. The men on the sand all stared up, their faces indistinguishable blurs from five hundred feet in the air. As the chopper slowed in its descent, dropping closer and closer, eyes and noses appeared, shadows filled the hollows and individual features began to define themselves. It was like watching half a hundred Adams simultaneously taking shape out of formless clay. Now Ripley could see the sand whipped into a stinging blast back up the beach where it was dry.

As the chopper touched down, Ripley saw a tight knot of men pass between the two nearest buildings. They were milling around, and it was obvious that they were dragging something out onto the sand. Behind the boiling mass, two men, both wearing uniforms and officer's caps, strutted with their hands behind their backs.

Ripley jumped down to the sand, and Karp landed right beside him. Turning to the COS, Ripley asked, "What the hell is going on?"

"Wait."

The knot of soldiers began to break apart, and Ripley saw that they had in fact been dragging a heavy burden. Four men, their hands tied, and their legs roped at the ankles, scraped through the sand, each towed by the arms by a pair of men. Skirting the men arranged in ranks, the new arrivals dragged their captives to the water's edge, set them on their feet and backed away. One of the captives, unable to keep his balance, buckled at the knees and swayed there, kneeling on the beach. A wave rushed toward the four prisoners, foamed and hissed as it broke a few feet behind them, then swept past, their ankles sending curls of water shooting up their calves.

The two men in officer's garb, both sporting mirrored sunglasses, split apart, one walking to the left end of the front rank, the other taking an identical position on the right. The taller of the two barked a sharp command in Portuguese. *"Prontidao!"*

The front rank dropped to one knee, shouldering rifles at the same time. The men in the rear rank shouldered their own weapons.

"What the hell is going on?" Ripley asked a second time. "A firing squad? What . . . ?"

Grabbing Karp by the shoulder, Ripley dragged him a couple of steps toward the four captives. He jabbed a finger in their direction. "Who are those men?"

"MLF," Karp said. He laughed, a raucous bark like that of a sea lion.

"But . . ."

"Apontar!" Another command echoed across the sand. Ripley turned toward the firing squad then back to the four prisoners. The captives stared at him, their faces blank. One was bleeding heavily from a long gash that had laid one cheek open. The bright red oozing from the gash caught the morning sunlight, and it looked for a moment as if he had been daubed with liquid silver. The other three sported a collection of knots and bruises on their faces. Their eyes were almost swollen shut, lips bulged grotesquely, as if the mouths of fat men had been carelessly grafted to their faces. Their clothes were dirty and blood-stained, and damp patches of urine darkened the khaki of their trousers.

"Why aren't you doing something to stop this, Karp?"

"It's not my business, David. Nor yours."

"Then why are we here?"

"Quiet!" He pointed toward the officer on the far side of the firing squad. At the same instant, the officer barked again.

"Fogo!"

The sudden thunder of automatic weapons exploded. Ripley glanced toward the captives again, but they were no longer standing. The rifles continued to chatter, and gouts of sand geysered up all around the four bodies. Pools of blood glistened on the damp beach. Another wave foamed up the sand and swirled around the bodies as the last of the firing died away.

The officer barked once more, and the kneeling men got to their feet. He said something to the second officer who issued a sharp command. The men turned, and marched off. The two officers swaggered across the beach, the taller of them rubbing one leathery cheek with delicate fingers.

"Senhor Karp," he said, a broad smile creasing his face.

Ripley looked at Karp, who said, "David, meet the Commandante. Jorge Caulfield."

Ripley felt his jaw go slack.

TEN

❖

Caulfield smiled. Or at least Ripley thought he did. Under the shiny lenses, Caulfield's cheeks seemed to bunch for a moment, and teeth suddenly appeared as if a zipper had been soundlessly opened.

"Mister Ripley," he said. He glanced at Karp, and the gash on his chin zipped closed again. "I've been looking forward to meeting you. We have much to talk about."

"You bet your ass we do," Ripley snapped. "What the hell just happened here?" It was all he could do to keep himself from going after the smug little bastard.

Caulfield shrugged. "One of the unfortunate necessities of war."

"Is that right?"

Caulfield shook his head. "Sometimes one has to do things that he is not proud of. It is a question of priorities, you see. And I know what my priorities are."

"Do they include cold-blooded murder?"

"Political crimes require political punishment. Those men were enemies of Mawindi and its people. It is unfortunate, but they made their choice. And now they pay the price." He looked past Ripley's shoulder, and Ripley turned to see two men taking one of the victims by the arms and legs. They dragged him toward the waves, waded in up to their knees then, laughing like fraternity pranksters, swung the lifeless body back and forth to pick up momentum while a wave rushed toward them. The wave broke, soaking them to the waist, hissed on up the beach and as it began to recede the two men swung their burden once more toward the ocean, this time letting go.

The body landed with the resonant splash of a cannonball in a swimming pool and sank out of sight for a moment. Floating face down, arms spread, waving like kelp in the surging water, the body surfaced, drifted a few yards, then rose as another breaker bulled its way up the beach.

The two soldiers highstepped through the water and onto the sand, where they bent to retrieve their next victim.

"The sharks will take care of the mess," Caulfield said.

"You mean the evidence, don't you?" Ripley snapped.

"Evidence? That suggests that a crime has been committed. This was no crime." Caulfield waved a hand over the beach as if he were a real estate salesman commending its merits to a prospective purchaser. "The crime was theirs, Mister Ripley. I thought you would understand that. Mister Karp told me you were sympathetic to our cause."

"I don't care what Mister Karp told you. I'm here to see things for myself."

"So you are," Caulfield said, glaring at Karp. "And so you have."

"Look, let's go inside, out of the sun," Karp interjected. "I'm starting to sweat out here."

"Don't want to get perspiration stains on your underarms, do you, Bob?" Ripley said.

"David, give it a rest. Quit acting like a schoolboy. You know what's going on here. Why don't you stop pretending this can be neat and clean. It can't be. It never has been, and nobody knows that better than you do."

"Shut up, Bob," Ripley snapped.

Caulfield nodded his head. "Mister Karp is right. We should go someplace where we can be comfortable. Cool heads are necessary. There is a lot to talk about. I'm sure you have some questions. And I have some of my own."

Without waiting for an answer, he turned and

started up the beach. For a moment, Ripley thought about walking back to the helicopter and telling the pilot to get him out of there, but the pilot was Karp's man, not his, and it wouldn't do to make a fool of himself in front of the man he was supposed to control.

Karp stood there with his hands on his hips, scowling at Ripley. "Don't fuck this up, David. I'm warning you, now, don't fuck this up."

Ripley brushed past him like an angry commuter at rush hour, not really caring whether he made contact and secretly hoping Karp would start something. But the COS backed away from him, then fell in behind as Ripley stalked up the beach. Caulfield was already between two of the buildings. As he drew closer, Ripley could see how dilapidated the structures were, their shingles cracked and in a few places revealing the tarpaper beneath them. They had been painted over, but the white paint was peeling away in long strips that looked like snakeskin, almost transparent, and showing the grain of the wood in their wispy curls.

Caulfield turned left and disappeared, so Ripley sprinted after him. The Commandante was just ducking into a doorway when Ripley turned the corner. He followed Caulfield inside. The gloom was thick, and it took a moment for Ripley's eyes to adjust after the glare of sun on white sand.

Karp entered and Caulfield nodded to him. Taking a seat on a canvas-backed chair, the

Commandante pointed to a pair of identical chairs and said, "Gentlemen, please sit down."

Ripley waited for Karp to take a seat, then dropped into the chair beside him. Caulfield leaned forward. A bare bulb dangling overhead provided the only illumination. It sparkled dully on the lenses of the sunglasses. The wall behind Caulfield was sprinkled with pin-pricks of white sunlight where the shingles had fallen away outside.

The Commandante was thin, and his arms looked like sticks in short sleeves, but they were thickly corded with tendons and prominent veins wriggled like snakes as the muscles flexed beneath them. His skin was a soft brown, and Ripley guessed he was probably a mestico, with a Portuguese limb or two somewhere on his family tree. His tongue flicked at his lips, then he tucked the lower lip under the upper and started to rock in his chair. "So, Mister Ripley," he said, "we have upset you this morning, have we?"

"You could say that."

"I understand from Mister Karp that you are no stranger to the uglier obligations of command. I am sorry if you are upset, but I would have thought that your experience in Asia would have inured you to violence, necessary or otherwise."

"You thought wrong, Mister Caulfield."

"Perhaps I can change your mind. Perhaps, when you have a chance to . . . how shall I say it? . . . educate yourself on the grim realities of Mawindi at this perilous time in her history, you will be a little more understanding."

"What did those men do? Why was it necessary to . . ."

"They were Joshua Bandolo's men, MLF soldiers, traitors who sold their souls. In a word—communists. There is no room for such men in Mawindi."

"That's it? They picked the wrong team, and you blow them away?"

"What should I have done? Should I have taken them into my home, adopted them, fed them from my own table?"

"You know damn well that's not what I'm suggesting. But you have to realize that cold-blooded execution won't win you any friends, Mister Caulfield. And a man in your situation is nothing without friends."

"Mister Karp is my friend. I hope that you, too, will be a friend in time, after you learn the terrible problems I have to confront."

"You have friends in Peking, too, don't you, Mister Caulfield?"

"Perhaps."

"And does that make you, too, a communist? Or don't the rules apply to you?"

"The first thing you have to learn about Mawindi, Mister Ripley, is that there are no rules. None."

"Then by what logic do you execute four men on that beach out there? If there are no rules, they broke none. If they broke no rules, they don't deserve to die."

"But they are already dead, Mister Ripley. That is not a rule, but it *is* a fact. I don't want to spar with you, though. I want you to ask me the questions you have come so far to ask. I will answer them to the best of my ability. Then, you will make up your mind whether you are with me or not. Does that seem fair? Am I too brusque?"

Ripley nodded. "All right, tell me this. You claim there was a four day pitched battle in Santo Cruzeiro, involving MLF troops backed by tanks and APC's. Is that correct?"

"It is."

"You also claim that your people defeated the MLF, inflicting heavy losses, including on the armored vehicles..."

"Yes."

"You are now in control of Santo Cruzeiro?"

"Yes."

"Then why is there no evidence of that battle? Where is the damage to the town? You don't take out modern armor with peashooters, Mister Caulfield. And if you take it out, it lays there in the weeds, turning to rusty junk. Yet there was no sign of armor, damaged or otherwise, in Santo Cruzeiro. There were no tread tracks in the mud. There were no heavy weapons shell casings. There were no dead bodies. There was no blood. In short, there was nothing to indicate that anything like the battle you described to Mister Karp ever took place. Why is that?"

"It took place, Mister Ripley."

"Prove it."

"You will have to take my word. Or that of Mister Karp."

"But Mister Karp wasn't there."

Caulfield shook his head. "Oh, but he was."

Ripley snapped his head around.

Karp was nodding. "That's right, David."

"You're lying, both of you."

"Wait just a goddamn minute, Ripley. You can't . . ." Karp spluttered.

Raising a hand to interrupt, Caulfield smiled. "Why do you say that, Mister Ripley?"

For a fleeting moment, Ripley thought about telling him about the Blackbird photos, but decided against it. That would be his hole card. Instead, he smiled back. "I already told you. There was no sign. How could there have been a battle like the one you describe without damage?"

Caulfield tilted his head to one side. "Metal is a scarce commodity in a backward country like Mawindi, Mister Ripley. Perhaps the people gathered the shell casings. Perhaps it rained and washed away the tracks you didn't see. I say didn't see, because surely they were there. The tanks were there. The APC's were there. So the tracks were there. But if it rained . . ." He shrugged, his smile broadening.

"Are you trying to tell me that people took apart a few Russian tanks and carried them off for scrap metal?"

"No, not at all. I'm just telling you that just because

you didn't see ephemeral signs of the battle doesn't mean there was no battle. Only that the signs are no longer there. There must have been bullet holes in some of the buildings. Did you see any?"

"A few."

"There you are. Even the most ingenious person has no use for bullet holes. That's why they were left behind."

"What about all the troops you're supposed to have, Mister Caulfield?"

"What about them?"

"Where are they? Santo Cruzeiro was deserted. If you control it, where are your men? I'm told you have more than fifty thousand troops in the Pan-African Movement. Where the fuck are they?"

Caulfield pointed to the door. Getting to his feet, he said, "Come. You want to see soldiers? I will show you soldiers."

As Ripley was getting to his feet, a figure appeared in the doorway. Despite the fact that it was little more than a shadow against the bright light outside, Ripley knew it was the second officer he'd seen at the execution.

The man stepped inside and Caulfield nodded to him. "Mister Ripley," he said, "this is my second in command, Colonel Reynaldo Carvalho. Colonel Carvalho will accompany us on our little sightseeing tour."

Ripley looked at the man's stony visage. Where the eyes should have been, he saw only a pair of lightbulbs mirrored in the lenses of sunglasses.

Carvalho scowled, then spun on his heels and stepped back into the light outside. Now that he could be seen clearly in the sunlight, it seemed to Ripley that he could have been a slightly reduced Xerox of the Commandante. The thought made him shiver.

Karp shoved Ripley toward the door. "Come on, David, I want to be back in Salazar before nightfall."

Ripley glanced at him. "What's the matter, afraid of the dark?" He suspected the real question should have been whether Caulfield truly controlled the area or whether Bandolo had free run after sundown, the way the VC were masters of the Vietnamese night. But he knew that Karp would not tell him so, even if his suspicion were correct.

Caulfield stepped into the sunlight, and strode briskly past the Americans to lead the way to the helicopter. The pilot, at a wave from Karp, cranked up the Huey, and by the time the four men reached the beach, sand was swirling in every direction, forcing even the Ray-Banned guerrilla leaders to shield their eyes as they ducked under the rotors and sprinted for the Huey's open door.

Once inside, Karp slipped on a headset and ordered the pilot to take off. The Huey started to lift as Ripley tumbled in. The chopper climbed straight up, and as the small camp fell away beneath it, Ripley stood in the open doorway. The buildings had shrunk until they reminded him of a childhood train set. He half expected to see a tiny engine puff along the rusted rails that slashed northward toward Salazar.

Turning to Karp, he shouted, "Where are we going?"

"Santo Emiliano," Karp yelled back. "Reynaldo will fill you in."

Ripley nodded. He knew the name. It was supposed to be one of three strongholds Caulfield used as staging areas. He squeezed his eyes closed, trying to sift through the names and numbers floating in his memory like confetti in a wind tunnel. If he remembered rightly, Santo Emiliano was supposed to be the largest of the three, with a garrison in the neighborhood of ten thousand men, and as many more in the field, relying on it as a supply base. More than half of the CIA's covert arms shipments had been earmarked for the base.

Ripley looked at Carvalho, who might have been watching him closely, but behind the shiny glasses, it was hard to tell. He thought about taking a seat next to the Colonel, but decided against it. Yelling at the top of his lungs was more trouble than it was worth. And he doubted that Carvalho would tell him anything useful in any case.

For a half hour, the chopper glided along the shoreline, keeping below the level of the forest canopy. Ripley wondered why the pilot was being so careful. If Caulfield were as firmly in control as he alleged, there should be no danger, but it seemed almost as if the pilot wanted to avoid being seen.

By the time Santo Emiliano came into view, it was nearly noon. Laid out in a large square, two sides gapped at their centers where a road snaked out of the forest and slithered through the town, Santo Emiliano looked promising. As the chopper swooped toward the large open square in the town's center, Ripley noticed several elaborate buildings on hills along the shoreline. They looked like villas on the Spanish Riviera. Apparently, the town had a prosperous past.

When the Huey touched down, Ripley dropped to the ground and started moving toward the nearest building. Several of the simple rectangular buildings had obviously been built long before. Others, almost duplicates, bore the marks of recent construction. Conscious of footsteps close behind him, he turned to see Carvalho dogging him.

The colonel pointed to the older buildings. "Those were worker barracks," he said. "Santo Emiliano used to be a plantation. Actually, several. You noticed the houses on the coast?"

Ripley nodded.

"They belonged to the Portuguese who owned the plantations. Most of them lived in Portugal, but they wanted nice places to stay when they visited the land they owned here. And the people."

"How many soldiers do you have based here?"

"Many."

"How many?"

"Thousands."

"How *many* thousands," Ripley snapped, not

bothering to conceal the exasperation in his voice.

Carvalho shrugged. "It is hard to say. It changes every week."

He took Ripley's arm and led him toward one of the barracks. Pushing open the door, he stepped inside, and Ripley followed him in. The place stank of urine and perspiration. Double bunks lined the two long walls. At a quick count, Ripley guessed maybe fifty. Half of them were empty. On the other half, men lounged around in various stages of undress. Their clothing was ragged, and he wondered what had happened to the uniform allotments he had seen on shipment inventories.

"Don't they have uniforms?"

Carvalho shook his head. "They do, but they don't like to wear them."

"Why not?"

"They say they don't like to seem separate from the people. It is what the Portuguese used to do, swagger around in their army uniforms. It brings back bad memories."

Ripley backed out of the barracks and headed toward another. It was one of the newer buildings, but when he stepped inside, he noticed that it had the same oppressive stink. A handful of men were sitting at a table playing some sort of game, moving smooth stones from place to place in a long wooden bowl. They glanced up for a moment, but if they recognized Carvalho, they were not overly impressed.

One man, sitting alone on a lower bunk, a *kalimba* in his lap, plucked out a monotonous melody that consisted of five notes repeated over and over. He looked piercingly at Carvalho for a second, then turned his eyes to Ripley. They went blank, and he stopped plucking the keys of the thumb piano for an instant, nodded, then resumed his recital.

Barracks after barracks was the same. The magazine was the largest building in the town, but when Ripley stepped inside and clicked on the light, he saw that there was little of value currently stored there. A few open crates that had once held rifles were stacked haphazardly in one corner. The air smelled of excelsior and gun oil. Tall stacks of ration crates, and several rows of boxes marked "shirts" and "pants" lined one wall. A few boxes of ammunition and two crates marked "grenades" completed the inventory. No mortars, no artillery rounds, no machine guns. Mentally ticking off the list in his head, Ripley found himself wondering if the C-130's that came into Kinshasa from South Carolina routinely dumped their cargo out over the Atlantic.

And there was another, much darker, explanation, but Ripley knew he had to keep it to himself. At least for now.

ELEVEN

❖

Michelle listened while Ripley ranted. He had come in fuming, and the smoke continued to pour out of his ears. "Caulfield's a fraud. I can't believe Karp believes in this guy. As near as I can tell, not one damn thing he's been telling us is true. He doesn't have the men he claims to have. He claimed there was a battle in Santo Cruzeiro, but there's not a single piece of evidence to support him. He's—"

She held up her hand to get a word in. "David, David, slow down. Relax! You've told me all this half a dozen times. It doesn't matter how many times you say it, nothing will change."

"I can't relax, dammit. Karp is going to screw

this thing up. It's going to be Vietnam all over again. I don't know why he's lying about Caulfield, but I know he is."

"How can you know that?"

"Because when I challenged Caulfield on what happened or didn't happen at Santo Cruzeiro, he told me Karp was there. Karp backed him up."

"Maybe he *was* there. Did you ever think of that?"

"Yeah, I thought of it. But it's not true. They're both lying, and I know it."

"How can you possibly know that? You weren't even in Mawindi when it was supposed to have happened. Isn't that so?"

"Yeah, it's so. But it doesn't matter. They're lying and I can prove it."

"How?"

"I can't tell you that."

Michelle shook her head, reached for Ripley's pack of Marlboros on the night table beside the bed, and tapped one out of the pack. She lit it with a match, tossed the pack onto the table again and slapped the matchbook down beside it. She let the smoke out in a long, thin stream, and Ripley knew she was angry. And the anger seemed to be directed at him, for reasons he didn't understand.

"What's the matter?" he asked. "Look, just because Karp flaps his gums, doesn't mean I have to. Michelle, if there is something going on here that I should know about, then I have to cover my ass any way I can. I can't afford to be playing my hole card too early in the game."

"David, you're too conspiratorial minded. You think Karp and Caulfield are in cahoots, but you don't know why. You think they're cutting Oscar Nkele out of the action, but you don't know about that, either, not for sure. And you haven't even met Oscar Nkele. Maybe he's exactly what Karp says he is."

"Maybe. But you don't believe that. I read your book, remember? And as far as meeting Nkele is concerned, I'll take care of that. And I'll make up my mind when I meet Nkele. Until then, I give him the benefit of the doubt, just like I gave Caulfield."

"Don't you have to give Karp the same benefit? I mean, if he knows something you don't know, then maybe he's doing what he thinks he has to do."

"Then why won't he tell me about it? We're supposed to be on the same side, for Christ's sake. If he's keeping secrets from me, he's . . ." Waving a hand, Ripley sat up in disgust. He leaned across Michelle to grab the Marlboros. She draped an arm around his neck and pulled him down. Her breath smelled like tobacco when she pecked him on the cheek. He could feel her breasts press against him, the thin sheet doing little to insulate him from her heat.

Snatching the Marlboro pack, he rolled back away from her and lay on his back. When he'd lit his own cigarette, he reached for the ashtray on the floor and balanced it on bent knees. She sat up then, letting the sheet slide away, and he shifted the cigarette to his left hand and reached out idly with his right to cradle the weight of a breast in his palm, letting his thumb trace small circles around the nipple.

She covered his hand with her own, pressing the thumb to keep it still. "What time is it?" she asked.

He checked his watch, accidentally stabbing the sheet with the lit end of the cigarette. He jumped up then, flailing at the sheet. He saw the dark circle, its inner edge glowing a dull orange as he slapped at the burn. "Jesus Christ! I've been smoking for fifteen years. You'd think I'd know how to do it by now."

"Smoking is the least of your problems," Michelle said, swinging her legs over the side of the bed. She repeated her question. "What time is it?"

"Quarter to eleven," Ripley said, slapping once more at the hole in the sheet, then wetting a fingertip and applying it to the small charred circle.

"You'd better get dressed. We're having company." She grabbed a work shirt from the back of a chair beside the bed and swung it over her shoulders, then slipped her arms into the sleeves. Standing, she snatched her jeans from the chair and slipped them on, tugging to get them over her hips.

"What's going on?" Ripley asked.

"You'll see."

Ripley asked again, and again she gave the same cryptic answer, cracked a grin, and said, "Spies aren't the only people with connections, you know. Journalists have pipelines, too."

BLACK MAMBA

Ripley dressed quickly, watching Michelle the whole time, hoping she would relent, but she just kept the Cheshire smile pasted on her face. At eleven, a knock on the door goaded him to tuck in his shirt, and he walked to the door with his shirt tail sticking out, cradling the Browning in his right hand and opening the peephole with his left.

"Who is it?"

The answer came from behind him. "Open the door, David," Michelle said.

He turned to look at her, and she waved her arms. "Go on, open it."

Ripley did as he was told, unlatched the chain and clicked the lock, backing away from the doorway as he pulled the door open. Oscar Nkele stood there, his eyes fixed on the Browning.

"Come on in, Oscar," Michelle said. "David, put that damned gun away."

Ripley looked at Nkele, then at Michelle, and finally back at the leader of the African People's Party. He tucked the gun into his belt and stood aside. As Nkele entered, Ripley noticed two other men standing in the hall. One of them followed Nkele inside while the other man made no move to enter. Nkele closed the door. He stuck out a massive hand and Ripley shook it gingerly, fearful that he might find his fingers mashed into pulp.

"I thought I would see you before now, Mister Ripley," Nkele said.

Ripley took a deep breath. Now that the man he was interested in meeting was standing there in his hotel room, he wasn't quite sure what he wanted to say. "I planned to see you in the next couple of days. Things seem to take longer than I'm used to, in Mawindi."

"That was by design, I'm sure," Nkele said. "Senhor Caulfield seems able to monopolize American attention as well as American arms."

"Senhor Caulfield is only part of the problem, Mister Nkele."

"Oscar," he said. "And yes, I think I know what you mean. But I am here now, and it would be good if we could talk a little before we go."

"Go? Go where?"

"You are on a fact-finding mission, are you not?"

Ripley nodded.

"Facts are hard to come by in hotel rooms. Especially in Mawindi. I want to take you out to the countryside, and show you what we have been doing."

"All right. Suppose you tell me what you think I should know."

"Suppose you tell me what you think you need to know." Nkele laughed. It was a deep, resonant sound. The man stood nearly six feet four. His upper torso was massive, and his forearms looked like ebony fence posts where they dangled from the sleeves of a colorful *dashiki*. On his head he wore an elaborately embroidered kepi at a jaunty angle. Even in the dim light of the hotel room, his black skin had a high gloss, as if he had been polished with oil or coated with polyurethane.

"I need to know everything there is to know, Oscar," Ripley said. "Let's start with your current situation."

Nkele grunted. "Not good. I have nearly fifteen thousand men under arms, but modern arms for only a third of them. Many are forced to use outdated weapons, old rifles from the Portuguese armories, weapons the army did not think worth keeping. Many of them are of World War I vintage. Parts are not easy to find for such old weapons, and there is little money, even if we can manage to find the replacements."

"What about the countryside? How much of it is under your control?"

Nkele shrugged. "Who can say? Loyalty is a variable thing. The people are frightened. They seem to support whoever is nearby, or whoever has the most guns. Even my own people, the Orobundu, do not know where their future is most secure. They are afraid of Bandolo, and they fear Caulfield. So . . ." he shrugged. "I suppose you could say their hearts are in limbo, waiting to see what happens in the next few weeks."

"You sound as if you don't believe you have a chance to win."

"That is because I don't believe anyone in Mawindi wins a civil war. It is always the people who suffer. I have seen enough suffering in my time. Even when I was away in Europe, I could see that it would be the people who would bear the brunt of the war. I had hoped that I could get assistance from your government, but Mister Karp does not seem disposed to offer much more than words of encouragement. And words are no match for bullets, Mister Ripley."

"Joshua Bandolo doesn't seem to think that way."

"He is a fine poet. But he has thousands of soldiers, and modern weapons for them all. It is easy to wage a war of words when you have firepower to back them up. Even a bad poet can win in such circumstances. All I can do is make speeches and tour the globe with my hand out like a beggar. And no one cares much what happens to beggars."

"Can Bandolo win?"

Nkele nodded. "Yes, he can."

"Will he?"

"That depends on whether the west decides to help us. I know about the arms coming in through Kinshasa, but they are few, and Caulfield doesn't know what to do with them."

"I didn't see much to contradict that," Ripley said.

"There isn't much to contradict it, Mister Ripley. For every shipment that reaches Kinshasa, at least half is kept by the Zairians. Mobutu takes the cream, and we are left with skim milk."

"Where are the weapons that do get through going?"

"You are asking the wrong man. I have seen very little. From time to time, Mister Karp throws me a crumb, but crumbs and skim milk are no diet for an army. And it is not just weapons. To get the people on our side, we will have to offer them more than guns. They need medical help, they need education, they need food, and they need to know that somebody cares about their troubles."

"You care, don't you?"

Nkele smiled sadly. "I do, sometimes I think I care too much. But I have nothing but commiseration to offer them."

"How much of the country would you say is under Caulfield's control?"

"It is difficult to say. Pockets here and there, certainly. But it is hard to sift the few kernels of truth from a bushel of half-truths and outright lies. I know that he has not been given as much as he needs. Even Alexander would have a difficult time waging war with the pitiful equipment the Americans have supplied. I don't blame him. I suppose he is sincere. I used to know him fairly well, although I think he has changed since I knew him. I used to belong to the Pan-African Movement many years ago."

"What about Bandolo?"

Nkele shrugged. "I know that he believes in what he is doing. But I think he is wrong. He thinks he can be his own man once he consolidates his power. But he will be dependent on the Russians. And if he tries to make decisions for himself, well, let's just say that the Russians are not noted for encouraging satellite governments to think for themselves. I know of no reason why Joshua would be treated any differently."

"You sound as if you know him, too."

"I do. There was a time when Mawindi refused to allow a black man to be educated. The Portuguese made much of their *lusotropicalism*. 'Look at Brazil,' they would tell us. 'Be patient. Your time will come.' But it was a cruel joke. It was not even permitted to teach the Portuguese constitution to black children, in case they might want to exercise the rights they supposedly had. Many of us were lucky enough to make our way to Europe, where there were people willing to help us get an education. Scholarships, subsidies, stipends, whatever we could scrape together. Joshua did that, the same as I did. We were in Paris together for two years, although I did not always agree with him even then."

"I don't know how much I'll be able to help you. You have to understand that, Oscar."

The big man shrugged again. "I understand. But I have to try. Just as you have to look, see, and learn. Perhaps if you look hard enough, see enough and learn enough, you will understand what needs to be done. My father was a teacher for many years, before the Portuguese threw him in prison where he died. And I hope I learned enough from him that I will be able to teach you what I think you need to know."

"But suppose I decide that it is Jorge Caulfield who has the best chance to win? That a PAM victory will be best for Mawindi?"

"First of all, let us understand that you will not be deciding what is best for the United States. I have to make you see that they are one and the same. And I will do my best. If you make an honest decision, then I will learn to live with it, whatever you decide."

"And if not?"

"How will I know, Mister Ripley?"

"Fair enough. Then suppose I think we should shift our support to you and I am unable to convince my government to do it?"

"I will be no worse off than I am now. But it is Mawindi that will suffer, Mawindi and its people. And I think they have suffered enough. Four hundred years of Portuguese oppression ought to be enough suffering for any people. It is getting late, and we should go."

"All right, but I want to ask you one more thing before we leave. I understand that you have been getting help from the North Koreans. At least that is the rumor."

"It is no rumor."

"Why? Why the North Koreans?"

"Because they offered to help. And I will take help from anyone, black or white or yellow, to help my country. I would work with Satan himself, if I thought it could make a difference. But there are two things I will not do."

"And what are they?"

"I will not work with the Portuguese under any circumstances, not even mercenaries. And I will not sell my soul. Not to anyone."

TWELVE

❖

The van was waiting behind the hotel. Nkele led the way out through the kitchen, where he was stopped by a knot of kitchen workers who gathered around, chattering excitedly and shaking his hand. Nkele was patient, had a good word for each of them, and beamed like a schoolboy. The two men with him stood aside shaking their heads, as if they were used to such things but didn't quite understand why they happened.

Finally tearing himself away, Nkele wrapped an arm around Ripley's shoulder and squeezed before pulling him toward the rear entrance. Once out in the alley, where the heat was even more oppressive than that of the kitchen, Nkele said, "I'm sorry for the delay, but . . ."

"Never mind," Ripley told him. "Does that happen often?"

Nkele shook his head. "Not often, no, but it is gratifying when it does happen. It's what gives me the strength to continue. Knowing that at least some people think I'm on the right track helps me over those rough spots, those nights when I think maybe I'm just tilting at windmills. When the people believe in you, it's easier to believe in yourself. Not easy, but . . ." He shrugged. ". . . it helps."

They piled into the battered Chevy van, one of the bodyguards climbing into the driver's seat and starting the engine. As they moved down the alley behind the Continental, the driver left the lights off. He was watching the rearview mirror, and when Ripley noticed, he turned to look out through the rear window, which was cracked and slightly yellowed, whether from dirt or age, Ripley wasn't sure.

Michelle Harkness, coming along despite Ripley's protest, was in the rearmost of the three seats. She, too, turned to look. "What is it, David? What did you see?"

"Not sure. I thought I saw something, a light, maybe a cigarette flare, I'm not sure."

Without turning around, the driver said, "It was a cigarette. They follow us all the time, but they don't know how to hide very well."

"Maybe they don't want to hide," Ripley suggested. "Maybe they want you to know they're there."

"That's what Oscar says," the driver mumbled. "But . . ."

"They do," Nkele boomed. "It is a war of nerves. I am supposed to be frightened, I think."

"Who are they?"

"I don't know. They are always there, like the pilot fish trailing the shark. Where you find me, you find them. But they have never caused trouble. I think maybe they just want to know where I am. Or to make sure I know that they know where I am. Whoever they are . . ."

"Bandolo's people?"

Nkele shook his head. "No, I don't think so."

"Caulfield's then?"

"Perhaps. But we will lose them once we get out of the city. James is quite a maniac behind the wheel. I think it is hostility of some kind. A good outlet for him, whatever it is." James laughed, and Nkele slapped him on the back. "Don't worry, Mister Ripley, we'll get you back safe and sound."

"Actually, I was more worried about you than I was about myself."

"I'm used to it. We all are. Even Miss Harkness. She has seen this before."

Ripley turned in his seat once more. Michelle's face was impassive, and he shook his head. Every day there was a new mystery about her. Just when he thought he had her figured out, she threw him a curve ball. He was constantly off balance, and never more than when he tried too hard to stuff her into one pigeon-hole or another.

As they pulled into the light traffic on Avenida Lisboa, James stomped on the gas and veered out into the fast lane. Ripley watched the mouth of the alley and spotted an old black Ford as it cut in front of a large delivery truck, accompanied by the squeal of tires and the belching of air-brakes as the truck lurched awkwardly and looked as if it might fall over. The driver of the Ford finally put his headlights on as the car cut out into the traffic.

The van's exterior was rusty and full of dents, but its engine was in racing form, and James handled the wheel with a casual mastery that looked almost effortless.

Nkele leaned over to Ripley and said, "In Salazar, I always have a shadow, even at midnight, but once we get into the countryside, I have none even at high noon." He laughed heartily, but Ripley didn't join him.

"It must be nerve wracking," he said.

"No. It only troubles me because I know that someone I trust must be telling them."

"Do you have any idea who it might be?"

Nkele shook his head. "No. But I hope that whoever it is will either make a mistake, in which case I will catch him, or he will realize that he has made a mistake, in which case he will confess, and I can put his mind at ease."

"What if you catch him?"

"I will have to send him away."

"That's all?"

"Of course."

Ripley nodded. "I see," he said.

They bored through the night as if they had been swallowed by a motorized mole, the headlights all but erased by the darkness as the road became narrower and more weathered. Traffic was non-existent now, as if the road, bad as it was, existed solely for Nkele's convenience. It was either that, Ripley thought, or that no one wanted to be abroad after dark.

Once, far to the east, a brilliant flash of light lit up the sky, and Ripley thought it must have been lightning. But when a throaty rumble washed in through the open window of the speeding van, he knew it was not thunder. There was a war out there, sporadic and low-key for the moment, but nonetheless a war. Nkele seemed lost in thought, and said little. Michelle was curled into a ball on the back seat, and Ripley envied her, wishing he too could sleep. But there was too much to think about, too many questions to get answered, and every time he closed his eyes, they flashed before him like a scrawl on a teleprompter, line after line, then word after word, faster and faster, until finally there was nothing but an endless skein of question marks that soon blurred into a solid black line. He knew then that he didn't even know what he should be asking, or of whom.

Ripley rested his head on one arm braced on the window frame, enduring the little bumps and sudden lurches as best he could. The sound of the air rushing past him, ruffling his hair and whistling from time to time, lulled him into a state of near sleep. He could hear everything, but his eyes registered little in the darkness. Now and then, as the van slowed to negotiate a particularly bad stretch of road, he could hear the sounds of the night, assorted chirps and buzzes from a myriad of insects, the whomp of a frog, and, once, the heart-stopping scream of a big cat.

"Leopard," Nkele said, leaning toward him and speaking softly, to keep from waking Michelle. "Beautiful animals, they are."

Ripley sat up then, and leaned forward to peer through the windshield. Far ahead, a faint smear of light seemed to wink and flicker. Nkele pointed toward it. "Not far now," he said. "Five miles, maybe less."

"Where are we?"

"South, almost to the border of South West Africa. Santa Isabella."

"That where you have your headquarters?"

"Such as they are," Nkele chuckled. "Such as they are. On my budget, one does not have headquarters. One has a place where one can hang his hat and, if he is lucky, a pillow for his weary head."

Ripley said nothing, leaned back in the seat and took a deep breath. "It'll be daylight, soon, I guess."

"An hour, maybe a little more."

The last five miles took nearly ten minutes. The road had deteriorated now to little more than dirt. They rolled up to a wooden gate, and two men armed with AK-47's stepped out of a small shack of rough wood, snapped crisp salutes and blocked the way. One of them trained his rifle on the driver while the other bent to peer into the van. When he recognized Nkele, he smiled. Straightening, he went to the gate, pulled it open, and waved the van on through while the other returned to the shack.

In the pre-dawn gray, Ripley noticed coils of razor wire snaking off into the jungle on either side of the gate. Several buildings, just blobs of dark gray, slowly took shape. One of them, a long low structure off to one side, was dimly lit, the only lights in the village. The driver rolled to a stop in front of it, and Nkele yanked open his door, putting a shoulder into it to make reluctant hinges behave.

Ripley turned to wake Michelle, shaking her gently, before stepping out. He waited for her as Nkele came around the van and clapped him on the shoulder. He waved a hand toward the few buildings. "It isn't much, but it's home," he said. "Or at least a home away from my home away from home."

The driver stood nearby, and Nkele turned to him and said, "Take Mister Ripley and Miss Harkness to their rooms." To Ripley, he said, "I have a few things to attend to. We can look around after sunrise, if you like."

"I'm not tired," Ripley said.

"I'm afraid what I have to do isn't very interesting," Nkele responded.

"If you don't mind, I'll tag along."

Michelle, who was still half asleep, shook her head emphatically as she stepped down from the van. "Me, too," she said.

Nkele shrugged. "Whatever you say."

He turned and headed for the low building with lights, and ducked through the doorless entrance. Ripley followed him in. The odor was unmistakable. Medicine, a hint of alcohol and the dank smell he associated with a jar of vitamins opened for the first time.

"What is this place?" he asked, whispering either because of the darkness or because of his suspicion.

"A clinic," Nkele said. "Medical care is not easily had, especially this far from Salazar. I was trained as a doctor, as I'm sure you know. This is one of the ways I can help my people."

A striking young black woman, the front of her white uniform wrinkled and stained with what could only have been blood, rose from a desk and rushed toward Nkele, her face suddenly creased into a smile. "It's about time you got back, Doctor," she said.

"Busy?" Nkele asked.

She nodded, suppressing a yawn. "As always."

"Anything I should look at?"

She nodded. "Room nine. He came in today. I'll show you." She turned on her heel and broke into a brisk walk, her sandals clacking on the wooden floor. She turned left at the end of the long, dark hall, reached into the darkness, and a rectangle of light spilled onto the floor before she ducked through a doorway. Nkele followed her in.

On a metal-frame bed, covered with clean but wrinkled sheets, a boy who couldn't have been more than ten lay with his body curled into a letter "C" while a woman who must have been his mother lay sleeping on a straw pallet on the floor beside it.

One of the boy's arms was heavily bandaged, and blood had soaked through the gauze in three or four places, dark brown where it had coagulated. An IV bottle dangled from a makeshift armature of bamboo.

"What happened to him?" Nkele asked.

The nurse shook her head. "He cut himself very badly. A chainsaw. He was trying to help his father, who has been sick and unable to work."

"How bad?"

"Very bad. The saw laid his forearm open from his wrist to his elbow. He lost a lot of blood, but Doctor Neto says he thinks there was no damage to tendons or major blood vessels. He's not sure about nerve damage, though."

"How are the antibiotics holding up?"

She shook her head. "Almost gone. We have to get more, Doctor Nkele."

"I'm trying, Rosa. I'm trying, but . . ." He walked to the bed, careful not to wake either the patient or his mother. Dropping to one knee, the huge man leaned over the frail child and rested one great hand on the boy's forehead.

Gently, Nkele brushed the boy's tight curls, then stood up. Holding a finger to his lips, he moved toward the doorway. Once outside, he waited for the nurse to leave, and pulled the door closed.

"How many patients . . . ?" Ripley started to ask.

Nkele shook his head. "Later," he whispered. Turning to the nurse, he said, "Rosa, please take Mister Ripley and Miss Harkness to the mess hall. There should be someone there who can make them some breakfast. I'll wait until you come back before I join them."

Ripley started to protest, but Nkele shook his head vehemently. "I insist. You are both exhausted, and there is much to see this morning before you return to Salazar."

Michelle took Ripley by the arm, and he had the distinct impression that she was somehow on Nkele's side. He thought back to her book. He had wondered how she had managed to have so much information about Nkele and the African People's Party and so little about Caulfield. And suddenly he understood that she had had access all along.

Halfway across the compound, he stopped in his tracks and took her by the arm. She snatched it away, and glared at him. "This is no accident, is it?"

"What are you talking about?"

"Nkele didn't show up last night by chance. You arranged it. This is a show for my benefit, isn't it?"

"Of course it is. You wanted, needed, to meet him. I could make it easier, so I did."

"Why didn't you tell me?"

"I should think it would have been obvious. What are you, some kind of nautilus? Are you buried so deeply in your shell you can't find the way out? For crying out loud, David, do you think you live in a vacuum? Or is it something worse, something more arrogant? Do you think you're the only person in Africa who can make things happen? Can your ignorance be that Olympian?"

"You're playing with people's lives, Michelle. You're—"

"Don't you lecture me about that. Don't you dare! I'm a journalist. I want to know things. I come. I look. I learn. But you, you think you're some kind of fucking Caesar . . . Veni! Vidi! Vici! . . . That's your goddamned motto, isn't it? You and all the other Bob Karps of this fucked up world. Only there's nothing here to conquer, David. There's nothing but misery. Misery that white men created, and now, not satisfied with that, they want to compound it by bombing the ruins back into molecules. They want to . . ."

"I want to help, dammit! That's why I'm here. No other reason."

"Maybe, but I don't think you know who you want to help. It's not Oscar, it's not Mawindi. You're trying to help yourself, trying to exorcise some personal demons, David. And you're using Mawindi as an excuse. Misery loves company, David. And you're one miserable sonofabitch."

Suddenly conscious of Rosa standing there

watching the argument, Ripley raised his hands in the air. "All right, all right, we'll talk about it later," he said.

He nodded to Rosa then, as if to tell her the fight was over, and she turned toward the mess hall again. Michelle looked as if she were not quite ready to give up the fight, but she scraped her lower lip with her teeth and turned to follow the nurse.

Several dozen men were already inside, dressed in crisp, clean uniforms. They were sitting at long tables, tin plates in front of them. It could have been a mess hall at a military school, if it hadn't been for the rifles arranged in neat pyramids at the end of each table. They were talking quietly among themselves and paid little attention to the newcomers. Rosa directed her charges to a separate table, then carried over two plates of synthetic scrambled eggs and sliced melon, set them on the table and, after pointing to a pitcher of water and an array of tin cups, she excused herself.

"Looks like Oscar has his shit together," Ripley said.

"Maybe you ought to watch him," Michelle suggested. "Maybe you'll learn something."

PART
TWO
❖

THIRTEEN

❖

August 5, 1975

Like lava, creeping so slowly it might not be moving at all, its leading edge black and silent, oozing inexorably closer, reaching foundations, welling up and then opening its white hot maw to vent its searing heat and slavering tongues of flame until it swallowed houses whole, the war eased closer and closer to Salazar. The capital had become a place where glacial calm and wild-eyed frenzy passed each other on the street, where life-long neighbors stared at one another with suspicion like small daggers flashing behind false smiles.

The Soviet weapons continued to pour like a flood into Joshua Bandolo's arsenal, while he continued to deny it, trying to fend off suspicion with a blizzard of poetry and press releases. And while Bandolo waged war with rockets and words as his weapons, Jorge Caulfield and the Pan-African Movement fell back a step, and then another and a third.

Like a spoiled child who needs his father to fight his battles for him, Caulfield kept running home to Robert Karp, and the Salazar COS matched every brilliant lyric of Bandolo's with a pedestrian cable of his own, its condensed language stripped of all color and image as if he wanted to show that Bandolo was hiding behind linguistic veils.

And the APP waged its own quiet war. Nkele knew about the weapons pouring in on Zairian transports, knew that mortars and automatic rifles, rockets and ammunition, were gushing in and that Caulfield was getting all of them. Ripley knew it bothered Nkele, but when they would meet, there was no reproach in Nkele's words or in his eyes, only bafflement. He didn't understand why he had been relegated to a second, stringless fiddle, and he didn't pretend to. Pretending was Ripley's job, and he was coming to hate it.

By force of will and an occasional firefight, the APP kept the Cardozo railroad open, and watched as the C-130's ferried arms from Kinshasa and freight cars full of weapons rattled in from Zambia to Caulfiled, and Nkele shook his head in wonderment all the while.

On August fifth, his three-day trip already a month old and changed now to indefinite, Ripley laid in bed staring at the ceiling, his eyes heavy but fixed as if he were paralyzed and unable to close them. Michelle lay beside him, a sheet pulled up just past her waist to ward off the chill of the air conditioner. He rested his hand on the curve of her hip, the cool skin taut as a drumhead over the bone. On the nightstand beside the bed, her tape recorder, its wires coiled in tangles like a nest of serpents, sat vigilantly, waiting for another of her fitful bursts of restless inspiration. Theirs had become an uneasy peace, at best.

In the shadows on the ceiling, Ripley kept seeing Jorge Caulfield, his crisp fatigues spotless and neatly tailored, his fifty-dollar sunglasses glinting in the sunlight, his eyes two bruised marbles hidden behind the dazzling lenses, his thin lips compressed into a faint smile. Caulfield would move, and the stiff cloth of his uniform would whisper, while Ripley tried desperately to understand.

But he didn't understand, and he wouldn't. Again and again, he'd gone over it all with Karp, and always it was the same—Caulfield's our man, Nkele's not trustworthy.

It was like some perverse mantra, words Karp used to put himself to sleep at night, and intoned again before his feet touched the polished tile floor of his residence in the morning. Or maybe they were the only words he knew and, rather than endure total silence, he repeated them just to feel their tingle on his lips. It didn't matter much whether they made sense or whether they were understood, and mattered even less whether anyone agreed. The words kept him sane and he would not let go of them.

But Ripley had come to believe that Caulfield was a clown. That was clear now. He lied about the size of his forces, their location and their ability. He made battles up out of whole cloth, spun luxuriant epics of imaginary victories like a spider seeing just how fanciful a web it could weave. At bottom, the leitmotif that held them all together was the number of MLF soldiers strewn around the battlefield when the smoke cleared. But Ripley had been down that road before. He'd seen enough of body counts. They were a bottomless pit, a yardstick without meaning, and he refused to listen to Caulfield's tales of MLF corpses stacked like cordwood.

The truth was that most of Caulfield's waking hours were spent plotting against the APP. He hated and feared Nkele, admitted to neither emotion, but never lost an opportunity to heap scorn on his putative ally. Not content to get the bulk of the aid the Agency was piecing together like a makeshift set of mismatched china, he kept agitating for Nkele to be taken off the Company teat altogether.

As it was, Nkele was clinging by his fingernails

to a handful of villages, none with a population of more than a few hundred, their only strategic significance their proximity to the railroad. To Ripley, it was as if Caulfield were an elephant, ignoring the hunter in the grass ahead of him to chase a single fly. There was no logic and less proportion in Caulfield's thinking.

Michelle stirred, then groaned while rolling onto her back. His hand became tangled in the thick bush between her legs, and he left it there, the fingers stroking gently for a few seconds then falling still. He turned on his side then to look at her, and he found himself wondering what she saw in him. He felt ineffectual, even impotent anyplace but in bed. He had a job to do, but it seemed to be beyond him.

Leaning over her, he brushed his lips against her left nipple, stiffened by the cool air. It felt like a cold pebble against his skin when he laid his cheek against her breast. She stirred again as he pulled back, brushing a hand across her chest for a moment, as if chasing a mosquito.

Ripley lay back again then, knowing that sleep would not be coming anytime soon, got off the bed and walked to the window. Looking out at the city, its lights pale through the soot-grayed windowpane, he wondered where Caulfield was at that moment. He had a momentary flash of the PAM leader sitting in Karp's living room, a bottle of brandy on the coffee table in front of him, sunglasses reflecting the indirect light from the ceiling, making his face look as if it had been fitted with a pair of windows on a tiny world where everything was slightly curved, slightly off kilter and impossibly small.

It would almost have been amusing if it were not for the slow but steady encroachment of the war. He remembered Saigon, how the rockets started to fall out of the blue like thunderbolts, tearing apart the haphazard amalgam of colonial elegance and colonized poverty, the palace and the shanty each reduced to rubble as the inexorable approach of the conquerors each day was signalled by another bite taken out of the city.

That was to be Salazar's fate, too. It was not far off, two months, maybe three, unless something could be done to halt Joshua Bandolo's relentless advance. The rules of the game were so simple—whoever controlled Salazar on Independence Day got to do what he wanted with Mawindi.

There were rumors now of Cuban soldiers, dressed in MLF uniforms, but speaking Spanish instead of Portuguese, their weapons newer, and deadlier, than the Czechoslovakian throwaways the Russians were feeding to Bandolo. It would be useful to know whether those rumors were true, Ripley thought, but certainty would change nothing either way. The truth was that the MLF was better armed than the APP, better trained and better led than the PAM. If Nkele had Caulfield's resources, or Caulfield had Nkele's ability, there might be a chance. As it was, each planeload of weapons unloaded at Salazar wasted a little more time and a lot more money, tipped the balance a little more in Bandolo's favor, and Ripley was coming to believe that that was how someone wanted it. It seemed almost as if someone in Langley *wanted* the MLF to win. It made no sense, and he didn't really believe it, but unless he had gone through the looking glass into a world where up was down and white was black . . . fuck it!

He snatched the pack of Marlboros from the window sill, tapped one into his trembling fingers and flicked the disposable lighter once, then again before he got the feeble flame to hold long enough to light the cigarette.

When he inhaled, the glow was bright enough to smear the window with an orange portrait. He studied the image in the glass for the split second, thinking that he recognized someone other than himself, some figure from another dimension, where eyes were sunken hollows full of midnight, and a mouth was a gaping, garish wound.

Exhaling, he watched the smoke hurl itself against the glass, flatten, then falter and curl away and he saw another image of himself in the futility. There had to be something he could do, but what?

He stubbed out the cigarette, and leaned forward with his hands on the sill, watching the city. It lay quiet, either dignified or resigned, like a patient in a terminal ward, not yet feeling pain or already anesthetized. It all amounted to the same thing. Again he came back to Saigon. He carried somewhere deep inside him a set of images which he could run and rerun at will. And like an intern carefully checking a list of symptoms, matching it against a list of diseases, he found match after match after match. And, still unsure, he checked again. But it came out the same way every time.

The rampant inflation, the brisk traffic in contraband, the flourishing black market, each had an analog in Vietnam. Salazar was dying one building at a time, its population declining almost daily, family by family. Every day, it seemed another shop had closed, its proprietor nailing plywood over his windows, then packing wife, children and bank account onto the next plane out. And the day after, the boards would come down and someone new would sit behind the grimy glass, his sleeves rolled up, his eyes shifty, as he peddled blue jeans and cigarettes from packing crates.

Caulfield's soldiers were everywhere, traveling in pairs and, in some places where pairs were not enough, in jeeploads, the safeties off their rifles, their hands white knuckled and eyes restless. And every day there would be a bomb or two. One day a bank, the next a bus or restaurant would be reduced to rubble in the twinkling of an eye, quick as the Big Bang. The destruction was announced as if by the thundrous clap of a pair of gigantic hands, a puff of smoke and an expanding universe of razor-edged shards of shattered glass.

There would be bloodstains on the asphalt for

two days or three or four. They would slowly fade, reminders as mute and terrible as the nuclear shadows on the walls of Hiroshima, until the friction of passing feet and two days of rain rubbed and washed the blood away. Then more boards would be nailed in place and when the blood was gone, those who didn't know would wonder whether the shop had simply been closed or blown away.

Ripley saw it every day. And every day, he thought that Karp would see the parallel for himself. There were beggars in the street who pulled his coat and should remind him. There were children selling themselves which should get his attention and make him think. There were men with missing limbs, their armless sleeves and wooden legs strewn in his path, who should force him to see. But Karp's mind was elsewhere, like a souvenir scorpion in a block of clear plastic. He seemed to see nothing at all. He remained oblivious.

That couldn't be by chance. And it couldn't be allowed to continue. He would have to make Karp see what was happening, jolt him from his lethargy, slap him on both cheeks the way John Wayne would slap a shell-shocked rookie. "Snap out of it soldier! Pull yourself together," the Duke would say.

Talking to Caulfield would do no good. The man was obsessed with his image. Nothing else mattered to him. Talking to Karp would probably be just as useless, but he would try once more, and if he failed, then he would have to improvise. There wasn't enough time for him to dick around with egos. This was about more than that, more than who got the most press, who had the highest profile, who commanded more stateside air time. Caulfield was the hands down winner in all three categories anyway.

The more he thought about it, the more convinced Ripley became that Oscar Nkele was the best man for the job. And the man least likely to get it. And he knew, with all the terrible certainty of Gethsemane, that if something were to be done before it was too late, he would have to do it himself.

But Jack Devereaux had changed the rules on him. Now under Karp's control, he no longer had the freedom he had wanted, and thought he had been given. Now he was locked in, his hands tied, moving when they moved only with the help of strings and sticks almost invisible against the scrim. It was Karp as Buffalo Bob, pulling strings, barely bothering to change his voice and changing his mind not at all. Ripley was a puppet, and he wanted desperately to tear loose, to jerk the strings until they snapped with a sound like pistol shots in an empty theater. He wondered whether his legs would carry him or if, when the strings parted, he would collapse into an impotent heap of wood and plastic, the articulated joints of knees and hips, wrists and elbows, folding in on themselves like Japanese fans. Would he lie there then, able to see and hear and feel, but not to speak or move?

Lighting another cigarette, he saw himself again momentarily reflected in the glass, an orange ghost floating in the pitch black night over Salazar. He leaned toward the glass until he pressed his forehead against it, the smooth surface cool on his skin, making him wonder whether he were fevered, whether he were thinking clearly or merely juggling delusions.

He leaned back away from the glass, turned and sat in the tall wicker chair half hidden by the open drapes. He could barely make out Michelle on the bed, her body a shadowy French curve, dark against the ghostly off-white of the sheets. He wanted to go to her, to lie down beside her, to whisper to her everything that terrified him, but not because he believed she could help. Not even because he believed she cared, because he didn't believe that, but simply because he had to tell someone or go crazy.

But morning would come, he thought, and the sun would rise, and he would not have to be so afraid for a while.

FOURTEEN

❖

August 6, 1975

Bob Karp was in his office. Ripley could hear him on the telephone, the voice just a murmur through the thick walnut door. Sitting there reminded him of waiting in a dentist's office. He kept waiting for the whirring of the drill, then the soft moan triggered by a struck nerve. There was no doubt that Karp was one of those who would short weight the novocaine, just to give him the opportuinty to practice insincerity. "That hurt, did it? Sorry. We'll try again, and if it still hurts, maybe another shot. Don't want to spoil you though, do we?"

The embassy was silent. It had the same ghostly stillness of Karp's home. The two nights he had stayed there, Ripley had the sensation that the house was haunted. It was as if Karp lived there alone, but Ripley was always conscious that somewhere, hidden in one of its countless rooms, Betty Karp was probably sleeping off another bout with the booze. She made no secret of the fact that she hated Salazar, and hated Mawindi. If Ripley had to bet, he'd bet that she hated Karp, too. That was the way it was. Like politicians, Agency climbers were concerned about the proprieties. How would it look if a man couldn't hold his own family together? How could you possibly count on him to keep a government together?

The embassy had that same cold stillness. Below, in the basement, Ronny Lang and Rick Brown were busy watching their machines, the LED's twinkling in Rick's eyeglasses, and Lang was humming to himself as he monitored incoming cable traffic. Like Tweedledee and Tweedledum, they were inseparable.

Ripley didn't belong anymore, and he felt powerless. He was a fifth wheel, and a gelding. He was a kid in a toy museum now, free to roam when and where he would, so long as he touched nothing. It was all too familiar, too incredibly self aggrandizing and, ultimately, too fucking silly to be believed. He knew that now. It hadn't always been that way, or at least he hadn't always felt this way. There had been a time when the inaudible hum of the comm gear would have registered on some sensitive antennae long since attenuated. He would have glowed as steadily as one of Brown's LED's at the notion that he was doing important work, saving democracy from a fate worse than death. But what was he doing, *really*?

Twisting his face into a wry grin at the question, he moved his mouth to shape the words on soundless lips. It felt good to ask it, even though he had no answer. Once more, this time just loud enough to make the skin on his lips vibrate, he whispered it, then once more, this time in a subversive hiss. "What am I doing? What am I doing? What am I doing?" Over and over, the question trembled, its sibilant echo trailing away like the dying buzz of a retreating fly. "What am I doing?"

Before he could even try to frame an answer, the gleaming walnut door of Karp's office opened, and Bob Karp, his glasses pushed back on his thinning hair, his impossibly starched sleeves rolled up nearly to the elbows, where the folds looked stiff as meringue, gestured impatiently.

Ripley gnawed on his lower lip as he got to his feet. Karp fanned his arms to hurry him, and Ripley dragged his feet a little to show the COS the limits of his authority.

Once over the threshold, he walked straight to a chair, leaving Karp to close the heavy door with a soft thud and the staccato click of the latch, definite as a pistol cock.

Karp crossed the deep-piled carpet, the uppers of his new shoes squeaking like mice until he reached the high-backed leather chair, sat down, and arranged his hands on the paperless desk top as if they were a priceless pair of dueling pistols he wanted to sell.

"You wanted to see me, Davey?" he asked.

Ripley nodded. "Yeah, I do." He stared past Karp at the huge vivarium, its non-reflecting glass looking just the least bit smokey. The black mamba was drowsing in one corner, curled into a ball of gleaming jet, its lidless eyes motionless where they fixed on Karp as if wondering, from wherever it went when it dreamed, what it would be like to sink its fangs into Karp's flesh.

Sensing where Ripley's attention lay, Karp swivelled in the chair and leaned forward to tap the glass. The dull black tongue flicked once, then again, and the flat head shifted a fraction of an inch. "Beautiful, isn't he?" Karp said, tapping the glass a second time. "Betty wants me to get rid of it. Not that she ever comes here."

"I know. You told me. And for what it's worth, I think Betty's right."

"She doesn't understand why I keep it," Karp went on, as if he hadn't heard what Ripley said, or didn't think it worth responding to. "It's not like I keep it in the house. She just doesn't understand."

"Neither do I."

"It's the power, Davey. The absolute power. That snake is about as deadly as anything on the planet. And it can't do a damn thing, because I'm in control. Total control. There was this Buddhist monk used to come to see me when I was in Prundit Pao, this godforsaken cesspool in Laos. Used to tell me that we couldn't hope to win because we didn't understand ourselves any more than we understood the Pathet Lao. He used to tell me that we become the things we own, and that we owned so much it clouded our brains. I don't know, maybe the old man was right. But I know one thing—I own this snake now, and if he *was* right, well . . . I think that's all right with me."

Karp tapped the glass again, this time with his ring. The metal cracked against the glass loud enough to startle the somnolent serpent, and it looked balefully at Karp for a moment, then slithered across the floor of the vivarium to coil itself again in some ferns, almost indistinguishable from the shadows.

"Now, what do you want to talk about? I've got to see the Portuguese ambassador in half an hour, so make it quick."

"I've been out in the boonies again."

"I know. I know all about it. So what?"

"I've seen a few things you might find very interesting."

"I know exactly what you're going to tell me. You're going to say that Jorge Caulfield is a blowhard, right? You're going to tell me that he pads his numbers. You're going to say that his troops just may be the poorest excuse for an army that you've ever seen. And all because you've seen Oscar Nkele's little dog and pony show. You think the African People's Party is better organized than PAM. You think we ought to give Nkele the push he needs. Am I right?"

Karp leaned back in his chair, a self-satisfied smile tugging at the corners of his mouth. "Well," he asked again, "am I?"

"If you know all this, then why in hell are you backing Caulfield instead of Nkele?"

"For precisely those reasons, Davey. Come on, you've been around the block a few times. You know how it works. You know human nature. Not as well as I do, maybe, but you'll get there."

Ripley interrupted. "What the hell does human nature and either your or my understanding of it have to do with the future of Mawindi?"

"Everything, Davey. Everything and more. Sure, I know the rap on Caulfield. The truth is he's probably even worse than you say he is. But that's precisely why we're putting all our eggs in his basket—because he's desperate, and because he needs us and because, if he wins, he'll be grateful. Grateful as all get out. To *us*, Davey, to the good old U.S. of A. And that's exactly what we want." He drew his hand like a dull sword across his throat. "I've had it up to here with these arrogant little sonsofbitches who stick out their hands for guns and bombs then spit in our faces when they win. I want to see somebody win who won't forget just exactly *why* he was able to win. I want somebody to win who will piss his pants at the very thought of U.S. aid being withdrawn, somebody who can't wipe his ass unless we unroll the paper for him. Got it? We're on Caulfield's side because he's pathetic, because he's a loser without us."

Ripley nodded dumbly. He couldn't believe what he was hearing. But he couldn't just sit there. He had to say something, anything, buy some time until he had a chance to recover. "And you really think he'll give a damn? You really believe that he sees himself that clearly, do you?"

"Hell yes, that's exactly what I believe."

"And what if, in spite of everything, he loses. Then what?"

Karp shrugged. "Then another one bites the dust. We pack up our marbles and go draw a circle in some other Third World back yard. What the hell do you think?"

"You don't give a shit about Mawindi, do you, Karp?"

The COS looked as if he'd just sat on a whoopee cushion. "Why should I give a shit about this place? For Christ's sake, Davey. Its principal exports are mosquitoes and malaria. Besides, I've seen what happens when you care too much— you get kicked in the balls. And that hurts whether the foot is the other guy's or belongs to somebody on your own team. Oh no, I won't live that nightmare again, Davey. Nobody's going to kick me in the nuts again. Not on your life."

"Then why the fuck are we here?" Ripley got up and leaned forward, his hands on Karp's desk. The wood was so slippery with lemon oil, that one hand slid away and he nearly crashed down on top of it.

"Because *they're* here, Davey, the Russians are here. Smell the coffee, dammit! *They're* here, so we have to be here, too. It doesn't matter whether we win or not, as long as we don't let them win too easily. It's all about momentum, Davey, that's all, just momentum. You think I give a rat's ass who runs this sinkhole? You think some moron in downtown Des Moines even knows where the fuck Mawindi is?"

"You're selling these people out, Karp. You're giving up on them and you haven't even tried. Bandolo doesn't have to win. Nkele can stop him."

"Nkele? Jesus Christ, Ripley, listen to yourself! You're making a goddamn hero out of the bastard. He's a politician like all the rest of them. Like you and me, for crying out loud. That's all we are—politicians. That's all this is about, just politics. And nobody cares."

"Give him a chance . . ."

"To do what, thumb his nose at us? You want me to help him win so he can kill chickens in the Saint Theresa Hotel, is that it? For Christ's sake . . ."

"You're afraid of him, aren't you? You know he can win and you'll do anything to see that he doesn't. That's it, isn't it?"

"Afraid of him? You're damn right I'm afraid of him. We helped Castro, and look at him now. There are Cubans sticking their noses into every damn Third World argument, pouring in by the planeload every time somebody yells 'Throw the rascals out!' or whatever the fuck the local equivalent might be. But I'll be damned if they'll come in here and help Nkele. I'll be damned if I sit back and make another Castro. Dr. Frankenstein made one monster, Davey, just one, and do you know why? Come on, dammit, you've seen the movie. Do you know why?" Karp slammed his fist on the desk. "Because he learned from his mistakes, that's why. And so have I. So should you. No way Nkele gets a chance to . . ."

"This isn't the movies, Bob. This is life. And real people are getting their heads blown off out there in the jungle."

Karp nodded. "I know they are. I know that. I know . . . and it's a goddamn shame. But you said it yourself, Davey. That's real life. It ain't pretty. It's more than a little messy, and there are no goddamned heroes anymore. None." Karp waved a finger under Ripley's nose. "You hear me? None. So don't you try to be a hero, Davey. Because I'll take you off at the knees, honest to God I will."

"I've been hearing rumors about Caulfield."

"I don't care what you've been hearing."

"I think we ought to listen, Bob. I think maybe we ought to try to find out whether there's anything to them."

Karp took a deep breath, then rubbed one hand across his brow. For a long moment, the only sound in the room was the rustle of skin on skin. Karp was breathing hard, and he seemed to be teetering on rubber legs as he straightened up behind his desk. He turned his back then and walked over to the vivarium.

Whirling suddenly, he stabbed a finger at the glass. In a flash, the mamba struck, and Ripley saw the gaping jaws as the fangs clacked against the glass he had forgotten was there for a moment. Stunned for a second, the snake coiled again, its head tapping against the thick plate glass three or four times.

"I feed him, and without me, he'd die," Karp said, his chest heaving, his palm pressed flat against the glass just beside the coiled viper. "And do you know what would happen if I let him loose in this room? He'd kill me in a flash. I feed him, I keep him alive, and he'd kill me anyway. Because that's what he does. That's what he *is*, dammit. No loyalty, no pity, no nothing." He clapped his hands together in a move that startled Ripley as much as the mamba's aborted strike. "No nothing. Bam! Just like that. Remember that, Ripley, the next time your heart starts to bleed for Oscar Nkele."

Ripley nodded. "I will. I'll remember that." He backed toward the door, his gaze drifting back and forth between the caged serpent and the COS. Groping blindly for the door, he found the knob, turned it and yanked the door open, hitting himself in the hip as he tried to get out.

Once out of the office, he closed the door softly, let his hand rest against the polished wood for a moment, then leaned his forehead against the coolness of the smooth walnut.

FIFTEEN

❖

August 7, 1975

"You can't use this, Michelle, not a word."

She looked at him curiously. Her head was canted to one side, almost birdlike, and her eyes were fixed on his. He wanted her to blink, to shake her head, anything, just so he wouldn't feel so naked. But she stayed motionless, waiting. He could see a mental pencil poised in her head. He knew she would remember everything, and wondered why he trusted her. Then he laughed.

"What's so funny?"

"I was just thinking . . ."

"About what? Tell me."

Ripley was nervous. He lit a cigarette and stared out the window. A single dark gray feather of smoke from the harbor waved in the wind. Beyond it, he could see the pale gray of the Atlantic, smears of sunlight glistening on the undulating surface. He sighed, took a puff on the Marlboro, and nodded. "I was wondering why I trust you," he said.

"Does that mean you definitely do? Trust me, I mean?"

"Yeah, it does."

"And did you decide why?"

He looked at her closely, wondering whether she were teasing him, but she seemed to be genuinely curious. "Yeah, I did."

"Tell me."

"Because you're the only one I *can* trust."

She leaned back then, arranged her long legs on the overstuffed sofa, and smiled. "You don't like Bob Karp very much, do you?"

"What's to like?"

"He's got a very difficult job."

Ripley shrugged his shoulders. "If he does it right, yes, he does."

"And you don't think he's doing it right?"

"I'm not sure he's doing it at all."

"Why do you say that?"

"Just a feeling. He told you who I was, didn't he? Why I was here? That's not exactly doing his job. He spends all his time scheming to put Caulfield at the head of the class."

"What's wrong with that?"

"Dammit, Michelle. You know as much about Caulfield as I do. Do you think that man is fit to run a country, any country at all, let alone one with the problems Mawindi has staring it in the face?"

"If countries were run only by men fit to run them, they'd all be run by women." She grinned, and it was hard to take offense. Her smile faded a bit, and she shook her head. "I know what you mean. But what is the alternative? Are we supposed to fold our tents and go home with our tails between our legs?"

He wondered about her choice of pronoun. It didn't seem to preserve the journalistic detachment of which she was so fond. But he chose not to mention it. "Why not?"

"Then why don't you do that? Why don't you go home, get out of this place and find something to do that makes sense to you?"

"I don't know, honestly. I just don't."

"*I* know, David. I know *exactly* why."

It was his turn to be curious. He sucked on the butt, blew the smoke out through his nose, and stubbed it out, before asking, "And why is that?"

"Because you care what happens here. That's the difference between you and Bob Karp. You care and he doesn't."

Ripley laughed. It was not a pleasant sound. "Oh, really?"

"Yes, really. And unfortunately for your chosen

career, caring is not a useful skill. In fact, it's an impediment."

"And what makes you think you know so much about my career, leaving aside for the moment whether or not I chose it."

"Didn't you? Didn't you choose it? Didn't you jump at the chance to make a contribution, to do something useful, something that would change things for the better somewhere, somehow?"

"Suppose I did?"

She ignored the question to bore in with her impeccable logic. "And now you feel betrayed. You think the job has turned its back on you, you think the Agency is full of cynical, calculating, dime store Machiavellis who care more about their next paygrade and their next assignment than they do about the people they are supposedly protecting from the communist menace. Isn't that right?"

"Something like that, I suppose, yes."

"Grow up, David! The job you accepted hasn't changed. Not one bit. It's *you* who've changed. You'll just have to accept that."

"You mean I should be more like Karp, is that it?"

"No, not necessarily. I just mean you should stop whining and make a decision."

"And what decision is that?"

"How the fuck should I know? It's *your* decision. You have to make it."

The profanity seemed almost musical on her

lips, and he wondered why he wasn't shocked. He had never heard her curse before, but he wasn't surprised. He realized then that he believed she was tougher than she seemed, that under the soft curves there was more than just a bear-trap of a brain, there was a skeleton of stainless steel.

Ripley lit another cigarette. He nodded. "You're right," he said. "You're right."

"So, what are you going to do?"

"I don't know. I'll have to think about it."

Getting off the sofa, she crossed to him, turned and lowered herself into his lap. She snuggled down, rested her head on his shoulder, and he leaned toward her. The scent of her shampoo tickled his nostrils. It smelled like a mountain meadow full of flowers, the perfume present, but overwhelmed by the open space and the brisk air. It was just right. He took a few strands of her honey-colored hair between his lips and moved his head, feeling the hair slide against his skin.

"You know," she said, "I once read, maybe it was in *Believe It or Not* . . . you're no relation are you?" She looked at him out of the corner of her eye, and when he shook his head, she continued, "that human hair was so strong that, if you started slowly enough, and gradually worked your way up, you could pull a battleship with a single strand. Of course, they didn't tell you that it would take a thousand years or something like that to get up to two knots." She laughed then, and it was an odd sound, almost detached, contemplative.

"That's always the bitch of it, isn't it—the things they don't bother to tell you. I suppose you're feeling a bit like that right now, aren't you?"

"I guess."

She turned then and kissed him on the tip of the nose. "Poor baby. I wish there was something I could say to make it better, but . . ."

"That's okay. You're right. It's up to me."

She got up then, with apparent reluctance, and when she was on her feet, she leaned over to kiss him again, this time full on the mouth. He felt the damp insistence of her tongue against his lips, but he didn't respond. He felt too helpless, too vulnerable. Her tongue seemed too much like a violation.

Straightening, she said, "I have to go out."

"So late?"

She nodded. "Will you be all right?"

"I'll be fine. Where are you going? Do you want me to go with you?"

She shook her head. "It's work. And the truth of the matter is I don't know whether my source will even show. He sure as hell won't if he sees you."

"You can tell him I'm your brother."

She laughed. "The way you kissed me, I think he'd believe it. Trouble is, there isn't anybody in Salazar who matters who doesn't already know who you are."

"Thanks to Mister Karp." He made no attempt to conceal the bitterness.

"Yes," she said. "Thanks to Mister Karp. But it's

done, David. Whatever else you're going to do, there's nothing you can do about that."

He sat at the window while she showered. He heard her curse when the water acted up, the temperature changing sometimes twenty or thirty degrees with no warning, and when she came out of the bathroom, she was pink all over.

"Too hot?" he asked.

She looked down at her skin. "How did you ever guess? I thought I would be saving money moving in here with you. Fancy digs, and all that. And I thought you might have some clout. Enough to keep the goddamn water running, anyway."

"Sorry. I don't seem to have control over much, these days."

She dressed hurriedly, and he watched her quietly, feeling almost like a voyeur as she tugged on a pair of pink cotton panties, her heavy breasts swaying as she leaned forward. And when those same perfect breasts disappeared into her bra, he felt a pain in his chest, as if dimly recollecting some terrible loss buried deep in his memory.

She packed her tape recorder, tossed a couple of extra tapes into her purse, and clicked it closed. "I'll be back as soon as I can, and we can talk more, if you feel up to it."

"We'll see," he said. "But thanks."

She slipped the bag onto her shoulder, crossed the room once more to kiss him good-bye. He watched her leave, as if mesmerized by the sway of her hips. The door closed softly behind her.

As soon as she was gone, Ripley changed hurriedly, afraid that any delay would cause him to reconsider. He was afraid, too, that Michelle might return before he left, and that she would try to talk him out of his plan. He had no idea whether she would or not, but his own second thoughts kept bouncing around in his head like Roller Derby skaters, colliding in mindless ricochets, skidding along the floor of his skull with legs splayed and arms desperately waving. It was easier to suspect Michelle than to face up to his own uncertainty.

It was a long shot. He knew that. And he knew that people who bet long shots ended up in the poorhouse more often than not. Unless someone named Vinnie caught them on the way and broke their legs. That could happen. And if he screwed up, a lot worse could happen, and almost certainly would.

He slipped on a light jacket, just enough to conceal the Browning in a sling. He thought for a moment about leaving the gun behind, but he was feeling uneasy, besieged. It would be better to have the comfort of the weapon, even if he were unlikely to need it. Its weight under his arm would anchor him somehow.

He didn't want to place his call from the hotel, so he went down to the lobby and out into the muggy street. Salazar had few public phones, and he had to walk several blocks before he found a drugstore that advertised the presence of one inside. There was no booth, just a phone hanging on the wall in one corner, a small plywood partition creating a segregated but decidedly insecure space for conversation.

He waited a long time, counting the rings in his head as if turning aside fingers. He was just about to hang up when someone picked up, surprising him by speaking English.

"Hello."

"Senhor Texeira, please?"

"Who shall I say is calling?"

"Mister Reilly."

"Does he know . . . ?"

"He'll know. Please put him on."

He heard Nkele's resonant baritone in the background as he finished a sentence, apparently approaching the phone as he did so. When he got on, he wasted no time. "What do you want?"

"I have to see you tonight. I need to discuss some things with you."

"That is why the telephone was invented, Mister Reilly."

"Not for this sort of discussion, it wasn't."

"Where are you?"

Ripley realized he didn't know the address. "A drugstore, down the street from the hotel, about six or seven blocks, I think. I'll wait outside."

"No, stay inside. We'll find you."

SIXTEEN

❖

The woman seemed to know who it was she was looking for. She headed straight toward him, her eyes darting around the cluttered drugstore for a moment as if suspecting some sort of trap.

Satisfied, she planted herself directly in front of Ripley, legs slightly apart, like a boxer setting up to deliver a crushing roundhouse. She leaned toward him, one hand extended. "Mister Reilly?" Her voice had a pleasant lilt, almost Celtic, as if she might have studied in Dublin.

He nodded. "Yes." He took the hand, felt the coolness of the skin, the smooth palm somehow soothing. "You're from Senhor Texeira?"

"Yes. Come with me, please."

He followed her into the street. He noticed the broad hips, their sway, the set of muscular, but very trim, legs as she turned slightly to open the door and hold it for him.

A battered black Ford, its rocker panels coated with reddish mud, sat a few yards up the street, its exhaust puffing white feathers in the twilight humidity. The woman made for the Ford, and both doors on the passenger side swung open before she reached it.

She ducked into the front and slammed the door as he sat down, pulled his legs into the rear, and yanked the door closed with a squeal from its protesting hinge.

The woman nodded to the driver, and the car pulled away as she turned to face him over the back of her seat. "It'll be fifteen minutes or so," she said.

"Who are you?" he asked.

She gave him a dazzling smile. Her teeth looked white as Chiclets in the dim light, but she said nothing. The driver was the same one who'd driven the van, the one Nkele called James. He was a big man. A roll bulged over his tight collar, and Ripley could tell it was anything but fat. The Ford followed the twisting streets, turning left and right and right and left, seemingly at random. It was apparent the driver was concerned about surveillance, and was doing his best to shake off any pursuit, seen or unseen.

Ripley felt just the least bit foolish. He didn't know who these people were, not really, and he had no idea where they were taking him. He remembered the Browning under his arm, but it gave him no comfort. They hadn't bothered to frisk him, and he wondered why.

Leaning back in the seat and letting his breath out in a great gust, he closed his eyes for a moment, and when he opened them, the woman was looking at him. Her face was almost perfect, an elongated oval, its softness tempered by an aquiline nose, the color of mahogany. Her eyes were a dark brown that was nearly opalescent. In the dimness, their fire must have come from somewhere inside her, he thought. There wasn't enough ambient light to explain the glow.

For a moment, he imagined there was a sheet of Plexiglas between them, as if he were a specimen in a cage, and he smiled. She smiled back at him, but maintained her silence.

Turning to the window, Ripley watched a stream of shanties, their sides covered with tar paper held in place by nails, the rusted heads trailing brown stains down the black paper. Most of them were dark, and he looked for some source of electricity, but found none. The sun was ahead and slightly to the left, and he realized they were heading northwest, toward the ocean.

In other circumstances, he realized, the determined silence of his escort would have been unsettling, even ominous, but he welcomed the quiet. He was able to think if he chose, or blot things out of his mind altogether, which seemed the more attractive option. The sun was gone a moment later, so abruptly that he steeled himself to wait for the thud when it landed somewhere below the horizon. There was none, of course, and the arrival of night made the silence all around him that much deeper.

He still didn't know why he had called Nkele. There was no news, none good, at any rate, but he felt as if he had something to say, as if somewhere deep inside him, insulated from his brain by bone and gristle, he carried an important message, one so secret, even he didn't know what it was. He would have to haul it up, a man tugging on a fishing line to drag something out of the depths, maybe a piece of junk, maybe a coelacanth. He wouldn't know until it hung there in front of his eyes still dripping ooze from the bottom, where it came from.

They were heading back toward Salazar now, using the shore road. Off to the right, he could see breakers cresting, their ridges outlined in phosphorescent foam. He rolled down the window, the sudden pumping of his arm prompting James to turn and glare at him. "Don't do that without you warn me first, man."

The accent floored him. It was pure U.S.A., probably Philly. He wondered whether to mention it, or if acknowledging it would invite disaster by breaching some unsuspected agreement. He watched the woman for a moment to see whether she seemed alarmed, but she continued to face ahead as if the driver hadn't even spoken.

"Just wanted to listen to the surf," Ripley said. "Sorry I startled you."

"Long as you don't listen to no surf music. That shit's too white for me, man."

This time the temptation was too strong. "Where you from, James?" Ripley asked.

"Everywhere, man. I belong to the fucking planet. If there's a place to hang my hat, that's where I'd be home. If I wore a hat. But I don't wear no hats, man. Hats mess with your head."

He ran a hand through the tight curls, so shiny they were tinted green by light reflected from the dash panel. He laughed then, a deep, resonant sound centered somewhere between his spine and his sternum, from the very center of him.

Ripley thought that was the end of it, but after a few moments, the driver said, "Where you from?"

"Montana."

"I been there. Wherebouts?"

"Not too far from the Wyoming border. Place called Powderville."

"All white folks there, am I right?"

"Pretty much."

The driver laughed again. "At least they don't have no surf music there. Them cowboys don't like no Beach Boys. That's got to be a plus."

"You been with Mister Nkele long?"

"Three years. I come over here, back to the motherland you might say, a long time ago. Looking for my roots. Found out I didn't have none, but I liked it, so I stayed. Mawindi was a pretty place back then."

Ripley leaned toward the open window now, and rested his head on the window frame. The breeze was warm, but at least it was moving air, and he listened to the humming of the tires on one of the few good roads he'd seen since his arrival. The surf was pounding, and it drew him to it the way only something alien can draw you. For a boy from the Big Sky country, nothing on earth was more alien than the sea.

There were buildings on the left now, long, low buildings that looked like warehouses, with their corrugated doors and concrete piers. Train tracks glistened under an occasional floodlamp, where a cone of light widened out toward the ground, splattering on the wall on its way down. To the right, a strip of brush no more than fifteen or twenty yards wide scaled down to a broad, gently sloping white beach. And beyond it, the dark waters grumbled, tossing off glowing curls of foam. He tried to imagine swimming in it, and wondered just how long he'd last before something older than mankind swallowed him whole.

The car began to move more slowly now, the smooth humming of the tires rasping now on blown sand. He could hear the dull throb of a leaky muffler, its rumble when James backed off the gas to coast into a turn, and for the first time he noticed the vibration of the floor beneath his feet. It brought him back to the joy of his first car, a '57 Chevy with a four-barrel carb and dual glasspacks. That little 283 V-8 seemed like the most powerful machine on the planet then and now, even with Apollo rockets and B-52's, it still held first place in a corner of his heart, the love tucked away where nothing could dislodge that first impression.

The driver turned off his lights, and the car continued to roll, just the sound of its muttering engine signalling its passage through the humid night. To the right, the funnels and masts of freighters clogged the skyline. The breakers were gone, having given way to the grumbling swells of the deep water harbor.

Like most waterfronts, Salazar's smelled damp, musty. Under the sound of the waves slapping against pilings, Ripley knew there was the almost inaudible skitter of rat feet on the creosote soaked docking, the scraping whisper of those same feet along hawsers. During the day, the sky would be littered with the tumbling skip of gulls floating like white rags on the shifting air currents. But now, the sky was dark.

The car turned left into an alleyway between two warehouses, leaving the harbor behind. Between the tall brick walls, the magnified rumble of the Ford sounded like thunder. Ripley rolled up the window to block it out. The woman turned now, and rested her left arm on the seat back, then rested her chin on her forearm. She seemed to be watching him closely, but her eyes were motionless, only the flutter of her ebony lids to tell him she was not a statue.

James killed the engine, letting the car roll into a turn and slowly stop behind the warehouse on the left. "Wait here, man," he said, and got out of the car. The woman smiled.

"What's your name?" Ripley asked.

"No need for you to know that," she said.

A hinge creaked, and Ripley glanced toward the back wall of the warehouse. He saw the oblique shape of a partially opened door and, beyond it, the dim glow of a small light. Two shapes blocked the light for a moment as two men approached the car. "It's time," the woman said, opening her door. Ripley noticed that the domelight did not go on, and he realized that it was by design, not poor maintenance.

He could see that both of the men were armed. One stood back, an automatic rifle, probably an AK-47, held at hip level and braced with a sling over his shoulder. The other came around to the passenger side and opened Ripley's door. He said nothing, but gestured with his own rifle, and Ripley got out. He closed the door softly behind him, leaning on it to engage the latch. The soldier moved around in front of the car, and Ripley followed him. The other armed man pivoted on the balls of his feet, the AK following Ripley as he moved past, then fell in behind.

The woman went into the warehouse, leading the three men in the pathetic parade. The door creaked again as someone swung it closed. Ripley, conscious of the gun behind him, did not want to turn around. Hands grabbed him then, and he felt himself being patted down. He held his hands up to make it easier, and when the Browning was lifted from the shoulder holster, he breathed a sigh of relief, as if he'd just received some sort of dispensation.

A hand pushed him then, and he started forward. He saw Nkele sitting at a makeshift desk of plywood and packing crates. For a chair, Nkele used another crate, cloth draped over its top.

The guards positioned themselves in the shadows, far enough away that their presence was unobtrusive, but close enough that Ripley couldn't forget for a second that they were there.

Nkele leaned forward, one great hand extended. "Mister Ripley," he said, "what is so urgent?"

It was typical of Nkele's no-bullshit style that he would get right to the point. Ripley looked around at the guards, then pulled another empty crate close to the desk and sat down. "I promised I would try to get you more weapons."

Nkele nodded. His face was impassive, gave no trace of whether he expected good news or bad. Inside him, Ripley thought, there must be a maelstrom, but he's too controlled to betray its presence. He waited for a question and when none came, Ripley went on. "I spoke to Karp yesterday. He says you're too unreliable. He doesn't like your connections."

"All this we have already considered. I assume, then, that he will not give us what we need?"

Ripley nodded. "That's right."

"None of it? Not even the non-military items? The medicine?"

"Nothing."

Nkele rocked back and forth a little, for all the world like a CEO in an imported leather chair. "I see," he said. Once more, he extended a hand. "Thank you for coming, Mister Ripley. I appreciate what you have tried to do. I'm just sorry that you had so little success."

He watched then, expecting Ripley to get up, but Ripley stayed on the crate and leaned forward a little closer. "There are four planeloads of weapons and ammunition coming in tomorrow night."

Nkele shrugged. "If they are not for me, I see no reason . . ."

"That's my point, Oscar. They *can* be."

Nkele looked confused for a moment. "Are you suggesting that I take them by force?"

"That's exactly what I'm suggesting. It's the only way you'll ever get the support you need. And, in my judgment, it's the only way to prevent Bandolo from capturing the capital before independence. Caulfield can't stop him, not with ten times the guns and money he's already received. And there isn't that much in the budget anyway."

"But if I do what you suggest, it will foreclose the possibility that Washington will change its' mind. They will never reconsider. I will be an outlaw, as far as they are concerned."

"Look, Oscar, as far as they are concerned, you're already an outlaw. Which is better, being an outlaw with guns or being one without them?"

"Will you forgive me if I . . ." He glanced at the guards, and said, "Marcello, will you and Augustinho leave us alone for a bit, please?"

When the guards were out of earshot, he finished the question as if it had never been suspended. ". . . suggest that that sounds very much like provocation to me?"

Ripley smiled. "Of course. I know what it sounds like, and I don't blame you, but I'm telling you that this is your only chance, and Mawindi's only chance. If you think about it, I know you'll agree."

"If I do what you are suggesting, it will be difficult to conceal my role in it, and it will not be long before your own part becomes known."

"I'm at the point where I don't give a fuck."

"What possible reason can you have for caring about this, to take such a risk with your career, possibly with your life?"

Ripley drew a long breath, held it for a long moment, then slowly expelled it. "I wondered about that, but I think I know the answer."

"And that is . . . ?"

"I'm tired, Oscar, tired of all the bullshit, tired of all the double-dealing, the manipulation, the abuse of trust, the . . . hell, tired of it all. I was sent here to do a job, but I've since come to understand that my job was not what I was told. I'm not here to help your side win, or Caulfield's side either. I'm just here to make sure it takes Bandolo a while longer to win. It's exactly the way we got into Vietnam and it makes no sense, no goddamn sense at all. I lived through that nightmare and I refuse to live through another one just like it."

Nkele covered his face with his hands and massaged his eyes with his fingertips. Then, tilting his head back, he stroked the whiskers under his chin, caressed his throat as if he were a vampire assessing a victim, then nodded. "And if I say yes?"

"We'll take our chances."

"Your risk is small, Mr. Ripley, just a personal one. I'm risking the future of my country."

"I know that, but it's the only chance you have, Oscar. If you don't take it, your country doesn't *have* a future."

SEVENTEEN

❖

August 9, 1975

Ripley stood on the apron, just outside the reach of floodlights hanging from the eaves of a hangar. Anxiously, he searched the skies looking for signs of the flight of C-130's. The big Hercules transports were already a half-hour overdue. Glancing to the east, Ripley thought he could already see the first gray stains seeping across the sky as the sun came closer and closer to the edge of the world.

He was nervous, and he was angry. Nervous because nothing in Mawindi was what it was supposed to be, and even angrier for the same reason. Safe in Zaire, a teat firmly grasped in each greedy hand, Joseph Mobutu had been milking QTHONEY for all it was worth. Holding a gun to the State Department's head, he had been demanding more and more compensation for his continued cooperation. He claimed he was taking risks that he had to keep secret even from his own men, lest he end up in the trunk of a car, like Patrice Lumumba, his bones broken, bleeding from every orifice. He was willing to help defeat the MLF, but he sure as hell didn't want to go out too soon, and have nothing to show for his pain but a university that bore his name in some foreign capital.

Where the hell were the planes? The flight from Kinshasa only took two hours. It was only a hundred and fifty fucking miles, after all. Even the poorly trained Zairian pilots should be able to go that far without getting lost.

Ripley began to pace, walking all the way to the end of the hangar and peering around its corner into the pitch blackness behind it, a blackness in which only figures out of Conrad could possibly feel secure. Africa had changed, more than he could have imagined, more than he could even understand. He was beginning to wonder whether or not he might be cut from the same cloth as the Portuguese and the limeys and the frogs. Maybe the Africa that floated somewhere in the center of his brain was a white man's Africa and, now that it was becoming the black man's continent again, he was feeling lost, maybe even betrayed, and more than a little afraid. It was irrational and at the very least disingenuous of him to harbor such feelings, but he was reeling. Everything he had ever known about Africa now seemed centuries out of date. He was starting to think he had no clearer an understanding of this place than would Sophocles were he to find himself in Athens when the sun rose tomorrow.

Looking to the northeast, he strained his eyes, even shielding them despite the fact that the nearest floodlight was a hundred yards behind him, its illumination all but nonexistent for the last fifty yards of that distance. He was staring across a hundred and fifty miles of rainforest, across one of the world's major rivers, and into the pitch black night of the dark continent. It was a wonder that he could see anything at all, he thought, let alone four tiny points thousands of feet in the air.

He strained to pick up the sound of the C-130s' big turboprop engines, but heard nothing but the whirring of a million insect wings and the irregular drip of dew from the eaves, landing with sudden splashes in the puddles at the base of the hangar wall. For a brief moment, he imagined that this must be what it was like floating in one of Lilly's sensory deprivation tanks, drifting aimlessly, his body in some sort of limbo, balanced between sinking and swimming at the perfect crest of that eternal moment of choice. It was equilibrium of a sort, with all of the awesome implications of the state, when the least investment of energy would translate into the most perilous of all human actions—a change of course.

He wanted to hear something, anything, that he recognized, the chirp of crickets out beyond the outfield fence on a summer night, just as the lights went on, the distant flutter of an owl's wings as it swept earthward in search of a mouse, the feet of that mouse scraping desperately on dry soil as it tried to hide. But he heard nothing but the bugs, because there was nothing else to hear.

To cover his uncertainty, he started to hum, running through an asortment of Charlie Parker riffs, fucking up "Dewey Square," "Scrapple from the Apple," "Parker's Mood" and "Confirmation" in short order, then pursing his dry lips and trying to wet them with a tongue that felt like a razor strop.

That was when he saw the initial burst of illumination far to the north, as the first of the C-130's kicked on its landing lights. He could hear the engines then, sounding as if they were a hundred miles behind the twin lances stabbing through the darkness of the night sky. A moment later a second pair, then a third and finally the fourth. Ripley took a deep breath, held it for a moment, wondering whether that pain in his chest was indigestion, or something worse, until it faded.

Watching the planes glide in, their engines rumbling, the sound growing louder and louder as the massive transports fell out of the sky, he watched the first C-130 touch down, but not until he heard the screech of its huge tires on the runway did he start to move. Then he ran to his jeep and jumped in. Cranking up the engine, he sped across the apron to the railroad siding where work lamps on aluminum stanchions cast a stark white light on the waiting boxcars, their open doors black rectangles in the peeling wooden sides.

The second plane had hit the runway now, and the first was taxiing toward the freight apron, where a half-dozen forklifts lurched, their squat bodies looking topheavy under the square engine housings. He could see the traffic control tower, its windows smeared with pale green light far across the strip of grass between runways. Several men raced on foot after the forklifts, looking like men chasing strange metallic beetles.

Ripley heard the third plane touch down, and backed off on the engine to let the jeep coast toward the end of the raggedy looking train, hit the brakes and skidded to a halt.

The first transport was already turning in place, its cargo doors starting to crack like a clam deciding whether it was safe to peek out. The ground traffic controller waved a pair of colored paddles edged with phosphorescent tape that glowed whitely, almost as if nothing were there. The pilot backed off on the engines but left them on. As the overworked whine of the Hercules' engines dwindled down, the plane's wheels were chocked. When the cargo bay was all the way open, the gangway in place, the first forklift lurched up into the gaping maw.

One by one, the planes fell in, to wait their turn, the forklifts grinding gears all the way up into the bay, disappearing deeper and deeper inside, then staggering back, huge pallets of weapons and ammunition teetering precariously as they tilted forward and started down the ramp. It looked as if some mammoth insect queen were being serviced by orange drones, their sides striped with carbon where the diesels wheezed and choked their thick smoke.

In his jacket, Ripley had a sheaf of bills of lading, but there was no time to check the shipment now. He wanted the planes back in Kinshasa before daybreak, and the train well on its way toward the sunrise. He stood near the first plane watching the last two pallets drawing groans from the lumbering forklifts. Spotting the shipping labels that identified the CIA arsenal in South Carolina, all he could do was shake his head. Anyone watching, and he hoped no one had a camera, would have no doubt where the shipments originated. Some asshole had forgotten the weapons were supposed to be deniable. He would have blown a gasket if it would have made a difference, but it was too damn late now, and the idiot responsible had six thousand miles and an ocean's worth of buffer. And as it was, there didn't seem to be a soul in Salazar who didn't know where the weapons were coming from.

Ripley kept glancing at the sky, then at his watch, and back. The offloading seemed to be proceeding in slow motion, as if the world had suddenly been covered with clear jelly to a depth of fifty feet. He wondered whether any moment he might realize that he couldn't breathe and suddenly find himself drowning in the transparent goo.

It was nearly three-thirty before the last plane had been emptied. He watched it taxi away, so anxious to be airborne that its cargo doors finally fluttered closed as it nosed into the end of the runway. The doors of the last freight car rolled shut on metal wheels, the thump of the huge wooden panels echoing along the silent siding.

Steam vented with a watery gush as Ripley scrambled on board the quivering caboose. A dozen silent men in fatigues barely glanced up at him. They seemed to resent him, as if somehow they blamed him for their unwelcome duty. It had been Caulfield's idea, and they were Caulfield's men, allegedly some of his best trained troops. They were a wrinkle he hadn't counted on. It would make things difficult, as if they weren't barely possible as it was. And Ripley knew that armed confrontation between Caulfield's men and

Nkele's could lead to an open war, guaranteeing that the MLF would end up on top.

He watched the men silently, worried about them, worried they might have families, worried they might turn on him if something went wrong and, most of all, worried what would happen to Mawindi if they and their leader were to win the civil war. Their AK-47's rattled against the metal seats as the engine spurted, drawing its train taut with a chain of thuds as coupling after coupling lost its slack and finally the caboose began to move.

Ripley walked to the bench seat in the back and sat down. Later, he would go forward and ride in the engine, but not until the train reached the main line of the Cardozo rail link that probed across the coastal flats, climbed the escarpments of the Transition Zone, then speared arrow straight all the way to the heart of Zambia, more than halfway across the continent. It was the principal rail link of all of Central Africa, and the shipment of the raw materials of three countries depended exclusively on its existence. Once they reached the Cardozo, Caulfield himself would join him. Or at least that was Caulfield's notion of the plan. But if things worked the way they were supposed to, the train would never get to the rendezvous. Then again, not much had gone according to plan lately, and Ripley was getting used to frustrated expectation.

As the train grumbled through the thickening forest, the supreme irony of the situation dawned on Ripley. The load of weapons and ammunition in the freight cars up ahead was destined for Caulfield's PAM, but if it weren't for Oscar Nkele's African People's Party, the Cardozo rail link would long since have been shut down. It might be overstating the significance of the APP's accomplishment in preserving the integrity of the railroad, but Ripley was hard-pressed to find anything that the PAM forces had done which came anywhere close. If there were any justice, Ripley thought, then there'd . . . But he stopped. What was the point in dwelling on it? There was no justice, there was only luck, and precious little of that, either.

He got up and walked to the rear door of the caboose, tried it, and when it rumbled to the side, he stepped out on the rear platform, letting the door slide shut behind him. He lit a cigarette, hanging on to the iron ladder leading to the roof. To the rear, he saw the last vestiges of light disappear among the trees. The skyline of Salazar was long gone, and the silence of the jungle was broken now only by the rumble of the train and the clack of its worn wheels on the rails.

The smoke soothed him a little, and the breeze on the platform made the oppressive heat and humidity tolerable if not pleasant. The forty-mile run to the junction at Malaka shouldn't take more than an hour, and he couldn't wait. He wanted nothing more than to hand over the armaments and head back to Salazar. The more he saw of Jorge Caulfield, the more troubled he became. The man had more than a bit of the charlatan in him, and it was almost as if he were some peculiar hybrid of Mussolini and medicine show barker. He was showy, but there wasn't much beyond the gaudy exterior and the lavish attendance to public relations.

Nkele, on the other hand, seemed to have a vision, or at least a blueprint for the future. It might be sketchy, the lines a little blurred, the paper tattered, but at least it was a plan. Ripley tried to turn the train of thought aside, knowing that part of him was trying to convince the rest of him that the substantial risk he was about to take was for the good of Mawindi, whether anyone knew it or not. And at the moment, he more than half believed the only one in the country who might believe it was Oscar Nkele himself.

The right of way was littered on either side with mounds of brush and severed tree limbs. The forest was so aggressive that it required constant pruning to keep the growth at bay. Left alone, it would grow right down to the gravel railbed in a month. The mounds were just bulky shadows under the sliver of moon barely riding above the canopy, as if skimming on the leaves. The rails weakly reflected the pale light, and they looked as if they were made of newly shaved lead, the almost silver gleam faint among the shadows.

He looked at his watch again, drumming his

fingers on the ladder railing, sucked on the cigarette once more, then crushed it in his fingers and tossed it into the slip stream where it glowed brightly as one wisp of paper burned to ash then winked out. He could smell the cloud of oily smoke from the diesel engine which seemed to hang in the greenwalled tunnel like water in a sluice, a thick gray filament payed out by the engine like silk from a spider's spinneret. The turbulence of the slip stream made the smoke swirl in place until it looked like a rotating rod of dark gray suspended just above the roof of the caboose.

The deep rumble of the explosion echoed from the forest on all sides, and the train immediately locked its wheels as the engineer sought to bring it to a halt. The piercing shriek of metal on metal sliced through the darkness, and sparks showered out behind the caboose. Nearly thrown off balance, Ripley grabbed the ladder and swung out over the side of the platform. He wrenched his elbow and shoulder in the process, and stared at the strange beauty of the cascading sparks all the way forward to the engine, past clouds of steam from the brakes glowing from the sparks as if full of tiny, darting comets or frenzied fireflies.

This is it, he thought, and released the safety on his AR-15 before jumping off the side of the platform before the train came to a complete halt. He heard shouting voices up ahead, then wands of orange light swept out of the jungle and slashed every which way. There was a flurry of gunshots as he sprinted, and he realized that he'd better take it easy lest he run into a stray slug.

Behind him, Caulfield's men were spilling out of the caboose like soldier ants from an anthill. He heard their boots crunch on the gravel as they raced toward him, then more gunshots from up ahead. Tracers lasered into the sky, and it was apparent that whoever was firing was hoping the noise alone would accomplish his purpose.

More feet crunched on the gravel and suddenly lights speared out of the jungle. He saw headlights and only then did he recognize the shape of the jeep draped in cut boughs leaving only its headlights exposed. Ahead, three more jeeps were similarly disguised. Ducking under a coupling between two cars he found the other side of the train also impaled by twin beams from several hidden jeeps.

Racing toward the front of the train, he found the trunk of a huge tree across the tracks and against the tree line, saw a gaping hole in the earth where the explosion had torn the shallowly rooted tree loose. Caulfield's men were in a panic, firing blindly, emptying clips into the trees on either side of the train. One pair of headlights went out, and the hiss of steam from a punctured radiator sounded as if a huge serpent, black as the night itself, were slithering out of the jungle intent on swallowing everything in sight.

A moment later, someone bellowed over a loudhailer in Portuguese, the words at first buried under the rapid fire of PAM's AK-47's. For a moment, Ripley thought that something had gone desperately wrong. But as the words gradually emerged from the chaos, his fears subsided.

"Throw down your weapons," the disembodied voice commanded, "and you will not be harmed."

EIGHTEEN
❖

The loudhailer barked again. Caulfield's men froze like jacked deer, their limbs arrested in motion leaving them in awkward poses, a leg suspended in mid-air, toes pointed toward the gravel, an arm half raised and with the fluidity of movement gone looking as if it were in a cast after a particularly bad fracture. One man had a cigarette clamped in his jaws, and it seemed that even the smoke had frozen in its ascent.

"Throw down your weapons!" The bell of the loudhailer gave the voice resonance, and it seemed to echo down along the train, bouncing in and out of the spaces between the cars before being swallowed by the thick green walls of jungle on either side.

Like the others, Ripley stood stock still. He knew he couldn't keep his part in the hijacking quiet forever, but if it were to work smoothly, he had to maintain the fiction at least for a while. He sensed that Caulfield's men were looking to him for guidance, and turned his head. The PAM soldiers, rigid as Segal sculptures in faded fatigues, moved only their eyes. Ripley could see them glittering in the glare of the headlights as they watched him.

Nodding his head, he raised his hands a little, as if to reassure the unseen captors that he meant no harm, and let his AR-15 fall to the ground. It cracked against the gravel, its stock sounding as if it had split in two. Then it rained AK-47's as the rest of the men dropped their rifles and raised their hands.

"Line up against the train," the hidden commander barked. "Face the cars. Hands overhead on the freight cars."

The engine belched steam, and then sighed as a cloud of white swirled around Ripley for a moment, beading on his skin and leaving him feeling damp and limp. He turned and walked to the train, listening to the crunch of two dozen pairs of boots on the gravel rail bed.

He was just behind the tender and moved to the rear a bit until he reached the front of the first freight car, then spread his legs and leaned forward, letting his flattened palms take the bulk of his weight.

Glancing back along the freight car, he saw the rest of the men following his example. He could hear the subdued muttering of men who felt foolish, but who were too frightened to be angry at themselves or at anyone else. For a long moment the only sound was the throbbing of the great engine, and it seemed to Ripley as if he were leaning against a huge beast, its heart pounding. He could feel the vibrations ripple down his arms and rattle his shoulders until they seemed loose in their sockets.

A rush of foliage being swept aside signalled that the captors were about to make their presence felt more immediately, and he steeled himself, still not certain that it was Nkele and his men who had sprung the trap. Information was worth its weight in gold in the burgeoning civil war, and anyone who had known that four planeloads of munitions and weapons were on the move might easily have cut himself a deal.

Ripley heard the approach of several men, how many he couldn't tell. For a moment he worried that Nkele would give himself away, but he knew that a shrewd commander would not expose all his forces in any event. It was almost certain that more men were hidden among the trees behind the jeeps. It was also likely that there were machine guns mounted on some of the jeeps, no doubt trained just about hip high on the captives. It was how he would have played it. And an itchy trigger finger wouldn't need much provocation to slice from one end of the car to the other, cutting all of them in half in less time than it would take for the idea of prayer to crystallize in his dying brain.

Someone stood directly behind him now, patted him down, removed the Browning from his hip and, satisfied that he had no concealed weapons, jerked him bodily away from the train.

He stood there watching as four men made their way along the line of captives, frisking each in turn then pulling him away and moving on. Looking around him, trying not to move his head, he saw several more men, each armed with an assault rifle and wearing the Soviet made uniform of the MLF. Once more, the thought that there might have been a leak, that Bandolo had learned of the plan and turned the tables crept through his skull on crablike claws.

Where the hell was Nkele, he wondered. What the fuck was going on?

But the quick search was almost over, and as the last of Caulfield's men was yanked away from the train, the loudhailer barked once more. "Line up!"

Ripley looked toward the trees, hoping to spot Nkele, then realized that he would not reveal himself in order to preserve the flimsy fiction, at least for a little while. Ripley was first in line, and searched the small knot of armed men anxiously, trying to decide who was in charge. He felt the jostling of the men behind him as the line closed up, each man pressing as close as he could against the one in front, as if trying to hide himself in borrowed flesh.

The knot uncoiled, and the small band of men in MLF garb spaced themselves evenly along a line parallel to that of their captives. One of them, a squat, beetle-like man with a bushy mustache, said, "We ought to shoot them all. We have plenty of bullets now." He laughed the barking laugh of a sea lion, and shifted an AK nervously in his stubby fingers.

Further down the line, another echoed the sentiment, and took a step toward the captives. He raised his rifle overhead and brought it down sharply. The dull thump of the heavy wooden stock on meat over bone sounded like a melon splitting open.

Ripley turned to the rear of the line, and the squat man raised his rifle a few inches, shaking his head. This wasn't supposed to happen, Ripley thought. There was not supposed to be bloodshed.

He sorted through the past twenty-four hours, just shards of time, as if someone had shattered a clock and left minutes and seconds in a mound on the floor. Nothing jumped at him, and he sifted the detritus blindly, looking for some hint that

Oscar Nkele was not what he had seemed to be. Had there been some nervous tic to indicate a lie? Had a word accidentally found expression, one that would have aroused caution in a more attentive man? Maybe Nkele's gaze had fluttered around the room like a terrified moth, afraid to land anywhere long enough to fall victim to the lizard. Was he to fall victim to his own plan, go down in flames like some overreaching Icarus?

But no, there had been nothing like that. Nkele's eyes had been bold and unwavering. His words had been simple and direct, his face animated but open. The man was what he appeared to be, he had to be, because anything else was unthinkable.

The man who had been bludgeoned lay on the ground now, moaning, both hands clasped over a collar bone that surely had been broken. Ripley said, "Let me have a look at him." Without waiting for an answer, he turned in place, stepped out of the line and started toward the stricken man.

A burst of gunfire shattered the uneasy silence. The slugs ripped an arc through the gravel, each shattering several small stones and scattering sparks as they plowed into the earth not twelve inches from Ripley's feet. "Back in line," the beetle-like soldier said. "Now!"

Ripley stared at the ground as if stunned. This couldn't be happening, not to him. It was his plan, a creature of his own convoluted brain, and it had to work. It *would* work, dammit!

As if in response to that thought, a burst of machine gun fire exploded down the line a bit, and tracers slashed through the humid air, narrowly missing the roof of the engine and tender. The loudhailer erupted again, its coarse bellow strangely soothing, almost serene, in the aftermath of the gunfire. "Get those men in the cars, quickly. Quickly!"

The men in MLF mufti, if that's what it was, exploded into frenzied activity, some running toward the rear of the train and yanking open the doors of several of the freight cars until they found an empty one. The others forced their captives to about face and prodded them with AK muzzles to march back along the train.

Instinctively, Ripley looked at the sky, like a man who thinks he may never see it again. One by one, the captives were hoisted up into the train, their comrades reaching down now to help, as if asserting their right to have some little control over events. Ripley had one hand extended and was starting to raise his right knee to haul himself aboard when the squat soldier clapped a heavy hand on his shoulder and pulled him back. "Not you!" he barked.

Ripley watched as the door was rolled shut, and a padlock rammed through the latch and forcefully clicked shut. "Come with me," the squat man said. He headed back the way they had come, his banty legs give him a rolling gait that would have been comical if it hadn't been for the muzzle of the AK jutting past his left hip, glinting in the headlights still spearing out from the undergrowth.

A schizoid shadow suddenly spilled from the brush as someone moved in front of one of the jeeps, blocking the headlights. Smeared on the side of the train, it looked to Ripley like the figure of a circus freak, a two-headed man, with two torsos joined at the hip, supported by four stick-like legs and sprouting a welter of arms.

He turned to peer into the darkness, where the figure was haloed for a moment by the light, then turned obsidian, but he was unable to see the approaching man's face. He didn't have to. He recognized the confident stride of Oscar Nkele.

"I thought you'd never . . ." Ripley blurted, then stopped when Nkele held a finger to his lips. He reached Ripley, put an arm around his shoulder and pulled him toward the front of the train. The squat man was already climbing up into the engineer's compartment, and two more men climbed in after him.

"What the hell is going on?" Ripley hissed.

Nkele shrugged. "I wanted to spare you the embarrassment of discovery," he said. "It wouldn't do to have Caulfield learn that you are helping me this way. I thought it best to take the masquerade all the way to its logical conclusion."

"You scared the hell out of me."

Nkele grunted. He looked back toward the rear of the train, raised a hand, and said, "And them, too. That was the idea. It had to look convincing, and it did, don't you think?"

"But those men were in fear for their lives. They might have gotten desperate, done anything. There could have been real bloodshed."

Nkele shrugged again. "There wasn't," he said.

"But dammit, there could have been."

"This is a war, Mister Ripley. A war that either no one wants and everyone has to fight, or a war that everyone wants and no one wants to fight. I don't know which."

Ripley took a deep breath. He wanted to say something more, something to make his displeasure unmistakable, but he had nothing to say. And he knew that Nkele was right.

Suddenly the cough, sputter, and finally the snarl, of chainsaws echoed down along the train. One of the jeeps lurched out of its camouflage and spun into position with its tail toward the fallen tree. The spurt of the released chain signalled that the first cut was completed, then another, and the whine of winch joined the uproar as a cable was payed out. Ripley watched as the first section of the fallen tree was hauled off the tracks.

The APP leader studied him in silence a long time, then nodded as if to himself before asking, "Which do you think it is, Mister Ripley?"

"I think it's a war everybody needs, Oscar. Don't ask me why they need it, but I think they do. And I think they're going to get their wish. And I don't want to be around when somebody finally sits down to tally the cost. And I don't mean in dollars."

Nkele nodded again. "You are probably right." There was genuine sadness in his voice.

This was no war lover, Ripley thought, not like Caulfield, and not like Karp. This was a man who knew the human cost of the war that seemed to be creeping unseen through an entire country, the way an electrical fire can creep through the walls of a house unnoticed while its inhabitants sleep, until someone opens a door and the rush of oxygen sends it roaring out into the night, tearing off the roof and leveling the walls in one gargantuan explosion.

Before Ripley could respond, one shrill blast of the train whistle tore the night apart, and he looked up at the sky, now dark gray and seeming to brighten even as he watched.

"We have to go," Nkele said. "Once the train is late, they will come looking for it. We have to get to Malaka, get off the main line, unload and get the train back before sunrise."

Already, soldiers were tearing the camouflage from the jeeps and throwing it aside. The engine started to throb and Nkele swung up onto the steps and climbed into the engine. Ripley followed him as the train started to move.

The sun seemed to vault over the horizon dead ahead, and suddenly it was morning. The train was making good time, but there was still fifteen miles before the junction with the spur to Malaka, where the shipment could be unloaded and carted away. Then the train would be brought back to the main line and run back to the scene of the hijack where another tree would be felled across the tracks. It might keep Caulfield guessing for a few more hours, if they were lucky. And by then, there would be nothing he could do about it.

"What about the prisoners?" Ripley shouted over the pounding of the engine.

"What about them?"

"What are you going to do with them?"

Nkele smiled. "Don't worry. Nothing will happen to them. That would be the most expedient thing, but I am not interested in seeing Mawindi lose any more men than necessary. When this is all over, we will need all the help we can get to rebuild."

"That doesn't answer my question."

Nkele sighed. "They will be given the opportunity to join us."

"And if they refuse?"

"I'll think of something."

"I want your word that no harm will come to them."

"I am not God, Mister Ripley. And you know as well as I do that harm comes to us all one day."

"I want your word . . ."

Nkele nodded. Ripley wasn't satisfied, but it would do. It would have to, if only because there had to be someone he could trust in this damn country.

NINETEEN

August 13, 1975

Ripley hoisted himself up the last twenty feet of the tree, trying to ignore the insistent shredding of his skin where the ants swarmed over his hands and wrists, their tiny pincers tearing at him, the sear of formic acid raising welts and turning the exposed areas to masses of red bumps.

It was nearly nightfall, and the firing had subsided a bit, but there was no question that Bandolo's forces outnumbered the APP unit by three or four to one. For two days now, Oscar Nkele had remained calm, sending small units in a series of hit and run attacks, seemingly content to harass the MLF rather than confront it head on.

In theory, Nkele's approach was sound—infiltrating his men through the MLF lines. The troops had been hand picked and armed with the cream of the stolen weapons shipment. Getting into position had been the easy part, but executing the rest of the plan promised to be a major headache. Caulfield had arranged his own forces in a broad arc fifty miles outside of Salazar. They weren't disciplined and they weren't organized. Their leaders were less than competent. But they had guns and plenty of them. They had mortars and they had all the bullets they could use. They were enough to slow Bandolo's approach, but nowhere near enough to stop it, as long as the MLF was free to concentrate its attention on a single objective.

When Nkele had first broached the flanking strategy, Ripley had been opposed.

"You'll divide your forces. You pull everyone out of Salazar and even if you win you lose, because then PAM is in control of the only city that really counts. You're barely hanging on there as it is."

"I don't worry about Senhor Caulfield, David. He is a fool, but at least he wants something close to what I want. If he wins, then Mawindi is better off than if we both lose, and we *will* lose unless we can find some way to slow the MLF down, at least long enough to convince the United States that we are serious, that we can win, and that it is better for the United States and Mawindi both that Joshua Bandolo loses."

"They don't care whether he wins or not, Oscar. Dammit, how many times do I have to tell you that?"

"But they *must* care. They would not spend money for this war if they did not care who won it."

"They would and that is in fact what they *are* doing."

Nkele nodded impatiently. "But they will change their minds when they see they can win. I know what is wrong with Washington. They lost in Vietnam and they are afraid to try again. It is too soon, and your people will not permit another war like that. But if this one can be won, and I believe, no, I *know*," and he thumped one huge fist on his chest with the sound of a hammer striking a barrel, "that it *can* be won, then they will change their minds. All we have to do is show them."

"Oscar, they won't change their minds. I promise you, they won't change their minds. Don't you understand, they don't care, dammit, they don't care."

"You don't know that for sure. No one has told you this. No one has said that the president wants us to lose."

"No, no one has told me any of those things.

But the handwriting is on the wall. You don't understand what's going on. The Congress is investigating the Central Intelligence Agency. The Congress is angry and the people are angry, and that anger will put handcuffs on everyone. The CIA can't do what it wants to do, Oscar. There is no will to win. They just don't care."

"I will teach them to care. I will show them that there are men who can be depended on to keep the promises they make."

"I've talked to Bob Karp until I'm blue in the face, and he won't change his mind. He won't listen. He doesn't even hear me anymore, for Christ's sake. They don't want your promises."

"They already have them. And I will keep them. You will see tomorrow."

That had been three days ago. After a tense meeting with Bob Karp, Ripley had left without telling anyone, not even Michelle, where he was going. He'd left a note for her saying that he'd be back in a week or ten days, and not to worry. But he had barely been able to keep his own hand from trembling as he scribbled the note. He was worried then, and he had seen nothing in the last three days to calm his fears.

Clinging to the tree, he kept thinking back over the last couple of weeks. He had the feeling that he was locked into a course from which no deviation was possible. Somewhere along the way he had made a decision, but that decision had involved relinquishing the ability to make another. He felt helpless, like the observer he was supposed to be, powerless to do anything but watch. Under the illusion of decisive action, he had completely sacrificed the ability to act.

Near the top of the canopy, he could see several columns of black, oily smoke rising over the veldt half a mile away. In the southwestern corner of Mawindi, where the descent of the Transition Zone was less abrupt, the forest gave way to grasslands in fits and starts. Pockets of forest still dotted the open plains for another fifty miles eastward, but they were small and grew more and more rare.

He could hear the crump of an occasional mortar shell, but it seemed now as if combat were dwindling away, just as it had the two previous evenings. It was almost as if the war had become a relic of a more gentlemanly time, a time when soldiers rose and set with the sun. Maybe, Ripley thought, that was the way it should be. Maybe it ought to be a requirement that wars only be fought in the glare of midday, when the spilled blood and the ends of broken bones would glisten on the battlefield for all to see.

And Ripley shook his head at the notion, knowing that most wars now were fought because the men who fought them had secrets. The light of day was an antiseptic, and the modern warmakers were more at home in their anonymity. It was war made by creatures that hid behind desks and mounds of paper, the way slugs hid under rocks in the dank and slimy darkness. With a rueful grimace, he realized that such men included him among their number. He wondered whether Oscar Nkele were also at home in the subterranean labyrinth where life and death decisions were made for millions. It seemed almost too much to be asked to believe that the man be exactly what he seemed.

He heard another mortar shell and saw the gust of dirty air where it had detonated, then the writhing snake of black smoke that signified a hit. The MLF had started with more than two dozen armored cars and six tanks. Those numbers had been reduced, but not by much. What Nkele needed was more sophisticated weapons. LAWS rockets maybe, for the armor. Maybe even the Redeye. But even Caulfield wasn't getting Redeyes. As usual, there was a lag in the rate at which new technology made it into the international arms trade. Only weapons readily available to anyone with enough cash could be convincingly denied. The Redeye was too easily traceable to its source. There were only two, Israel and the U.S. itself, and everyone knew that if Israel parted with modern weapons, it did so with the blessing, overt or otherwise, of the original source. And there could be no doubt as to who that original source might be.

Ripley was disappointed with the view. The canopy was so thick, all he could do was look over the top of the green carpet, already beginning to darken as the light began to fade. It was like looking across a table top and trying to see what was on the floor on the opposite side. He was tempted to stay in the tree, because it made him feel secure, almost comfortable, despite the fire ants making a feast of his limbs. He found himself wondering whether it had been like that two million years and a continent away. Why had men bothered to come down from the trees? What was it about the ground that seemed so attractive? He wondered whether that had been the temptation of the serpent. Had it not been an apple after all, but an enticement to come down out of the trees, the hands, freed from the necessity of clinging to rough bark, now free to wreak havoc? And had that first tentative step onto terra firma been original sin?

He started to work his way back down, and the earth seemed to be pulling him almost angrily, as if it feared that he had been about to break free, as if he had come so close to the point of no return that earth would lose its hold on him and, free at least of its immense gravity, he might find that the way to paradise lay not back through garden gates but in a leap toward pearly ones, soaring above the ground with its terrible pull, free to rise as high as he might, perhaps so high that he could not come back even if he wanted to.

When he dropped most of the way down, and the last and least layer of brush began to claw at his clothes, he let himself fall like a stone, landing in a crouch and feeling the shock all the way up through his skeleton, every bone passing on the shudder to the next until his skull threatened to rattle free of his spine.

A sudden flurry of small arms fire punctuated the gathering darkness. Instinctively, he dropped to the ground. He could hear voices shouting in three languages, none of them English, as he lay there trying to orient himself to the source of the exchange. It was sporadic, and when the next burst, a little closer than the first, chattered, its sharpness attenuated by the thick undergrowth, he turned toward the sound slowly, precisely, as if he were an automaton homing in.

Ripley glanced over his shoulder, back toward the small camp where Nkele directed his forces by radio. He wanted to run, and he didn't know which way to go. If he ran toward the firing, and the MLF were making a last twilight assault, he might run right into them. But if he ran the other way, he might give Nkele the wrong idea. After all his brave talk, it would look foolish, if not downright cowardly, to explode out of the brush in full flight.

He was no stranger to jungle warfare. Two tours in the Marines in Vietnam and two more in the same hellhole as an Agency man had taught him the one lesson that a survivor most needed to learn—watch every fucking step, it could be your last.

He made the only decison he could make, the

only one he could live with—dying was better than losing face—and started toward the gunfire. More voices slithered through the brush, their origin buried in green, and he zigzagged among the brush clumps, holding the AR-15 at an angle to plow through the insistent wall. It crossed his mind that he was surrounded by life on all sides, a million forms, most of them insects, the likely inheritors of all that would survive after mankind played out his option.

The deeper into the jungle he pushed, the faster he tried to run, like a magnet drawn by an opposing pole. He thought of those little toys, the black and white terriers on magnetic pedestals, that had so fascinated him as a child, how one would draw the other, how you could use one to tease the other, get it spinning until it didn't know which way was up. And he ran still faster, keeping his ears open, but not caring how much noise he made as he plunged on.

Then, off to his left, a short burst, close enough that he could see tracers lancing through the brush. He hit the deck and skidded for several feet on the damp compost underfoot until his shoulder slammed into the trunk of a huge tree. He thought for a moment he'd broken his collarbone, and massaged the aching bruise gingerly. The bone seemed intact, and he shrugged off the pain, hauling himself up with his spine against the rough bark.

More tracers speared past him, several bullets

slamming with resonant thwacks against the tree behind him. Mentally, he gauged the thickness of the trunk and wondered how close to through and through the bullets had come. He could envision the shattered noses of half a dozen metal-jacketed slugs poking like curious copper grubs through the bark and for a moment was tempted to look for traces with his fingers, like a blind man feeling for the braille on an elevator control panel.

Ripley slid the safety off the AR and checked to make sure he had a full magazine. He was baffled by the firing, wondering what the target had been. No one could have seen him, he was sure of that. And then he remembered his breakneck charge and realized that the racket must have drawn the fire his way. He slid back down the trunk of the tree, then rolled onto his stomach and crawled on elbows and knees a good twenty yards to his left.

He stopped to listen then, and heard the far off chatter of men on the verge of hysteria shouting to one another. It seemed to be in Spanish, although the brush dampened the yelling enough that he couldn't be certain it wasn't Portuguese.

His breathing sounded impossibly loud in his ears. His throat felt raw, as if he had been screaming, and every breath seemed to send a sheet of flame down into his lungs. He was out of shape, for sure, and his instincts were rusty. He wished for a moment he'd chosen to run the other way.

The firing immediately in front of him had

stopped. There wasn't a sound now. Even the distant yelling had died away. But somewhere ahead of him, not a hundred yards away, someone lay in wait. He couldn't decide whether to play the same game, or take the dare, confront the challenge head on. The thought of staying there until dawn, letting the jungle and its welter of bloodcurdling night music tear his nerves to shreds, was more than he could stand.

He started slowly, easing out away from the nearest cover. Instinctively, he glanced up toward the canopy, where smears of charcoal sky told him he didn't have much daylight left. Already, the jungle floor was full of shadows that seemed to thicken as he crept ahead. Every few yards, he stopped to wait, to listen, and each time, he heard nothing at all.

As he crawled, his mind seemed to reprogram itself. He forgot all about Oscar Nkele, about Joshua Bandolo. He was alone now, one man against the universe and everything in it that breathed. A single bird could give him away, a single tendril of vine be his complete undoing. He was going native, maybe even further back in time, reverting, as if by some unknown chemical process, back to a primal state, taking on the mindset of the untrammeled forest. It was either that, he thought, or take a slug in the head and litter the moldering carpet with brain tissue and skull fragments. Whether by friend or foe would make no difference.

He'd gone about thirty yards when he heard a

whisper. It came from off to his right, but he couldn't be sure how far away. He lay still, mouth breathing to cut down on the noise. Someone answered the whisper, and it sounded as if the reply came from almost the same spot. At least two, he thought, and close together. But how many more were there?

After three or four minutes of silence, he inched forward again. The smell of the mold and rotting vegetation just under his nose was making him gag, but he swallowed hard and kept his head turned to one side, trying to keep his gorge in check. The brush grew low to the ground, and every trembling leaf sounded like crashing cymbals to his ears. Rolling on his side for a moment, he looked up at the sky once more. The darkness around him had grown still deeper, and there were wisps of reddish orange trailing across the few holes in the canopy far above him. It couldn't be more than fifteen minutes to sunset.

Then he caught a break. Peering along the ground, he saw something move. At first he wasn't sure what it was, but as it moved again, he caught the distinct shape of a combat boot. Screwing his eyelids wide open, he strained to see the other foot. Suddenly, the toe of the boot was pointed straight at him as it moved again. Then the other boot was planted a few inches ahead of the first.

He couldn't see any sign of the second man, and still didn't know whether they were friendlies.

He didn't want to fire blindly through the brush on the off chance that the men were on his team. He'd have to wait. Moving to one side to avoid getting stepped on, he crept backward under some thick, rubbery leaves. Water showered down on him and went down his collar. He felt something squirm, and for a moment he remembered the ubiquitous leeches of Southeast Asia. He reached up, found the lump under his shirt and pressed down hard with his fingertips. Something sharp stabbed into him, then he heard the distinctive crunch of a hard shell—a beetle.

The feet were two yards away now, and they weren't alone. Another pair had joined them, a few feet behind. He took a deep breath and prayed there were no more. He saw fingers curl around the edge of a tall frond, pulled it aside, and a shoulder materialized out of the gloom, followed by a swarthy face, floating above the distinctive gray-green of a Cuban Army uniform.

He felt his trigger finger twitch, and brought the rifle up, its barrel showering more water out of the leaves above him. It had been a long time since he'd shot at a man, longer still since he'd been close enough to see whether he'd hit his target. He wanted to squeeze the trigger, but couldn't do it. If only the second man would expose himself, he could get the drop on them.

The first man was in the open now, looking back over his shoulder, one hand raised as if to call his companion forward. Ripley waited . . . and waited . . . and, finally, the second man stepped into the clear. It was time.

"Frio!" Ripley barked, squeezing off a short burst to freeze the men in their tracks and see whether the gunfire provoked a response from the brush behind his prey.

If God had noticed the crossed fingers, he chose to ignore them. The man in the rear took a step back, and Ripley fired again, this time for effect. The first man turned to see what had happened, his gun rising as he raised his arms, then falling to the ground, its metallic clack dampened by the thick, soft compost underfoot.

Ripley scrambled to his feet, waving the muzzle of his AR back and forth, his eyes fixed on the man's midsection. If the Cuban moved, no matter which way, he was a goner.

TWENTY

◆

It was four o'clock in the morning.

The prisoners were frightened. Nkele sat across from them, a single lantern dangling from the cross bar of the command post tent dripping orange light on his tight, glossy curls and smearing his beard. Ripley sat back against the canvas wall on a folding stool, the pale light from the lantern making his welted skin look jaundiced. He watched Nkele, and marveled at the man's patience as he tried once more to get something from his captives.

"How many Cuban soldiers are there in Mawindi?"

Neither man spoke. They looked at one another without appearing to do so, their eyes swivelling into the corners of their sockets until the pupils almost vanished inside their skulls. Then they looked at the large black man across the table from them and shook their heads.

"How long have you been here?"

The same response.

"Are there many troops in the area?"

And again, the eyeballs swivelled like well-oiled ball bearings, and nothing was said.

Ripley remembered the countless interrogations he had conducted or witnessed. He remembered the rasp of the generator crank, the sudden spurt of urine as testicles jumped and quivered under the prod of the electrodes. He remembered the roar of the wind in the Huey's open door, the pounding engines and whomp of the rotors making everyone shout to be heard. And most of all, he remembered the curiously thin scream as one more uncooperative Vietnamese, political affiliation unknown, arced out and away, the body pinwheeling with arms flailing like broken propellers until it sank out of sight beneath the forest canopy far below, the wail lingering for a few moments in the air until the rotor wash swept it away the way an eraser wiped out a single chalk line, leaving only a blurred swath of a clean blackboard behind it.

He wondered whether Nkele had ever gone so far to get so little. And as he watched the large, patient man slowly rearrange his features, sigh loudly and begin again, Ripley guessed that he had not.

Two of Nkele's men hovered in the entrance to the tent, their eyes hard as marbles as they watched the interrogation. But neither one made a move to bring pressure on the prisoners. There was not going to be any good cop–bad cop routine here. The Cubans would respond of their own free will, or they would say nothing.

For another twenty minutes, Nkele went over the same half-dozen questions, sometimes rephrasing them slightly, sometimes reasking them word for word. And always the response was the same. It became like a litany, all that was missing was the reiterative refrain. Instead of "Have mercy on our souls," or "Pray for our salvation," there was simply silence and the slow swivelling of frightened eyes over and back, over and back, over once more and back once again.

Finally, leaning back in his chair, he faced the fact that his prisoners were not prepared to tell him anything. He nodded slowly, as if to say, so that's how it's going to be. Crooking a finger to the two men in the entrance, he said, "Give them something to eat and then make sure they're secure."

The prisoners looked at Nkele in disbelief, tiny smiles just beginning to tug at the corners of their mouths. Their shoulders went slack for the first time since they'd entered the tent. Ripley lit a cigarette and waited for the guards to escort the two captives away.

"That was a waste of time," Nkele said. "But it always is."

"You could have put more pressure on them," Ripley suggested.

"Sure I could have. But when you squeeze a man too hard, you break his ribs. And you never know how much pressure is too much. Maybe they don't really know anything anyway. The problem with interrogation is that you have to proceed on the assumption that your prisoner knows everything you want to know. More often than not, he doesn't. So you squash him like a bug and get nothing for your efforts. Except a reputation . . ." he smiled sadly.

Then, while Ripley was still off balance, Nkele looked him in the eye. "What would you have done?" he asked.

Ripley shrugged. "I don't know."

"I have heard stories about . . ."

Ripley shook his head. "Those days are gone."

"But the stories are true, aren't they?"

"It depends on what you've heard."

"You know the stories. You've heard more of them than I have. Are they true?"

Ripley nodded. He wondered whether he was being asked about Caulfield or about himself, and realized that the answer was the same in either case. He realized that Karp had probably made no secret of his own experiences in Asia. And there was no reason the COS should have stopped there. He could have, probably did, include Ripley in some of his tales. Karp liked the idea of terror, thought it a useful tool, and often argued that if people thought you were willing to do anything to get what you wanted, as often as not you didn't have to do much more than threaten. But there had been times when threatening hadn't been enough, not nearly enough. And Bob Karp didn't mind rehashing such times in all their grisly detail. But he never embellished. There was no need to.

"How long have you known about the Cubans, Oscar?" Ripley asked.

"I didn't know until you brought them in."

"But you weren't surprised . . ."

Nkele looked up sharply. The tip of his tongue appeared in the corner of his mouth as he scrutinized the American. "No, I wasn't surprised. Bob Karp told me they were coming. He didn't say how he knew, and I didn't ask. But he seemed certain. Now I see why."

"This might change things, you know, maybe drastically."

"If you mean with Karp, I don't think so. If he had intelligence, I'm sure he didn't keep it to himself. Your State Department must know, even the president must know. Such information would not be concealed."

Nkele was quiet for a long moment. He seemed to be lost in thought. When he spoke, it came as a surprise. "There is talk of a truce, David."

"What kind of talk? Who's talking?"

"Nothing concrete, just . . . talk."

"Would you participate?"

Nkele shrugged. "The way things are, I think I would have to. I am already nearly a pariah, a prophet without honor . . . a warrior without weapons . . . yes, I would participate."

"Why do you think Karp doesn't trust you? Is there something about you I should know?"

Nkele smiled sadly. "I have no secrets, Mister Ripley. I'm sure your Mister Karp knows everything there is to know."

"But he might not have told me everything."

Nkele didn't seem surprised. "No, he might not have told you everything. But that won't make any difference. If he is the one making the decisions, then . . ."

"It's my job to advise Langley. If he's wrong, maybe I can change their minds. But I don't want anything to blow up in my face. If you're . . ."

Nkele shook his head. "Not now. It's late, and I'm tired. So are you. We should get some rest. The two men you captured are not the only Cubans in the area, I'm sure of that. And where there are Cubans, there are modern weapons, better even than those Joshua has been given."

"Why do you say that?"

"Because it's obvious. It's the way it is. Joshua Bandolo is a black man, like me, like Jorge Caulfield. The Russians are white like you and Mister Karp. Color is more important than politics. White men don't give black men their best weapons. It's the weapons that make the difference, you see. If I have the same gun you have, then the best man will win. The Russians don't want that and neither do the Americans. Do you play chess, Mister Ripley?"

"Some."

"Then you know what I mean . . ." He looked at Ripley for a moment, as if trying to decide whether or not the American did know what he meant, but when he spoke again, all he said was, "Good night."

Ripley went to his tent, wondering whether Nkele was right. He didn't want to believe it, but he kept thinking of chess, the ease with which pawns were moved around the board. They were made for sacrifice, disposable objects tossed on a scrap heap, used to protect the more important pieces. And as he lay down on his cot, it dawned on him that Nkele had gotten it wrong. It was true that pawns were meant to be used. But politics was more important than color. And at that moment, he realized that he too was a pawn.

After an hour of fitful sleep, he got up and walked outside. That was when he heard it for the first time—a low rumbling sound, as if tectonic plates halfway around the earth were restless. He could feel the ground tremble under his feet and feeling just a little foolish, got down on all fours and pressed his ear to the ground. He could hear it clearly, the steady growling of large machinery. Turning his head, he saw the stars far overhead, tiny points of light against the pitch black sky. The contrast was so stark they seemed less like things floating in deep, limitless space than like holes in a flat plane, like pinpricks in black paper shielding him from some brilliant light on the other side.

A burst of static crackled from the direction of Nkele's tent, and he got to his feet. Running toward the tent, he heard another burst, then accented English half buried in electrical disturbance. Instinctively, he looked to the sky again, half expecting to see advancing clouds, a flash of lightning. But the sky was clear, and empty of everything but those points of light, impossibly tiny against the hugeness of the night.

He pushed into the tent just as Nkele turned off the radio. The APP leader turned to him then, his face thoughtful. "I thought you were going to get some sleep."

Ripley shook his head. "What was that just now?"

Nkele looked at the radio before answering. "The radio, you mean?"

"Dammit, Oscar, you know that's what I mean. What was it? Who were you talking to?"

"Friends, Mister Ripley. Just friends."

"What sort of accent was that? It sounded like German, Dutch maybe."

Nkele nodded. "Yes, I suppose so."

The rumbling was growing more insistent now, and Ripley glanced at the open flap of Nkele's tent, as if he expected an answer to his question to come from outside. "What is that noise?"

"You will see for yourself very soon. Come with me." Nkele brushed past him. As he stepped through the entrance, an engine cranked outside, and Ripley followed him out. Two of Nkele's men were in the front seat of a jeep. Nkele moved toward the jeep, and its headlights slashed through the darkness as he climbed in. Patting the vacant seat beside him, Nkele said, "Come on, David. You want to know, and I want you to know. But it's easier if you see for yourself."

Ripley climbed in, and Nkele handed him an AK-47 but said nothing. The driver jerked the jeep in gear and it lurched ahead so suddenly that Ripley was thrown against the back of his seat. The driver rammed the jeep into the main road to Kalindu that gaped like open jaws in the green wall. Confined by the green tunnel of the forest, the headlights were impossibly bright. The leaves on either side glistened as if they had been oiled, and drops of dew glittered like handfuls of diamonds tossed into the undergrowth.

"Where are we going?" Ripley shouted.

"Not far." Nkele stared straight ahead. His face was almost stony, as if he had slipped on the death mask of someone who looked very much, but not quite exactly, like him. The noise of the jeep engine drowned out all other sound, and conversation was virtually impossible. Since Ripley was too confused to think clearly, and Nkele seemed undisposed to answer questions, the American stared straight ahead, as if whatever had made the rumbling he could no longer hear would suddenly rise up out of the road without warning.

The road veered toward the east, and suddenly they exploded onto the veldt. The thick undergrowth was gone now, and the jeep engine sounded thin and weak without the forest to channel its snarl. Ripley looked out over the grasslands ahead, but saw nothing to explain why they were here. The jeep reached a crossroad, a splintered wooden pole bearing two faded white arrows, one reading Salazar, the other, at right angles to the first, Kalindu, the black letters reduced by incessant sun to gray outlines and clumps of dark flecks on the peeling white.

Nkele tapped the driver on the shoulder and he pulled over, killed the lights, and then the engine. The silence flooded in around them like water into a cave, and Ripley wondered why he couldn't hear the thunder of it.

Then, off in the distance, he could hear the dull whomp of the rotors. A helicopter. He peered into the night, but there was nothing to see. The pilot was running without lights. And beneath the unceasing beat of the rotors, almost unnoticeable, but definitely there, like white noise, was the grumbling he had heard before. He stepped down out of the jeep, and immediately felt the trembling beneath his feet. And he knew what it was—armor!

He looked at Nkele, but Oscar was standing with his back to the jeep, staring up at the stars.

TWENTY-ONE

❖

Ripley walked around behind the jeep and leaned against the left quarter-panel. Nkele glanced at him, circled the jeep, and took up a place beside him, his arms folded across his chest. They stood there quietly, staring at the blackness, neither sure what the other might be expecting to materialize out of the sky.

One of Nkele's men lit a cigarette. The rasp of the match was followed by the sharp tang of phosphorous then the pungent tang of tobacco.

The rotors were growing louder, and there was no question that Nkele had come to meet the helicopter. Abruptly, the sound grew louder and a black blob swooped toward them, following the road. Its engine thundered, and a finger of light suddenly speared out of the darkness, swept along the road, past the jeep, momentarily bathing them in harsh light, then winked out.

Dropping like a stone, the chopper came to rest fifty yards away. Nkele pushed himself away from the jeep, glanced at Ripley and said, "You wanted to see. Come on."

He walked toward the waiting chopper. Ripley ran after him as a heavy door on the chopper rolled open, locking with a thud. The rotors continued to turn, but then the engine died, and coughed once as the rotors slowed and finally stopped. Ripley recognized the helicopter. It was a Sikorsky Night Hawk, but it was unmarked, and the man who stepped down from the open door was wearing nondescript fatigues. He stood with his arms folded as Nkele and Ripley approached, his face barely perceptible in the darkness until Ripley got within a few steps.

His clothing bore no signs of national origin or rank, but there was no mistaking the authority in his posture.

"Doctor Nkele," he said. It clearly wasn't a question. Ripley noticed the same accent he'd heard over the radio, but this time there was no mystery as to what it was. Ripley almost blurted it out, but bit his tongue as Nkele extended a hand.

"Colonel Voorster," he said.

Voorster took the hand without hesitation, shook it perfunctorily, and looked at Ripley, but addressed his question to Nkele. "Ripley, is it?"

Nkele nodded. Voorster extended his hand again, and Ripley shook it without quite knowing who he was greeting or why he was there.

Nkele explained. "Colonel Voorster is from the Bureau of State Security."

"BOSS? South African?"

Voorster gave him a thin smile. "Strange bedfellows, that what you're thinking Ripley?"

Ripley, still stunned, shook his head mutely. He turned to Nkele. "Oscar, what the fuck is going on?" Before Nkele could answer, Ripley took a couple of steps to one side and peered down the road toward the steadily increasing rumble of the armor. "Jesus Christ! That's South African armor, isn't it? Coming this way . . ."

Voorster smiled again. He nodded.

Once more, Ripley looked to Nkele for an explanation. "But why?"

Nkele seemed baffled by the question, and Voorster jumped in to fill the void. "He needs help and you haven't given him much, have you?"

Ripley shook his head. "No, I suppose not. But . . ."

"We're wasting time, Doctor Nkele. It'll be daylight soon. I have to be in position before then. You know the terms. Night travel only."

"Position for what?" Ripley demanded. He had meant the question to be forceful, but he was still reeling, and it sounded lame, even pathetic to his own ears.

Voorster noticed, and his grin was wide when he answered. "Doctor Nkele needs some help with some immigrants from the other side of the Atlantic. To be precise, he wants to send them back where they came from, the sooner the better."

"The Cubans?" Ripley asked.

"The Cubans, of course," Voorster said. "But they're just part of the problem. I don't know how much you know about the Soviet arms Bandolo is receiving, but compared to Doctor Nkele, David was a superpower when he confronted Goliath. And that, Mister Ripley, I know you know."

Instinctively, Ripley looked down the road once more. He could see a dim glow now and, behind it, a faint mass that could only be a cloud of dust. "How large is your column, Colonel?" he asked.

"Large enough."

To Nkele Ripley said, "Oscar, are you sure you want to do this?"

Nkele nodded. "Yes." He sighed, then added, "I don't really have a choice. I have to take help where and when I can find it."

"But—"

"Spare us your moral agonizing, Mister Ripley," Voorster snapped. "I know what you're going to say, but there is no time for such self-indulgence. Not now." He stepped up to Nkele. "You and I have to talk, Doctor." He took Nkele by the arm and tugged him away from Ripley, glaring over his shoulder at the American to make certain he didn't follow.

Ripley walked back to the jeep. He sat there on the running board, the sound of the approaching armored column an ominous rumble in his ears as he watched the unlikely allies deep in conversation. He felt rejected, like a kid watching his best girl on the way to the prom with his worst enemy. And there didn't seem to be a thing he could do about it. For one fleeting moment, he had a vision of himself lying in the road as the tanks and armored personnel carriers sat there stymied, clouds of diesel smoke swirling in the morning sunlight. And he laughed out loud, not just at the futility of the gesture, but at himself for even thinking about it.

The headlights of the approaching column were brighter now, and the rumble of the engines was making it hard to think. It seemed as if his head were gripped in an enormous vise and all he could think about was how soon his skull would succumb to the pressure, bursting like a melon and spilling gore into the dust. Glancing at the sky, he saw that daylight was little more than two hours away. And he knew that when the sun came up there would be no turning back. Oscar Nkele was taking an irreversible step, one that would make him hostage to the most despised regime on the continent, and ostracized by much of the rest of the world. The idea of a black

African freedom fighter aligning himself with the demons of apartheid seemed mad. What gain could there be that could possibly be worth the undeniable loss?

Voorster was still talking to Nkele, but he seemed to be staring over Oscar's shoulder, his eyes fixed on Ripley as if he expected some resistance, some desperate, last ditch attempt to abort the alliance before it got off the ground.

But Ripley was too numb to do anything even if there were something he could do. He cupped his chin in his hands, pressing his eyeballs back into their sockets with his fingertips, trying to stop the insistent pounding in the center of his skull. Voorster's face was slowly softening, as if he sensed that Ripley were defeated. By the time Nkele turned to walk back to the jeep, Voorster was wearing a broad grin.

Without a word, Nkele got into the jeep, lifting one long leg over Ripley's shoulder and using the back of the driver's seat to vault up and into the rear. Voorster nodded to Ripley, and his lips moved, but the armored column was so close, the words were drowned out. The colonel sprinted back to his helicopter then, and the pilot was already cranking his engines. The rotors trembled, wobbled, then started to revolve in stuttering fits for a few seconds before settling into a blur. The chopper lifted off, climbed nearly straight up, then slipped sidewise and sped off down the road toward Nkele's camp.

Nkele patted Ripley on the shoulder. "Time to go, David," he said. "Come on. Get in."

Ripley looked at him for a moment, trying to find some apology, or at least some hint of an explanation in the obsidian features, but Nkele's face was blank.

Nodding, Ripley got to his feet, walked around to the passenger side and climbed in. The driver started the engine, but it seemed to make no sound at all as the armor rolled up behind the jeep and thundered impatiently for it to get moving.

They rode in silence, letting the rumbling engines fill the huge void between them. Ripley kept shaking his head, a man suddenly asked to explain the inexplicable. He wondered whether Karp knew about the South African connection, but now wasn't the time to ask. And if Karp didn't know, what would he do when he found out? For a moment, he wondered whether Karp would use it to control Nkele, offer arms and silence in exchange for obedience. But from what he'd seen of the man sitting beside him, it would never work. Nkele was not about to toe anyone's mark, and most especially that of a man like Bob Karp. Nkele was too proud and too committed. He had ideals while Karp not only had none, but seemed constitutionally unable to understand the concept. There were only ends and means for Bob Karp.

The sky was brightening by the time the column neared Nkele's camp. Five miles beyond, on the very edge of the forest, was the small town of

Falanda, straddling the rail line to the coast. It burned Nkele that the MLF had captured the village and cut the rail link, because keeping the line open was the one indisputable achievement to which he could point, the one argument in favor of more support. With a hundred times the money, Caulfield and the Pan-African Movement had nothing that concrete to point to.

Now, with Bandolo in a position to interdict rail movements from the coast inland and vice versa, Nkele was facing loss of support from Kaunda in Zambia and Mobutu in Zaire. Neither man wanted Bandolo in power, but Nkele understood all too well that if he had nothing to offer them, they would swing toward Caulfield as the only viable option. As it was, they were under constant pressure from Karp and the U.S. Department of State to do just that. And Ripley knew that unless the MLF were dislodged from Falanda, they probably would.

As daylight grew closer, Ripley looked back over his shoulder. The column was too long for him to see the end of it, but he could count more than a half-dozen tanks, British made Centurions, and at least a dozen Saracen APC's, two of which were towing G5 155 mm howitzers. For all he knew, the column was twice that long, but he couldn't bring himself to ask. It was bad enough to have been taken by surprise, but to be reduced to begging for crumbs was beyond the pale.

The sun came up abruptly, a huge bloody eye

peering at the endless sweep of grass toward the Indian Ocean. It looked almost malignant to Ripley, the eye of a madman bent on mayhem. And the rumble of the armor kept reminding him that mayhem was already on the prowl. None of the pieces he could see bore markings, but it wouldn't take anyone smarter than the village idiot to figure out where white men in tanks called home on African soil.

When they reached the camp, Nkele's men were already on the move, straggling along the road in single file. They moved aside to give the tanks and APC's plenty of room, waving their hats and cheering, as the heavy vehicles clanked on past. In the bloody sunlight, the cloud of dust behind the column swirled like red tea in clear water.

They had gone three miles past the camp when a sudden chattering of small arms fire sent bullets snarling like angry hornets into the column. The pathetic pings of the slugs flattening themselves against the armor plate sounded like nothing so much as rain on a tin roof.

A moment later, one of the tanks swung off the road and roared ahead, its treads tearing huge divots out of the grass as it rumbled by. The hatch was open, and Ripley caught a glimpse of a tanker in his helmet, a microphone cord dangling beneath his chin, ratcheting his M-50 and firing a burst to make sure the weapon was clear.

A moment later, the tanker was chewing at the

brush alongside the road, and the hammer of the M-50, a glittering arc of spent shells curling up and away from the hatch, bounced inaudibly off the armor before vanishing in the grass. Ripley had the momentary glimpse of some future Leakey on hands and knees, scraping painstakingly at the earth with X-acto knife and paint brush, unearthing the string of strange artifacts.

There was some return fire, but it was light and sporadic. The MLF were running back toward Falanda. And suddenly the sky was full of terror. The road ahead erupted into columns of damp earth as a crescendo of explosions drowned out the roar of the engines, the chatter of the M-50, everything, swallowing all other sound in its convulsive jaws.

Ripley knew immediately what had happened. "Rockets," he shouted. "Get off the road! Get off the road!" The whoosh and thunder was unmistakable. Soviet made 122mm rockets had been a VC staple. They were light and they weren't very accurate, but two men could fire them from makeshift launchers, even a pair of sticks if they were desperate, and the explosive force was so great that accuracy was useful but not essential. But Ripley knew they were facing something far deadlier than two men with bamboo. The concentration of incoming rockets was tearing the ground into piles of earth like rudely plowed fields. There had to be a Stalin Organ somewhere up ahead, no doubt manned by Cubans; jeep mounted and therefore mobile, it could fire a salvo of the lethal rockets and move out before mortar teams or the G5 crews could zero in on it.

He grabbed the driver by the shoulder and pointed to the veldt off to the right.

The driver seemed not to understand, and another salvo of the 122's clawed at the road a hundred yards closer.

"They've targeted the road, Oscar. We have to get off."

Even as he said it, he glanced behind to see that the armor had reached the same conclusion. The tanks were out in front, their tracks clanking and ripping at the grass and the APC's rocked over a narrow ditch and out into the tall grass, their huge tires tearing gouts of sod free and scattering them in high arcs.

Ripley wondered whether Voorster still wore that smug expression. He'd be willing to bet he didn't. This was more than he'd bargained for. It had to be. And if Bandolo's forces had enough of the 122's, even the South African armor would be no match for them. The whole column would be turned into a junkyard in twenty minutes.

The jeep careened into the grass, the tall blades hissing and slashing at the men, swarms of bugs swirling, their angry buzz that of a runaway sawmill.

"If we get out of this alive," Ripley shouted, "I have to get back to Salazar—"

"We will, David, don't worry."

"And I'll have to tell Karp—"

"He already knows about the Cubans," Nkele reminded him.

"I didn't mean the Cubans, Oscar," Ripley yelled, ducking as another swarm of incoming 122's turned another stretch of road into a moonscape. "I meant the South Africans."

"He knows."

"No he doesn't. He can't."

Nkele laughed. "Whose idea do you think it was, David?"

TWENTY-TWO

❖

August 15, 1975

Ripley hated light planes. His childhood was scarred by memories of heroes disintegrating over cornfields like Buddy Holly, or slamming like Patsy Cline into mountains, and always it was a small plane, its pathetic propeller no more effective than that on a beanie, that had led to grief. But he had no choice. Sitting in the passenger seat of the Cessna, he felt his fingers cramp and knew without looking that his knuckles were whiter than the whites of his eyes.

Rocking over the dirt strip, the plane sounded

as if it would never get airborne at all and if, by some unforeseen freak of aerodynamics, it managed to, the shuddering beneath his feet convinced Ripley that the small plane would tear itself to pieces and shower down over the makeshift airstrip like a fistful of aluminum confetti. The pilot seemed unconcerned, but pilots were assholes, too cocky by half and so convinced of the sacredness of their calling, they believed they would live forever, floating away from a pinwheeling crash like a puff of milkweed.

All the way back to Salazar, Ripley kept framing his arguments. He had sent a dozen cables to Langley and was still waiting for an answer. Lang and Brown were supposed to be handling his communications with Jack Devereaux on the African desk, but he was starting to believe they just might be in Karp's pocket, or that they had been fed to the damned snake in Karp's vivarium. He was tempted to blame himself, thinking that his decision to cut the communicators out of the loop gave them *carte blanche*, the freedom to change their loyalties, and then he realized that he had never wondered about those loyalties to begin with. He had taken it on faith that Lang and Brown worked for him and that, because they did, they were in his corner. But he hadn't picked them. He didn't even know who did. For all he knew, it had been Karp and they had been his assets all along.

But that didn't matter. He was crawling way

out on a shaky limb now, and there was no room for anybody but him. He wasn't even sure it would take his weight, but he had to try. He was getting that familiar sinking feeling in the pit of his stomach. His nights were full of sleepless dreams and his sheets stank of night sweats. He was hanging on to a cliff by his fingernails, and he knew it. And the boot about to come down on his fingertips, sending him cartwheeling head over heels into a bottomless pit, belonged to Bob Karp. He was sure of that now. His only real chance lay in getting Langley on his side. He knew he couldn't get Karp relieved, but he had to push him a little, try to make him back off, at least long enough to regain a little momentum of his own.

Nkele had left the ruins of Falanda in a hurry, without saying where he was headed. Voorster's armor had taken a beating but managed to save itself, but not the town. It might not be too late to save Nkele from the mistake, but Karp's role in it troubled Ripley. The COS had to know that South African involvement would isolate Nkele even more from his potential African allies, few as they already were, and with public opinion in the States so volatile, if word leaked out, Congress would see to it that not another penny found its way into APP coffers. Ripley sensed that his control, vestigial at best, was eroding by the hour.

Watching the grassland below give way to arboreal clumps then to solid forest, he was beginning to understand that the continent sliding by beneath the frail wings that were the only things between him and death was not for nothing called dark. The men, white and black alike, who were in the convoluted process of deciding its fate were every bit as impenetrable as the deepest of its jungles. To wander into the tangled motives that surrounded them like spider webs was to ask for trouble. One of them would ensnare him and it wouldn't matter which. Once the delicate filaments began to wrap around him, someone would make a meal of him, suck the juice out of him and leave him there, draped in silk, rattling in the soft breeze like the dried husk of a beetle.

The pilot was a taciturn man who said not one word, and who looked at him only once, as if Ripley were some inverted Gorgon, crowned by a fearsome tangle of writhing serpents. But that was just as well. He was in no mood for idle chatter, and he had little enough time as it was to decide what his next step would be.

When Salazar's airport finally appeared out of the morning mist, Ripley felt as if every joint in his body had turned to stone. He was so tense that he wondered if his fingers would uncurl from the armrests of his seat. His legs felt as if they were made of cast iron, his elbows mortared over, his shoulders welded into immobility. As the plane began its long, slow descent, the crackle of the tower little more than gibberish to his uncomprehending ears, he flicked a piece of paper across his arid lips three times before he realized it was his own tongue.

Dead ahead, the end of the runway seemed to rush at him now, the white lines on either margin blurred into gray as the concrete sped upward and the plane fell until he was certain there was no way to land without total destruction. But the plane touched down lightly, the tires barely squealing as the pilot yanked back on the stick, and let the nose hang a bit before easing off, and then the nosegear made contact and they were home free.

The pilot taxied to the end of the freight terminal, where Ripley climbed down, closed the door and waved to the pilot who just stared at him through his mirrored shades. The plane moved off to refuel and Ripley headed through the yawning doors into the roar of a handtruck lurching toward a stack of wooden pallets, speared the bottommost, and jerked into reverse. He passed through the huge, nearly empty space and out through a glass door and onto a concrete walkway.

A taxi sat a hundred yards ahead and Ripley started to run. He reached the waiting cab just ahead of a large man dressed in a gray suit, the jacket draped over one shoulder and dark stains under the arms of his white shirt. The man's wispy white hair stuck out in clumps in every direction, and his pink skin was beaded with sweat. He glared at Ripley, who shrugged apologetically and pulled the cab door closed, leaned forward, and directed the driver to the Salazar Continental.

It was nearly noon, and the city streets were clogged with traffic. Open-backed vans were cheek by jowl with passenger cars and taxis. If he didn't know better, he would have thought Mawindi was just one more sleepy African nation on the verge of waking up both to freedom and to the painful dislocation of its arrival.

The driver, like most cabbies, had the soul of a kamikaze pilot, and made the battered Citroen dart like a hummingbird into spaces too small for a car half its size, escaping harm by the thickness of a human hair on three occasions, but sustaining no additional dents before pulling up at the curb in front of the hotel.

After paying the fare, Ripley went inside at a fast walk, stopped at the desk to check for messages and, when there were none, walked quickly to the elevator bank, pressed the call button and patted a nervous foot while he waited. When the car gaped open he stepped inside, pressed the button for his floor and backed into a corner to watch the doors wheeze closed. He could hear the whisper of air in the shaft as the car sped upward. When it bumped to a halt on the sixth floor, the car seemed to rock on its cable, a yo-yo in fretful sleep.

Out in the hall, he walked to the room, opened the door and stepped inside. "Michelle?"

he called. There was no answer, and he realized he was disappointed. He had been looking forward to seeing her again without realizing just how much. Her clothes were still in the closet, so at least she hadn't moved out. He checked the dresser for mail, but found none.

He took a quick shower, keeping his fingers crossed that the water would cooperate. He could feel the grit on his skin as the water stung his back with its needle spray. As the water ran down over his forehead, he caught just a hint of cordite, and for a moment his ears rang once more with the scream of the 122 mm rockets and the closed fist of the concussive detonations. He knew it was illusory, but for the briefest of moments, it happened again before his eyes, like a film run back in slow motion.

He grabbed two bars of soap and lathered himself all over to try to wash out the memories. He had thought that he was used to violent death, but the carnage at Falanda was too fresh, too real, and too fucking bloody for that fiction to stay intact. It had cracked like the most fragile of eggshells the moment the first Cuban rocket landed in the road, and now he was like a chick, terrified of the world outside, trying to hold the delicate pieces together to shield him for one more minute, one more hour.

But it was no use.

First on the agenda was a visit to Bob Karp. He wasn't looking forward to it, not because he was afraid of Karp, but because he was afraid of himself, afraid his control, already feeble at best, would desert him altogether. But there was no point in putting it off.

Once out of the shower, he felt less like a new man than like a newborn baby. It seemed almost as if the accumulated grime of the last few days had been a kind of armor and now, without it, he was defenseless. He dressed quickly, scribbled a note to Michelle, and left the hotel even more quickly than he had entered it.

Back out in the bright sun of midday, he hailed a cab and directed the driver to the American Embassy. Glancing at his watch he realized that Karp, a creature of meticulous habit, would just be leaving for lunch, but that was alright. It would give him a chance to descend into the whirring, humming bowels and collar either Lang or Brown and get off yet one more cable. And if there were a god in heaven, there just might be an answer to the dozen he'd already despatched. But he wouldn't hold his breath.

During the ride, he tried to compose himself, get his heart to stop racing and try to slow the whirling gears in his head before he threw something permanently out of alignment. He was perilously close to committing the cardinal sin of his profession—taking it personally.

At the embassy he nodded to the Marine guard, showed him his credentials, and waited for the gate to be opened by another Marine inside.

In order to give Karp a little extra time to go to lunch, he went straight to the comm center in the basement. The halls of the building were white and cold. Even the artwork, mostly recent abstracts that fought against the white expanses, were unable to warm the eye. The marble of the first floor lobby was so shiny it hurt his eyes where it reflected sun pouring through the huge windows, but it was a cold, heartless light.

He took the stairs down, and the walls seemed to tower over him in the confined space of the stairwell. The basement was less fashionably appointed. Tile floors instead of marble. There was no artwork, and the walls were light gray as if they had absorbed the shadows of those who passed through.

Ronny Lang was on duty in the communications center. He looked up as Ripley entered, nodded his head, and said, "I figured you'd be back sooner or later. Where the hell have you been?"

"Falanda."

"What the hell were you doing there?"

"My job, Ronny. My job."

"You'll be lucky if you still have one. Karp is ready to rip out your liver."

"Fuck Karp."

"Funny, that's exactly what he says about you. The only difference is, he's serious. He wants your head, man, and you'll be lucky if he doesn't get it."

"Ask me if I care, Ronny. On second thought,

don't. I want to send a cable first. Then ask me."

"What for? You must be communicating with a black hole, man. Everything goes in and nothing comes out. What the hell is going on?"

"That's what I want to know."

Ripley sat down at a table in the corner, pulled a legal pad toward him and grabbed a pencil from a small wooden vase full of them. Lang got up and stretched, but he gave Ripley room, yawning once, then going into the back room where the gear was set up.

Over and over again, Ripley wrote a sentence, at first using the curiously condensed, almost impenetrable language of cable-ese, drew a line through it, and tried once more, and then again. It took him twenty minutes to get it right. When he was finished, he sat back as if he had just drafted the Declaration of Independence, tapped the pad twice with the eraser end of his pencil, and stood up.

"All set, Ronny," he called.

"Be right there . . ." Lang came back to the front room a moment later. "Give it here," he said.

Ripley slid the pad across the table toward him, using the pencil instead of his fingers.

"That hot, is it?" Lang asked. "Can't touch it with your fingers. Better get my asbestos gloves."

"Just send it Ronny, and I want it sent FLASH. And you tell Rick, too, as soon as you get an answer, call me. I don't care if it's three in the morning. You get me on the horn."

Lang picked up the pad and read it aloud:

> *"Caulfield a liability. Insist Nkele get equivalent support, if not all. COS out of control. Urgently request immediate response."*

Looking at Ripley, he said, "Christ almighty, Karp'll go through the roof."

"Like I said."

"But I got to show him everything."

"Not this one, Ronny. You send it."

"It'll be my ass, if Karp finds out. And he *will* find out."

"I'll take the heat."

"There's plenty to go around, Davey. You won't be able to cover me on this one."

"Send it, Ronny or, as God is my witness, I'll rip out *your* liver."

"In plain language like this? Jesus . . ."

"Send it!"

"Okay."

"I'll tell him about it myself. I'm going to see him right after lunch."

"Watch out for that snake, Davey."

"Which one?" Ripley asked.

Lang didn't laugh.

TWENTY-THREE

❖

Ripley sat in Karp's chair, his feet up on the desk. He was tired, so tired he felt as if he'd never be able to sleep again, as if he had been launched into some endless orbit, doomed to circle the world in free fall forever, his eyes perpetually gaping and his brain forever spinning its helpless wheels. He was tempted to rifle the desk, see whether Karp was keeping secrets from him, but realized he already knew the answer to that question, and that those secrets would be meaningless to him even if he were to find them.

The desk top was a model of efficiency. The in-box was empty. The out-box was crammed with memos, a stack of envelopes, some interoffice and some outgoing. The desk set, a slab of polished onyx, its wells gleaming gold, stabbed up toward the ceiling, twin shafts of black, a single, tasteful band of gold circling the barrels midway between tip and top.

He could hear Karp's secretary banging away at her Selectric, and for a moment he imagined what it would be like to be that little ball that quivered and whirled, its cable-driven spinning so monotonous and contradictory. Turn this way, turn that, upper case, lower case, clack, clack, clack, ding, an endless field of white stretching out ahead of him. It was the perfect metaphor for his life.

He was still smiling when Karp walked in. The COS slammed the door. "Where the hell have you been, Ripley?"

"Out in the field." Ripley said, "And hello to you, too, Bob. How are you? Glad to see you."

"Don't you give me that crap, David. You know damn well you should have told me where you were going. I'm in charge here, in case you forget."

"How can I forget that, Bob? I mean, I send cable after cable after cable, and I never hear a blessed word in response. But silly me, it never occurred to me that you might be spiking the traffic. If anybody has a right to ask what the hell's going on, I'm the man."

Karp crossed the wide expanse to his desk. He looked at the empty chair in front of it, and for a moment Ripley thought he was going to sit in it. Instead, he covered the last ten feet in two strides, slapped Ripley's feet and said, "Get the hell out of my chair."

"Chairs are what this is all about, aren't they Bob? Nothing matters except who sits in what chair. This is your chair, and that makes you smarter than me. Isn't that right?"

Karp smiled. "Smarter?" He shrugged. "Who knows? More powerful, though, yeah. It does do that."

Ripley lowered his feet to the floor slowly, one at a time, got up and bowed in mock gallantry. He circled the desk, keeping it between him and Karp, then plopped down into the visitor's chair.

"That's better," Karp said, taking a seat. "Now, where were you?"

"Me first, Bob. I have a few questions I want answered."

"Like what?"

"Why did you kill my cables?"

"Who says I did?"

"Come on, Bob. Ronny told me you were screening all traffic. What did you do, tell Langley to disregard everything I sent? Or did you kill it altogether?"

"I don't owe you any explanations, David. I'm in charge here. And while you were off on your little vacation, somebody ripped off a whole goddamn shipment of weapons. You wouldn't know anything about that, would you?"

"Why would I know anything about it? You think I stashed the stuff in my hotel room, is that it?" Ripley yanked the room key from his pocket and tossed it across the desk. Karp missed, and the key cracked against the glass of the vivarium. There was a sudden flurry of motion behind the glass, and Ripley saw the gaping jaws of the mamba as it struck. The dull thud of the serpent's head, punctuated by the sharp tick of the fangs hitting the glass, made Karp spill out of his chair. He glared at Ripley then bent to snatch the key from the carpet.

"You arrogant sonofabitch, Ripley. If I . . ."

"If you what, Bob? Go ahead, finish it."

Karp ignored him. "I'm getting more arms. Eight more C-130's full. Post haste, as they say. A whole fucking train load of guns doesn't just disappear. Somebody got them, and when I find out who, I'll know how. If I find out you had anything to do with it . . ."

"That's that baboon in Ray-Bans you picked for your front runner, Bob. Caulfield couldn't find his ass with both hands, and you keep propping him up. He's like a goddamned clown in the dunk tank at a circus. Somebody throws a baseball and he gets wet. You drag his ass out of the water, set him back on the stool, and along comes another baseball. When the hell are you going to realize he's not the best man for the job?"

"Don't give me any more shit about Nkele. I

know what you think of Caulfield, but Nkele's no good. He's unreliable. We want him to hang in there, but that's all."

"For God's sake, Karp. The man can win, if you give him half a chance."

"If I give Oscar Nkele half a chance, he'll be sitting in Salazar in six months. Six months after that, we'll have another Cuba right here."

"For Christ's sake, Cuba was ninety miles off the coast. There's a whole ocean between us and Mawindi."

"I don't care. We're not backing Nkele."

"If you *don't* back him, Bandolo will be here, and you'll have the same thing."

"I rest my case. That's why it has to be Caulfield."

"You're wrong about Nkele."

"I don't give a damn. I have my orders. You have yours. We're here to take orders, not make policy."

"I don't have the faintest goddamned idea why you're here, but I'm here to make an assessment," Ripley snapped. "You're making policy without even having the facts."

"This is not about facts, Ripley. It's about life. We lost one, and nobody in State, and sure as hell nobody on the Hill, is going to get us into another one. Not now. Your man Nkele can't win without lots of help, and there isn't that much help in the budget."

"But he *can*. The people of Mawindi will follow him. And if we help, he'll be grateful. I'm not saying we can buy him, because we can't. He's not for sale. But—"

"Look, Ripley, you might as well know, I've already told Jack Devereaux that Nkele was behind the highjacking."

"You don't know that."

"I can't prove it, but I *know* it. And that's all that matters. I want you to stay away from him. Do you understand? Stay the fuck away from him."

"Did you tell Colonel Voorster the same thing?"

For a second, Karp was off balance. "How did . . . ? Who?"

"Come on, Bob. You know damn well what I'm talking about."

But the interview was over. "I'm very busy, David. You'll have to excuse me." Karp got to his feet and crossed the room, his new shoes squeaking. Ripley heard the crack of static electricity when Karp reached for the doorknob. Only when the door swung open did he turn.

Karp was standing there, one arm extended toward the open doorway. "I want to see you tomorrow," he said. "Nine o'clock sharp. Right here. Don't be late or I'll have your balls in a jar."

Ripley sighed in disgust. He got to his feet and stalked out without saying good-bye. He heard the door slam behind him, but he was expecting it so the loud bang didn't even slow him down.

He decided to walk back to the hotel. It was

only eight blocks, and it would do him good to burn off a little of the adrenaline coursing through his arteries. Three blocks up Cordeiro Boulevard, he turned left and headed into the bazaar. The streets were teeming with people, and the noise buffered him against the pounding in his temples.

He stopped at a little pushcart to buy a paper cone full of shaved ice. From the bewildering array of bottled flavors, he chose coconut and banana, watched as the vendor tilted both bottles simultaneously, the thick, sugary waters gurgling as they slopped into the ice and turned it the same pale chartreuse as the syrups. He paid with a handful of coins, not bothering to count out the correct price, then ambled deeper into the bazaar.

All around him, a wilderness of blurred colors seemed to swirl. The chattering of parrots, the chirp of smaller birds, all seemingly content in their bamboo cages, vied with the excited voices of hagglers. The air was filled with conflicting scents, the sharp tang of cinnamon warring with the overwhelming swirl of sugar.

Bolts of cloth were spread open on long tables. He stopped to watch one woman make her choice. Then the vendor, his movements so fluid and practiced that they seemed robotic, rolled the bolt open, exposing the burnt orange and dark red of the cloth, snatched a pair of large shears and sliced through with a blur of clicking blades.

On another stand, a blend of sausages and hot

peppers bubbled in a cauldron, the thick sauce popping like lava. Ripley ordered a bowlful over white rice, then sat on the curb to eat it. Looking around, he realized that his was one of the few white faces in the crowd. Most of the Portuguese who had the wherewithal had already left Salazar. He was the quintessential outsider here, and it soothed him in a way that he couldn't understand.

He caught a glimpse of a face that seemed familiar, but when he looked again, the man was gone. The sauce was hot, probably laced with tabasco, and he filled his mouth with rice to kill the pain. He tried the cone, but licking the ice didn't help, and he was losing control of both the cone and the paper plate.

Getting to his feet, he pushed on, heading down toward the waterfront. The air changed here. The tang of salt mixed with the stink of fresh fish. Wagons, their beds full of chipped ice, leaked fishy water onto the pavement, and it ran along the gutters. Flies swarmed around the smelly rivulets, their buzzing angry and insistent.

Leaning against the side of a canvas-covered stall, he finished the sausage and peppers, found a trash bin for the plate, then turned his attention to the cone. He watched the crowd, and once more caught a glimpse of that familiar face. This time, it looked almost as if the man had recognized him, too, and for some reason chose not to acknowledge him.

Was he being followed? Curious, Ripley

tossed the cone away, wiped his hands on a paper napkin which he balled up and tossed after the cone, then pushed into the throng again. He caught sight of the back of the man's head for a moment, still wondering where he'd seen him before. The glimpses had been too fleeting for a good look, but Ripley was sure he knew the man.

He was all the way out to the boulevard again, but the man was nowhere in sight. Shrugging, he started toward the hotel again, walking briskly now. He hoped Michelle would be there. He needed the reassurance of seeing her. It hadn't taken him too long to get attached to her, but that was always the way it was when you were stuck in the middle of some strange place you'd never been before and, most likely, would never see again. You grabbed onto something with both hands, and held on for dear life. With Michelle, he was even beginning to think it might be something more than that. But it was too soon to know, especially for Michelle herself. She was reserved, even reticent, even in bed, as if part of her had to be tucked away somewhere out of his reach.

When he spotted the marquee of the Continental, he quickened his pace. In the lobby, he felt the chill of the air conditioning and realized just how hot and sticky it had been outside. He checked at the desk for messages, then took the elevator up to his room. As he stepped off, Michelle was just locking the door. She turned as he approached her.

"There you are," she said. She slipped her bag over her shoulder and grabbed him by the hand. "Come on, we're going to be late."

"Late for what?"

"I'm not sure. Something hot. I really don't know the details, but I think you'll want to be there. Something big, that's all I know."

"What are you . . . ?"

"I'll tell you on the way. Come on, come on, dammit!"

TWENTY-FOUR

❖

The ballroom of the Salazar Hilton was buzzing. Camera crews from the major U.S. networks, BBC, and Soviet News Agency, as well as independent crews from several European and African countries, jockeyed for position. The stage at one end of the ballroom was backed by a heavy dark blue drape. The flag of Mawindi and the red, black and green flag of African solidarity hung from the ceiling, the colors clashing with the blue backing.

Four chairs, arranged with one facing the remaining three, occupied the right half. On the left was a gleaming wooden podium, a forest of microphones rooted precariously on its front. Dozens of cables trailed into the darkness at the foot of the stage, as if the podium were on some sort of elaborate life-support.

Two hundred folding chairs filled the ballroom floor, their neat rows already knocked askew by the milling reporters who gathered in knots, renewing old acquaintances, trading rumors, and filling the high-ceilinged room with a steady mutter.

Karp stood in one corner, Ripley and Michelle beside him. "I busted my butt to put this together," he muttered. "I hope to Christ it works."

"How can it?" Ripley asked. "Nothing's resolved. I'm amazed Bandolo even agreed to participate. He's winning the war as it is."

"The hell he is," Karp snapped. "It's a Mexican standoff. That's why he's here. It's Caulfield who's making the sacrifice. But public relations are half the battle in this kind of war, David, you ought to know that. Hell, in Vietnam, it was the press that beat us, not Charlie. I hope to Christ that doesn't happen again."

"You give the press too much credit, Mister Karp," Michelle said, giving him a thousand watt smile. He glowered at her, but didn't argue.

"How in the hell did you get Achebe to agree to sponsor this insanity?" Ripley asked.

It was Karp's turn to smile. "I got a friend at Exxon. Nigerian oil is big bucks. You push the right buttons, money stops. Push them again, and it starts. I pushed some buttons, made a couple of phone calls and the rest is about to become history."

"I'll believe it when it happens," Ripley said.

"Oh, it'll happen. You can take that to the bank."

Michelle watched Karp walk away, then turned to Ripley. "I have a bad feeling," he said.

"About what?"

He spread his arms to take in the undisciplined throng. "About this circus. If I had known, I would have tried to talk Oscar out of it. He mentioned something about a truce, but wouldn't say much. And he told me that anything that might stop the killing is worth consideration. I wonder why Karp didn't tell me anything about it."

"He never even mentioned it?"

Ripley shook his head. "Not a word. He just said he had places to go and people to see."

"He doesn't seem surprised that you're here, though. Or even annoyed."

"He's pretty well written me out of the will, I think. Right now, I'm the black sheep of the West Africa Division. I . . ."

"Look, there's Achebe." Michelle pointed to one corner of the stage, where Ripley saw three men in *dashikis*, talking quietly, just beyond the edge of the curtain. "He's an interesting man," she went on.

"You know him, too, do you?"

Michelle nodded. "I lived in Nigeria for a year, right after the Biafran War. It was just before he became president. I got to know him pretty well. Maybe he can pull this off, but I don't think so. Instead of Achebe, we ought to see Brezhnev and Ford in the wings. Maybe that would do it, but I'm not even sure of that."

"I smell a rat, anyhow, just like you do. I don't like it. It's too sudden. And too public. Things just don't happen like that."

"You're too cynical, David. You're so used to shaping the world from the corner of an abandoned warehouse, you mistrust anything that takes place under the glare of publicity. But that's where it all happens. People can and do say anything in the dark, because nobody can call them to account. You get up in front of the cameras, and the whole world watches. The truth needs daylight to survive."

"That sounds like typical journalistic hubris, to me. And besides, it didn't seem to bother Tricky Dick..."

Michelle gave him a look, then pinched him on the forearm. "See what I mean? Cynical to the core."

"Not cynical, Michelle, just realistic."

Someone Ripley didn't recognize moved out of the wings and toward the podium. "Do you know him, too, Michelle?"

She nodded. "That's Winston Okonga, the Zairian ambassador to the UN."

Okonga stopped at the podium, glanced toward the wings, then leaned forward to tap one of the microphones. The hollow echo of the live mike filled the ballroom, and Okonga looked once more toward the wings. He covered the mike and asked, "Are we ready?" Ripley didn't hear the response, but it must have been affirmative, because Okonga nodded, then leaned into the mike a second time.

"Ladies and gentlemen, we are about to begin. I'd appreciate it if you'd all take your seats." The ambassador waited a moment while the reporters scraped chairs closer to the stage, the camera crews jockeyed once more for position, which resulted in a shoving match for a few seconds, then cleared his throat.

"Let me make a few brief remarks about the purpose of this morning's press conference. As you all know, I'm sure, Mawindi has been wracked by civil war for several months. Since its independence will become official on November first of this year, there has been a certain amount of, shall I say, outside interference. And I think all but the most unrepentant of colonialists would agree, the people of Africa have had more than enough of such interference. Accordingly, the presidents of several nations, not coincidentally including those which share a common border with Mawindi, and by that I mean Zaire, Zambia and Angola, which has internal troubles of her own but nevertheless endorses what we are trying to accomplish here, have all agreed that Mawindi's problems are African problems, and Africans can and must solve them without interference from the super powers and the former colonial powers, who in the first instance bear the major portion of responsibility for the very existence of these problems."

Okonga looked out over the audience, then back toward the wings again. Once more, he nodded. "As a result of several weeks of intense negotiations, the presidents I referred to have, among themselves, devised what they believe will be a workable plan for immediate cessation of hostilities, to be followed by a peaceable and democratic transition to representative form of government for Mawindi. President Joseph Achebe of Nigeria has graciously agreed to present this plan to you in the hopes that you will disseminate it as widely and as quickly as possible, not only within Mawindi, but around the world. It is important that the entire world see that African peoples are not only deserving of the right of self-determination but more than ready to exert themselves toward that end." He turned again, this time waving. "Here is President Achebe of Nigeria, who will explain the details. President Achebe . . . ?" Okonga then walked to the single chair and sat down, folding his hands in his lap.

The room buzzed when Achebe appeared and the buzz grew louder while he walked to the podium.

"Ladies and gentlemen, good morning. Before I outline the plan for which, as Ambassador Okonga has told you, we have high hopes, I think I should introduce the three men whose cooperation is essential if our intentions, and our fervent hopes, are to be realized. Each has, in his own way, tried to do the best for Mawindi. As often happens when oppression ends, forces begin to develop which had been there all along but which, freed from pressure from above, become contentious and even violent. This is not to say that the men I am about to introduce are violent men, merely that they have the misfortune to live in violent times. First, let me introduce a man who is best known, in Africa and elsewhere, as one of the continent's best poets and as the leader of the Mawindi Liberation Front—Joshua Bandolo."

Bandolo appeared in the wings, walked across the stage with grace and confidence, a man practiced at public appearance and comfortable in the spotlight. He waved and took one of the three chairs.

"The next participant in this signifcant step toward peace is the leader of the Pan-African Movement. He has been in the forefront of the fight for independence for nearly twenty years—

Jorge Caulfield."

Ripley tensed as Caulfield, wearing fatigues as usual and, as usual, concealing his eyes behind dark lenses, strode across the stage without bothering to look at the audience. He ignored Bandolo's extended hand and dropped into one of the vacant chairs, folded his arms across his chest and looked at the ceiling.

"And finally," Achebe said, "a man who fought the longest of odds, the odds against a black man in a white man's world, and managed not only to get a medical degree from the University of Geneva, but who has unstintingly given Mawindi's people his considerable talent and energy as a physician as well as a politician, the leader of the African People's Party—Doctor Oscar Nkele."

Nkele strode out of the wings, his giant frame dominating the stage as soon as he appeared, and seeming to grow more impressive as the full glare of the lights caught him. He nodded to Bandolo and Caulfield. Bandolo returned the nod, but Caulfield continued to study the ceiling tile until Nkele sat down, then looked out at the audience.

"Now, just briefly, let me outline the terms of the cease fire which has already been negotiated and which the three men who represent the people of Mawindi have agreed is in her best interest. First, there will be an immediate cease fire. All hostilities are suspended as of seven o'clock this morning. The forces of the three contending political parties will stand down and remain in place."

Ripley watched as the reporters started scribbling furiously, and the camera crews moved closer, drawn as if to bloodshed.

"Second, there will be elections, first for parliament, to be held on September first, to create a general legislative body, and again on October first, when the people of Mawindi, for the first time in their history, will have both the considerable pleasure and the awesome responsibility of choosing their own leader without fear of reprisal from anyone for any reason. Third, and last, President Mobutu of Zaire, President Kenneth Kaunda of Zambia, and myself will stand as guarantors of this cease fire. Now, ladies and gentlemen, before we take your questions, each of the three leaders will make a brief statement. We'll start with Doctor Nkele."

The big man got to his feet and walked to the podium. Achebe shook his hand, and then Nkele leaned forward, one huge hand on either edge of the podium. "I have looked forward to peace and self determination ever since my father was arrested for teaching the true history of Mawindi, when I was a boy of ten. When I visited him in a Portuguese prison, not knowing that it was the last time I would ever see him, he told me once more, as he had told me a thousand times before, that one day we would all be free. That day is not yet come, but it is on the horizon, like a rising sun, and I look forward to a time when all the people, not just of Mawindi, but of all of Africa, can bask in that warm and welcome glow. Thank you."

Nkele turned to his two adversaries and waited for Bandolo to rise before stepping away from the podium.

Bandolo leaned closer to the microphone bank, adjusted the main mike, and nodded. "I have known Doctor Nkele for many years. We have much in common and we have had our differences, but until now, I never realized that it was he, and not I, who was the poet." The assemblage laughed, and Bandolo raised a thumb and glanced at Nkele before continuing. "There has been too much death, too much dying, too much misery for too many years. I, too, lost a father, not to a Portuguese prison like Doctor Nkele, but to another kind of prison, the prison of poverty and neglect. My work has been an attempt to seize the world by the eyelids, tear them open, and force the eyes to see. Perhaps that work is almost finished. I hope so."

He turned and walked back to his seat. All eyes were now on Jorge Caulfield, who got slowly to his feet, his sullen expression suddenly breaking into a grin. He walked briskly to the podium and leaned forward with hands on its edges, as if in emulation of Nkele. "Ladies and gentlemen . . . this is supposed to be a great day for Mawindi and its people. I wish . . . I wish that I could agree. But . . ." he pointed toward the rear of the ballroom, "if you will bear with me a moment, you will see why I cannot." He waved, and the twin doors at the rear of the ballroom swung open with such vehemence, they banged against the walls. A crowd mushroomed through the opening, several men in uniform, but it was dimly lit to the rear and Ripley couldn't see anything.

"Lights, please," Caulfield snapped, his voice hollow through the mike which began to feed back, and the house lights came up.

The knot of soldiers pushed on down the center of the ballroom, crossed in front of the buzzing reporters and mounted the stairs leading toward the stage. It was clear now what was going on, and Ripley started to get up, but Michelle grabbed him by the arm and dragged him back down. "Wait, David, don't . . ."

Caulfield raised a hand and waited for silence as the soldiers manipulated two men, clearly their prisoners, toward the podium. "These two men," Caulfield said, stepping toward the prisoners and bringing the microphone with him, "were captured early this morning near Santa Isabella. In case any of you don't recognize the uniform they wear, let me give you their names." Pointing at the nearer of the two, he said, "This man is Sergeant Willem van

Dyjkstra, and his comrade in arms is Private Pieter Voorman."

He walked back to the podium, set the microphone down with a dull thud that amplified the hollow echo of its impact with the wood, and nodded. "That's right, they are soldiers, as I am a soldier. But unlike me, they have no right to fight in Mawindi. They are soldiers in the army of the Republic of South Africa. That, in itself, is significant, but more significant still is why they are in Mawindi in the first place. They are here, they assure me, because they were invited to be here. Invited by Oscar Nkele who, even as we sit here, knows that an armored column of the South African army is pushing deeper and deeper into the heart of Mawindi, *my* country. And I will not have it! I will not enter in an agreement of any kind with a man who would betray his country for the sake of his own greed for power. As far as I am concerned, as of this moment, regrettably, the Pan-African Movement renounces its participation in the cease fire agreement. I say regrettably because it had been my wish that Mawindi begin to enjoy the peace of which Oscar Nkele spoke so glowingly . . . and so falsely. Now, if you'll excuse me, ladies and gentlemen, I have a war to win."

Ripley started for the stage, but the reporters were crushing in ahead of him, holding microphones and waving their pads to get Caulfield's attention. Shaking his head, Caulfield headed for the wings. The curtain moved aside, and Ripley caught a glimpse of Bob Karp, his hand just descending onto Caulfield's shoulder as the curtain swirled closed.

PART
THREE
❖

TWENTY-FIVE

❖

August 15, 1975

Ripley had gone straight to the hotel after the fiasco. His head spinning, outraged, and wanting nothing more than to go numb all over, he had proceeded to drink himself into a stupor. Michelle woke him at eight o'clock. He rubbed his eyes and sat up, letting his feet dangle over the edge of the bed.

"You look like hell," she said.

"I love you, too."

"You know what I'm talking about."

"You think I could get an ordinary night's

sleep after that circus yesterday?"

"You should have seen it coming."

Ripley slammed a fist into the mattress. "Dammit, Michelle, if you're so fucking smart, why didn't *you* see it coming?"

"Maybe I did."

"Yeah, and maybe I'm Henry Kissinger."

She smiled. "Trust me, you're not. That much I can tell you."

"Why, have you slept with him, too?"

She looked as if he'd slapped her. Turning away, she spoke to the wall. "That was uncalled for."

"I'm sorry. You're right, but . . ."

"No buts, damn you. Why don't you quit making excuses for yourself? Why don't you stop blaming Bob Karp for your problems? You're supposed to be a big boy. You should be able to make a decision on your own. But all you know how to do is run and hide. David, you're not here to play ringoleevio."

He rolled across the bed and put a hand on her hip. She seemed to shrink away from his touch for a moment, then relaxed. He let his hand stay where it was, the sharp prod of her bone against his palm strangely erotic. She wasn't wearing a bra, and he could see the curve of one breast as she turned slightly and reached down to pat the back of his hand.

"You did know didn't you?" he asked.

She looked at him then. "Know what?"

"You knew there would be a press conference,

that a truce was in the works. And you knew what Caulfield was going to do yesterday, didn't you. That's why you were in such a hurry."

"No, I didn't know. There were rumors. I heard some of them, that's all."

Ripley went on as if she hadn't disagreed. "And you knew about the South Africans, didn't you?"

This time, she nodded, tentatively at first, and then energetically.

"How did you know?"

"I can't tell you that."

"Did Karp tell you?"

"I can't tell you, I said."

"That means it was Karp." He looked at her thoughtfully. "Are you on the payroll, is that it? Are you one of Karp's people?"

She lay back on the bed, facing away from him. He tugged his hand free, and she rolled onto her stomach. He let his left hand lay flat against the small of her back, his fingers tracing the curve of a single vertebra with endless circles. If she minded, she didn't let on.

"You know what I think?" he asked.

Muffled by the pillow, her voice was barely audible when she asked, "What . . . ?"

"I think Karp engineeered the whole thing. He wanted Nkele to make the deal with the South Africans, that much I know, because Oscar told me so himself. But I think Karp wanted to isolate him, to make sure that nobody would help him.

That was the whole purpose. Achebe walks away. Mobutu cuts him off, Kaunda cuts him loose. Hell, I suppose Lumumba would have cut him loose, too, if we hadn't iced him fifteen years ago."

"You're getting very cynical in your old age, David. It's not becoming."

"Moi?"

"It's not funny."

"Babe, listen, this whole fucking business is an exercise in cynicism. I see that now. I see things I should have seen a long time ago." He lay back on the pillow and spoke as if to the ceiling above him. "You ever read 'The Purloined Letter'?"

She nodded her head against the pillow. "What does Poe have to do with . . . ?"

"You remember where the letter was?"

"On the dresser or something, right?"

"Yeah, in plain sight. The whole goddamn time they're looking high and low for it, it's right there under their noses. That's what I feel like. I spend half my life working in this damned business, and half of that wondering what the hell I'm doing. And all the while, the answer is right there under my nose."

"And what's the answer? What *have* you been doing all that time?"

"Nothing. Not a goddamned thing. It's political onanism. They send an asshole like me out in the field. We get diseases we'll carry to our graves. We get people killed. We kill people ourselves, people who trust us, and we use that trust to manipulate them until they're no longer useful, then we snuff out their lives the way other people swat flies. We sell our fucking souls, for God's sake, and all the while they're doing one thing while they got us doing another. Fools, that's what we are. Incredible, stupid fucking fools."

"Maybe you shouldn't be so hard on yourself, David. Maybe you're just..."

"Don't patronize me, Michelle. That just makes it hurt all the more."

She rolled over then, and held her arms out to him. He leaned over her, lay his head on her chest. She cupped a breast in one hand and raised the nipple to his lips, and he flicked it once with his tongue, but turned away. "No," he said.

"No what? What do you mean, honey?"

"I mean I'm not going to kid myself. Sex isn't a cure, it's an anesthetic. It's what people do when they don't want to feel anything real."

"That's not all it is. It's—"

"Don't give me any platitudes about sharing, about getting in touch with feelings, about comfort. What I have has no cure, Michelle. I'm terminal. I can't belive in anything anymore."

"What are you going to do?"

"I don't know. I'll think of something. I have to see Karp this morning. Maybe it'll depend on what he does. What he says."

"David, that's just crazy. You don't like him and you don't trust him. Why should he have anything to do with your decision?"

"Precisely because I don't trust him. Maybe he's what the Agency wants. Maybe I'm not. Maybe I can't work for an outfit that values a man like Bob Karp. Maybe that's something I should have realized a long time ago. Hell, I don't know, maybe it's something I did realize, but just never had the balls to do anything about. But I can't go on like this."

He got up and went into the bathroom. Michelle sat for a few minutes, listening to the hiss of the water. Getting up slowly, she seemed lost for a moment, then followed him in. The water was working for a change, and steam swirled out the door when she opened it. It tickled her nose, and filled the room with that damp smell that seemed to be the single most memorable thing about a hotel shower.

He was already in the tub and she knocked on the sliding glass door. "Can I come in?"

"Suit yourself," he said.

She rolled the door to one side, climbed in and pulled it closed behind her. He was rubbing himself with a washcloth as if he wanted to take his flesh right off the bone. The water was nearly scalding, and she yipped when he turned and the spray hit her.

"What are you trying to do, David, boil yourself alive?"

He grunted. Rubbing soap into his hair, he smiled at her. "Look, I don't mean to make this hard on you. I like you a lot. Probably I feel something even stronger than that, I don't know. But..."

She grabbed his arms and pulled them down, locking them behind her back. Reaching past him, she adjusted the water, adding enough cold to make it bearable. "You don't have to say anything," she said. "I just wanted to be in here with you. Just to be together. We haven't seen much of each other lately and..."

She leaned her head on his chest, and let the water course down over her body. His hands were soapy, and when he stroked her back, they felt slick on her skin. She felt him stirring, and backed away, holding him at arm's length and flashing a grin. "If I didn't know better, I'd think you were glad to see me."

She reached out and tickled his erection. It jumped under her touch like a live thing, and she grasped it and pulled him close. "What time did you say your meeting was?"

"Nine o'clock."

"Too bad."

He kissed the top of her head, burying his face in the damp hair. "You be here later?"

"I guess so. Why?"

"Why do you think?"

"Oh. Does that mean I have to let go now?"

"If I'm going to make my appointment on time, it does."

She squeezed, ran her fingernail along the length of him, and rolled the shower door open.

"I'll hold you to that," she said. The door rolled closed again and Ripley turned the cold down, sending more clouds of steam up over the shower stall.

She was back in bed when he came out. He dressed quickly, and she watched as he pulled on the shoulder harness for the Browning. "You don't think you need that, do you?"

"Michelle, I don't know what I need, or even what I think. But I'll tell you one thing, there's a lot more going on here than I understand. I'll take any edge I can get."

He leaned over the bed, pecked her on the lips, and left quickly, pulling his jacket on as he opened the door and disappeared in a swirl of empty arms.

It was eight forty-five when he pushed through the revolving door and out into the street. A cab was just disgorging a pair of tourists and he held the door for them as they climbed out. As the man leaned in the window to pay the cabbie, Ripley climbed into the back seat, pulled the door closed and waited until the tourist reached for his bags before saying, "The American Embassy, please."

The ride took ten minutes, and when Ripley stepped onto the pavement after paying the driver, he stopped for a moment to look around. It was a beautiful morning. The sky was deep blue, a single monstrous cumulus floating far off to the west. It was the kind of cloud a kid could watch for hours, finding everything from George Washington to Winnie the Pooh in its shapeshifting mass.

Tearing himself away, he hurried inside, took the elevator to Karp's floor and listened to the tapping of his feet on the hard tiles. Karp's door was open and the COS was waiting for him.

"Close the door, David," he said.

Ripley closed the heavy wooden door and sat down without being asked.

"You are one stubborn sonofabitch, do you know that?"

"What are you talking about?"

"What the hell do you mean sending a cable without my permission?"

"I wasn't aware I needed your permission."

"I'm Chief of Station. Who the hell's permission do you think you need?"

"I don't work for you, Bob. I work for Jack Devereaux. He made that clear before I took the job."

"Guess again, wiseguy." Karp leaned forward and shoved a cable across the desk. "Read it and weep."

Ripley snatched at the paper angrily. For a moment, he thought about crumpling it into a ball unread and tossing it into the vivarium. Instead, he snapped it once, then looked at it.

The cable was short and to the point. There were no loopholes, no ambiguities. It meant what it meant.

David,
Bob Karp in charge a/o 8-15-75.
Jack Devereaux

He read it twice to himself, then a third time, this time aloud. When he finished, he looked up. Karp was smiling. "How 'bout them horse apples, cowboy?"

"I can't accept this. I don't even know that it's genuine. I want to talk to Devereaux. I'll go back to Langley and get this sorted out."

"The hell you will. You work for me, and you'll do what I tell you to do, or you won't work at all."

"What difference does it make to you, Karp? Why are you so damned adamant about screwing Nkele?"

Karp snorted. "You know what your problem is, Davey? You think small. You have a small mind, full of small thoughts. You can't see the big picture."

"You know what I think, Karp?"

"Ask me if I give a shit."

Ripley ignored the taunt. "You're a goddamned five and dime Machiavelli. But you're not satisfied with fucking up a small part of the world. You want to fuck up as much as you can. All of it, if you can."

"Should I consider that insubordination, do you think?"

"Consider it resignation."

"I'll want that in writing. Maybe I'll accept it, maybe I won't."

"You want something to read, read the handwriting on the wall." Ripley turned to the door.

"You'll regret this, Ripley."

"Not as much as I regret taking the assignment in the first place."

"Call Jack if you want. He'll set you straight. Use a patch from downstairs. Tell Ronny I said it's okay. But you stay away from Nkele, or . . ."

Ripley whirled around. "Or what? What'll you do, Bob, have me shot? Turn your fucking snake loose? Is that what you'll do?"

He jerked the door open, and nearly wrenched his wrist as he tugged it closed behind him. Through the thick walnut, he could hear Karp shouting, but he couldn't make out the words.

And he didn't care.

TWENTY-SIX

❖

August 16, 1975

"Michelle, you've got to help me."

She shook her head, not so much to deny the request as to convey helplessness. "David, I . . . what can I possibly do? We're playing in your ballpark. I don't . . ."

"You know people. You have connections, you can get to people I can't get to."

"What good would that do? What can they possibly do that would make any difference to you? I don't even know what it is you *want* to do. And you don't either."

Ripley walked to the window to look out at the city. Every night, it seemed, there were fewer and fewer lights after dark. He remembered stories about World War II, about the blackouts, how life seemed to go daily into hibernation, and people moved around like grubs in the dark, driving without lights if they drove at all, covering windows with blackout curtains, making moles of themselves. His father used to tell him stories, and all he could think of was those fish that live in underground rivers. Fish with shallow bowls where their eyes should have been. Fish who had no eyes because there was no light. And he used to wonder if people would end up the same way if they lived long enough in the dark.

Now, it seemed that Salazar was slowly drifting in that direction. And he wondered if the war went on long enough, if the sun, too, would stop shining, if there would be endless night, where not even the moon bothered to show itself. He turned then and leaned against the window, enjoying the feel of the cold glass against his bare skin.

"I think," he said, "that maybe I've been going about it the wrong way. Instead of trying to convince Karp that Oscar is the right man, maybe I should be trying to convince him that Caulfield is the *wrong* man."

"But you said yourself that Karp doesn't even care who wins the war, as long as the MLF doesn't win easily, if it wins. It's almost like he *wants* Bandolo to win. You keep saying that, and I think I agree with you. So how could anything you do make a difference?"

Ripley wagged a finger. "All the difference in the world, if it's the *right* anything."

"Such as . . . ?"

"Karp is the ultimate bureaucrat. More than anything else in the world, he cares about how his superiors perceive him. The 40 Committee says fight, but not too hard? Okay, that's what he does. The president says no easy wins for the big bad Russkies? Fine, we'll make them sweat a little."

"So?"

"What's the one thing that matters most to the CIA right now?"

Michelle shrugged. "You tell me."

Ripley smiled. "Public opinion, Michelle. It's so damned obvious, I overlooked it. Like the Poe thing. I was looking in the wrong place for the right thing and in the right place for the wrong thing. Remember when we talked about it? Well, it's right here," he said, extending his arm and opening curled fingers, "in the palm of my hand."

"I still don't get it."

"Karp sandbagged Oscar with the South African gambit because American public opinion would be outraged. He put it together piece by piece, then let it blow up like the fucking *Hindenburg* with a hundred cameras rolling. In fact, he lit the match. I have to hand it to him. It was beautiful. And the thing about Karp is, he doesn't see anything wrong with it. He sees what he wants to see and does whatever he has to to make things happen his way. But two can play that game."

"You think he doesn't know that? You think you can run the same number on him? I doubt it."

"Not the same number, no. But the thing about guys like Karp is they're arrogant. So arrogant, they think they can't be outfoxed. And if I can get something on Caulfield, something genuine, something that'll stick, I have a chance. Maybe I can't get him to switch to Oscar, but I'll bet my ass I can at least level the playing field."

"I don't know . . ."

"There must be something. There has to be. I'm telling you, Michelle, I've seen this guy in action. I told you about the execution I witnessed. That can't be the only skeleton in his closet. But I need something big, something so big that Karp can't afford to walk away from it or try to sweep it under the carpet. It's got to be big enough that the press will sit up and take notice. Not just the leftists, either."

"My Lai, is that what you're looking for, something like that?"

Ripley shrugged. "I don't know. I'm like the guy with a lot of money who wants to buy a painting, the guy who doesn't know anything about art, but knows what he likes. I'll know it when I see it." He looked at her thoughtfully. "Why did you mention My Lai?"

Michelle lit a cigarette before answering. "I

don't know. I just thought, maybe there is something like that, that's all."

Ripley crossed to the bed where Michelle was leaning against the headboard, her knees elevated to hold her ashtray. Kneeling beside the bed, he said, "You've heard something, haven't you? Something like that. You told me before you were hearing rumors. That's the kind of rumor you've been hearing, isn't it?"

She blew out a plume of smoke and nodded. "Yes. That's the kind of rumor I've been hearing."

"Well?"

"Well what?"

"What about it? Is there anything to the rumors?"

She shook her head in exasperation. "David, I don't know. I've been looking, but . . ."

"Look harder, honey. You've got to . . ."

"Dammit, David, be realistic. Don't you think I have been? Don't you think I wouldn't like another Pulitzer nomination? And if there was anything like My Lai out there in the goddamned jungle, don't you think I'd bust my ass to get to it?"

Ripley took a deep breath. "Sorry. I guess I just . . . aww, hell, I don't know. Maybe it's just all wishful thinking. Maybe I *want* Caulfield to be a monster because I don't know any other way to . . ." He leaned his head on the edge of the mattress.

Running her fingers through his hair, almost like a mother comforting a child, she said, "Look, maybe I can make a few inquiries. There are still some people I can talk to, but . . . I can't make any promises."

Into the mattress, he said, "I don't want promises, Michelle. I just want . . . fuck, I don't even know what I want."

"It'll take some time, David. I can't just snap my fingers and get what you need, you know."

"I know . . . but will you try? That's all I'm asking. Just try. Please?"

"No promises . . ."

"Okay. No promises."

"What are you going to do in the meantime?"

"Talk to Nkele. Maybe he has something I can use."

"Do you know where he is?"

"No. But I know how to get a message to him. In fact, I already did."

"When?"

"Tonight. I'm supposed to meet someone at the drug store, the same as last time."

"That must mean he's in Salazar," Michelle said. "He's taking a big chance."

Ripley nodded.

"And you're going to go?"

"You bet I am."

Ripley dressed quickly, while Michelle sat on the edge of the bed, nearly catatonic. Her eyes seemed flat and distant as they followed his hurried movement. She was watching him, he knew, but she didn't seem to see him. When he was dressed, he strapped on the Browning holster, slipped on a seersucker jacket of blue and white stripes and pocketed an extra clip for the automatic.

"Do you need the gun?" she asked.

"I don't know, but I want it handy when I find out." He walked to the bed, leaned over and kissed her on the forehead. "Are you all right?" he asked.

She nodded.

"You'll still be here when I get back, won't you? Please?"

Again, she nodded her head. It was faint, but it was assent, and he smiled. "Good. We'll talk about all this garbage in the morning."

"Be careful..."

He walked to the door, glanced at her over his shoulder as he opened it, and watched her immobile face, thinking of Lot's wife as the door swung closed.

Downstairs, he took the elevator to the hotel garage, his hand patting the Browning through his jacket as if to reassure himself that it was still there.

When the elevator opened into the garage, he stood in the doorway for a moment, letting his eyes adjust to the dim light. He listened, but the huge space, full of cars silent as coffins, seemed to be deserted. The ping of a cooling engine tolled once, and he jerked his head toward it, dropping into a half-crouch. When he was certain there was no one there, he moved out into the garage, almost enjoying the smell of gasoline and motor oil, the tang of exhaust giving the sweetness a slight edge.

His rented car, a dark blue, three-year-old Chevy, was against the wall, a dented white Citroen parked beside it. He kept swivelling his head as he moved toward the Chevy, the keys dangling from his left hand, his index finger through the large ring that held them.

When he reached the Chevy, he inserted the key quickly, one hand inside his wrinkled jacket on the butt of the pistol. Ducking in, he cranked it up, pulled the door closed and backed away from the wall. Using only his parking lights, he rolled toward the main door. The electronic eye started the servo droning, and he could hear it as he cranked down the window. The Chevy's air conditioning was on its last legs, and he had never cared for the artificial coolness in a car in any case. Cars were supposed to be open to the air.

He rolled up the ramp, giving the stuttering engine some gas. Something knocked under the hood, maybe a lifter, maybe a loose motor mount, but he ignored the clatter and pulled out into the main street. It was nearly midnight, and the lights of Salazar, fewer every night, seemed to be flickering, as if the entire city were on the verge of going dark.

He parked a few doors from the drug store, which was closed, and sat there, waiting for some sign of what he was to do next. According to his phone contact, James, the driver from Philly, was to meet him at twelve on the button, and he had only three minutes to wait. In his rearview, he saw a pair of headlights approaching and hunched down in the seat, shifting his gaze to the external mirror, fiddling with the knob to adjust it as the car drew closer.

The headlights went out then, and Ripley rolled up his window. As he leaned over to lock the passenger door, a driver's habit as old as the Model A, the window of the driver's door exploded, and three holes were punched in the passenger door window.

Ripley screamed and covered his head with his hands as he heard the roar of an engine. As he started to raise his head, the windshield blew out, showering him with chunks of broken glass. He unlocked the passenger door, and crawled out onto the sidewalk as the car careened around a corner, its tires squealing. He got to his feet, tempted to run after the car, then stopped and looked back at the rented Chevy.

It had all happened too fast for him to notice much more than the general contours of the car. There had been no sound of gunfire, and he suddenly realized the gunman's weapon was silenced.

He was about to pull the Browning from his shoulder sling when he saw headlights again, coming from the same direction. He dropped to the ground and crept back along the row of parked cars. He worked the slide of the Browning to chamber a round. Releasing the safety with his thumb, he crept into the street, hunching between two cars a half dozen behind his own.

The approaching car slowed, rolled past, and he recognized James behind the wheel. The car stopped alongside the Chevy, and he saw the driver lean over, as if to get a better look, then open his door and get out. James circled his own car and ran to the Chevy, bent to peer inside and, when he realized it was empty, stood up straight, turning a full three hundred and sixty degrees, a man suddenly mystified.

Ripley moved out into the street, darted forward, and hissed, "Hold it right there, James."

The man turned, saw the gun and raised his hands. "Shit man, what're you doin'?"

"You see that car?" Ripley asked stabbing his left hand toward the wreckage.

"Yeah, I see it. What happened?"

"I suppose you don't know?"

"Hell no, I don't know. What the fuck are you talkin' about?"

"Somebody just tried to waste me, James."

Nkele's driver snorted. "And you think it was me? Let me tell you, my man, it was me, you'd be in there with all that glass all over your ass and blood on the seat cushions. Can't miss a man sitting like some dumb ass duck in a parked car."

"What are you doing here?"

"You want to see Oscar. And Oscar wants to see you. You already know that or you wouldn't be here now."

"Who else knew that?"

"How the fuck am I supposed to know?"

Waving the Browning, Ripley said, "Get in the car." As James moved around to the driver's side, Ripley opened the passenger door and dropped to one knee, keeping the pistol trained on James as he climbed behind the wheel.

Slipping into the back seat, Ripley pulled the door closed after him. James looked expectantly at his hostile passenger. Ripley tapped the Browning against the back of the driver's seat. "Drive," he said.

"Drive where, man?"

"Let's go see Oscar."

TWENTY-SEVEN
❖

"Where the fuck are you going?" Ripley demanded.

"You said you wanted to see Oscar. That's we're were going. He don't have no TV man, so you got to see him live, up close and personal like that dude on the Olympics, what's his name, Jim McKay, likes to say."

"This isn't the way to the warehouse."

James shrugged. He half turned, letting up on the gas a bit while he glared at Ripley over the back of his seat. "Man, you just don't get it, do you? You think the man can sit on his ass in one place forever? How long you think he'd last, he did that. Got to *move* man, keep 'em guessin'."

Ripley brought the gun up above the seat, and James flicked his gaze toward the Browning for a second, almost contemptuously, as if daring Ripley to shoot him, before turning back to watch where he was driving. Shaking his head, he said, "Man, I had a gun in my face before you was out of high school. That shit don't scare me. You want to shoot me, you go right ahead and pull the damn trigger. See how long it takes you to find the man then. You want to see him, shut the fuck up and let me take you to him. Otherwise, I can haul your sorry ass back to that raggedy Chevy you used to be rentin', and you can see can you get home in it."

Ripley didn't bother to answer. He knew James was right, but hated to admit it. It didn't make sense for Nkele to sit like a duck on a tiny pond. There were too many hunters and too little game. Move or die were the only choices.

They were south of Salazar fifteen minutes later, and as near as Ripley could tell, theirs was the only car on the road. There was nothing but blackness behind them, occasionally tinted red when James touched the brakes. Ahead, the twin augers of the sealed beams bored their way through the night. The flurry of insects caught for a moment in their glare looked like driven snow. The snap and crackle of their hard shells against the windshield sounded as if someone were pelting the car with small stones.

Once, James turned slightly, resting one arm on the back of the passenger seat as if he were cruising for burgers, and said, "Ain't far now, man. Be about ten minutes or so." The movement had taken Ripley by surprise, and he was embarrassed at how readily he tensed up. He thought for a moment he caught a glimpse of a smirk on James's face, but wondered whether it might just be his imagination.

Ten minutes later, just as James had predicted, a spit of land jutted out into the breakers a few hunrded yards ahead, its mass heavy and dark, making itself known less by its presence than by the absense of cresting breakers, disarming the surf before swallowing the whitecaps against its sandy sides the way a black hole swallows light.

James slowed, and Ripley could see a heavy wrought iron gate, open between two pillars of brick. Turning through the gate, James let the car coast into a grove of trees, its tires crunching loudly on a roadbed made of sea shells. The crushed shells glittered like sequins in the headlights.

"What is this place?" Ripley asked.

"Old hacienda or whatever the anchovy boys called it. Belongs to some rich dude who salves his colonial conscience by letting Oscar use it from time to time. Nice place, if you can afford the upkeep."

The car broke out of the grove, and the lane

curved to the left across a broad expanse of grass. In the headlights, Ripley could see that the place was well maintained, the huge lawn recently mowed, its grass almost magazine-ad green. The building itself appeared so suddenly it might have just risen from under the sea, like Atlantis surfacing after ten thousand years.

A broad piazza ran the full width of the three story house, which was considerable. High up, at the uppermost limits of the headlights' reach, reddish brown tiles crowned the steeply sloping roof, and the small "V's" that roofed a half-dozen gables. Wrought iron grillwork, its white paint recent and brilliant in the headlamps, filled the recesses of every window.

The lane became a semi-circular driveway, and James killed the engine halfway through, letting the car roll the rest of the way, the only sound its tires grinding mother of pearl to powder.

James parked the car and opened the door almost before Ripley realized what he was doing. Scrambling to get out himself, the gun making his movements awkward, he managed to open the passenger door, but James was just standing there, laughing.

"You are one sorry white boy," James said, shaking his head. "Don't know what Oscar sees in you, but it ain't my place, I guess."

"Where is he?"

Turning on his heel, James waved a hand like

a man leading a cavalry charge. "Come on, Mister Ripley," he said.

Their heels crunched on the broken shells as James led the way toward the piazza, up a low flight of broad steps, and toward the back door, which was open. Stepping inside, he nodded to two armed men who sat at a small table in one corner, the table and the chairs the only furniture in the large foyer.

Ripley followed him, noticing the gaze of the two guards, and looked down to see the Browning still in his hand. He had forgotten it was there, and tucked it back into his holster as James moved down a long hallway.

At the far end of the hall, broad glass panels seemed to look out on a hole in the universe. There appeared to be nothing but black beyond them, because the reflection of the hall's interior stopped the eye and held it.

Turning into the last doorway on the left, James disappeared and Ripley hurried to catch up. As he passed through the doorway, he found himself staring at a wall of books a good fifty feet away. To his right was a wall of glass, and it registered dimly that there must be a spectacular view of the ocean.

Oscar Nkele was sitting at a large wooden desk, papers stacked on one corner and a huge map spread out on its top. He looked up, then turned his attention back to the map. James nodded to Ripley, then left the library, a broad grin his only farewell.

"Oscar," Ripley said, "we have to talk."

"I'm listening," Nkele answered, still poring over the map. "Go ahead."

Ripley reached out and put his hand on the pen Nkele was using to make notes along a clear plastic ruler's edge. "Pay attention to me, Oscar, not the map."

Nodding, Nkele let the pen fall, backed up a step and sat down in a large leather chair. Folding his hands behind his head, he leaned back in the chair, cocking his head toward a settee to his left. "Sit down."

Ripley shook his head. "No need. I won't be here that long."

"From the looks of things, neither will I," Nkele said. "What do you want, David? I should have thought my usefulness to your CIA had been exhausted."

"Look, Oscar, I don't blame you for being angry. I just . . ."

"I'm not angry, David. Just perplexed. And more than a little sad. I don't understand why Mister Karp . . ."

"Forget about him for a moment, will you. It's Jorge Caulfield I want to talk about."

Nkele nodded. "As I said, I'm listening. But you don't seem to be saying much."

"I think we have one chance to undo what Karp has done."

"And what would that be?"

"Fight fire with fire. Get the press, and

through it public opinion, back on your side. It worked once, why not again?"

"Because it was I who accepted the South African aid, not Jorge."

"I'm not talking about that. What I'm talking about is Caulfield himself. There's more there than meets the eye, not much of it good. I'm convinced of that. The man has a bloodthirsty streak. Somewhere, there must be evidence of that. Something we can get our hands on, something we can use to force the press to be more critical of him, the European and U.S. press, I mean. You know what they're like. Jackals. If we find the raw meat, the dead bodies, they'll do the rest."

"Are you suggesting that we manufacture something for them? Because if you are, we have nothing to discuss. I will not even consider such an idea."

"You don't have to. I know the evidence is there, somewhere. I saw him execute four MLF men with my own eyes. I know what he's like, what he's capable of. This is not like Angola, Oscar. We're not talking about a choice between Roberto and Savimbi. We're talking about the very real possibility that my country, knowingly or not, has climbed into bed with a coldblooded killer. Where there are four bodies, there are bound to be more. There must be closets all over Mawindi with Caulfield's skeletons in them."

Nkele laughed. "Your country has never been particularly careful about its bedmates. I don't see why this time should be any different. I find myself in the rather unfortunate circumstance of having married a harlot and expecting her to be faithful. It is not in the cards."

"If we leave it to Karp, it won't be. If there is something, and I find it, I don't plan to go to Karp. I'll go straight to the press. Michelle can help me do that. She knows enough people in enough places that we're bound to get the story out."

"But you don't *have* a story, do you? And you're asking me to give one to you or, better yet, to make one up."

"No, not make it up. But if you know anything, anything at all, now's the time to tell me. This is your last chance to . . ."

Nkele shook his head. He rubbed his neck with both hands and for a moment, the only sound in the room was the hiss of his skin on whiskers. Beyond it, like the meaning of a parable, almost too subtle to notice, came the rumble of the surf from somewhere out beyond the wall of glass.

Looking out toward the ocean, Nkele said, "You know what they say about people who live in glass houses? Well, it applies as well to those who only rent them. It might be time for me to accept the fact that, for whatever reason, I have been unable to marshal the support I need. And if I have to choose between Joshua and Jorge, I think . . ."

"Go on, finish."

"No. I *am* finished. There is nothing more I can do for Mawindi. Here," he said, leaning forward, "look at this map."

With a finger, he traced a broad black line that surrounded Salazar from the Zairian border all the way around to the seacoast fifty miles to the south. "You see this line? This is where the MLF is located." Then, stabbing the same finger at another, much larger semi-circle, he continued, "And this is where they were just two weeks ago."

"The red circles, they're Caulfield's forces, am I right?"

"As nearly as I can figure it. And the small green blotches, mostly along the railroad, as you can see, are the areas I can safely say are under the control of the African People's Party. Not a pretty picture, is it? And it will be less pretty tomorrrow, and the day after and the day after that."

"You sound like you've given up, Oscar."

"No. I haven't given up. But as one advances in age, one learns that facts, no matter how painful, must be faced. You ignore them at your peril. Too many people depend on me. I am afraid, though, that they should no longer expect much from that dependence. They would be better served to look after themselves. Perhaps if they join the PAM forces, they might . . ."

"And if they don't?"

"Then Joshua Bandolo will surely be the first president of the Republic of Mawindi."

"You know, don't you, that Caulfield has been executing MLF prisoners."

"It would be like him to do so. I remember 1965 as well as the next man. He has changed since then, of course, but not for the better. Already, some of his soldiers have turned their attention to the small pockets of APP resistance, preferring, I think, a smaller, less significant war, one that will allow them to salvage something and, perhaps, to vent some of their frustration."

"You're saying you expect him to . . ."

"I'm saying that my hands are tied. Whatever will happen will happen. There is nothing I can do."

"But there is, Oscar, there is. If you know anything I can use against Caulfield, something to force the American support to shift toward you, there will never be a better time. This is your only chance."

"I wish I could help you, David. I know you mean well, but . . ." Nkele shrugged and looked once more at the wall of glass. "It is very dark out there," he said.

And Ripley knew he meant more than the night itself. He knew that Nkele was looking not just at space, but at time. And the future was, indeed, dark. "If you change your mind," he said, "you know where to reach me."

Nkele nodded. "James will take you back to Salazar."

TWENTY-EIGHT

❖

All the way back to Salazar, Ripley kept trying to understand. Oscar Nkele, a man whose energy was larger even than his enormous physique, and whose spirit had been larger still, seemed to have given up. It was as if the air had been let out of a great balloon. The man who had sat there, his hands crabbing over the map of the country that he loved more than life itself had been gutted, vacuumed, and now was a mere shell of the man he had been.

And Ripley kept telling himself that it was just temporary. It was the kind of deflation that sets you back on your heels for a day or week or even a month, but that doesn't take you down completely.

He knew the feeling only too well, because he had lived it himself in the aftermath of Vietnam. But there was a difference. David Ripley had the rest of his life to recover, but Oscar Nkele had ten weeks at the most, and, realistically, far less than that.

The MLF was slowly expanding its sphere of influence, and Jorge Caulfield, the only man with access to the firepower necessary to stop it, or at least to slow it down, was folding up like a worn-out road map. And Nkele didn't seem to have the will to jump in, to take up the slack, to fight, not just for his own survival, but for the survival of his dreams.

Slim as it was, there was still a chance, but if Nkele were to have that chance, Ripley knew that it was up to him, not Nkele, to seize it. And he was scared to death.

James was silent on the drive back, and the Ford was filled with the barely audible sound of bebop from a portable tape player lying on the front seat. From time to time, Ripley recognized one of the tunes, but he was in no mood to engage in idle chatter, even about jazz, the one thing in his life that mattered more than life itself.

When he climbed out of the car in front of the Continental, the morning was just beginning. The phrase "rosy-fingered dawn" kept running through his head, over and over and over, and try as he might, he could not place it. Homer maybe. Or Virgil. But he thought he knew what it must have been like to stand there on the plains of Troy, mouth agape, as warriors who were more than men and less than gods fought to the death, hacking at one another for reasons that were clear, simple, easily understood.

It seemed to him that Oscar Nkele, in another age, would have been there too, cheek by jowl with Hector and Ajax and Achilles. But that age was long gone, and Oscar Nkele had the terrible misfortune to live in a time when, instead of the heroes of the golden age rising above the ordinary by force or force of will, they were dragged down by the awful, crushing weight of the trivial, reduced to the banality of war in the age of paper and its pushers. Perhaps there no longer was room for a man so large. Not anymore.

He watched those rosy fingers tickle the sky until its single, unblinking eye was open, then pushed wearily into the hotel lobby, crossed to the elevator, just managing to squeeze between the closing doors, and pushed the button for six.

He leaned back against the rear of the car, his eyes closed, his body slowly dissolving in its own sinking spirits. When the car stopped, he pushed away from the back wall and started forward. When the doors wheezed open, Michelle was standing there, a heavy bag slung over her shoulder.

"There you are," she said. "Christ, I thought I was going to have to do this myself."

"Do what?"

"Your job."

"What are you talking about?"

She shook her head. "Not now. Let's get the

car. I'll tell you on the way." She stepped into the elevator and stabbed at the down button with a jittery finger, then turned to look at him. "Christ, you look like you've been up all night . . ."

"I have been."

She said nothing more until they reached the lobby. Only then did Ripley remember the car was in ruins a few blocks away. "We'll have to take a cab," he said.

"Why?"

"It's a long story."

"We'll take my car, then. You drive." She led the way to the elevator down to the garage, fishing in her purse for the keys to her rented car. Tugging them free with a tissue trailing like the tail of a comet, she flipped them to Ripley as she stepped into the garage.

The car was a replica of his own, as if the rental agencies in Salazar imported one make and one model. Ripley slid behind the wheel and Michelle was urging him to get moving even before she climbed into the passenger seat.

"What the hell's your hurry?" he asked, peeling rubber. The squeal of the tires sounded deafening in the underground garage. He gunned the engine and roared up the ramp and out into the street, narrowly missing a crowded bus and frightening several people clinging to its rear bumper.

"I got a phone call a few minutes ago from an old friend of mine."

"I suppose that's exciting, but—"

"Shut up David. Shut up and listen. I did what you asked. I made some inquiries, a couple of phone calls, cashed in a few chips . . . anyway, Pete Fletcher is a stringer for Reuters. He ran into an old friend of his, a guy named Gerard de Beauville. Gerard is a free-lance documentary producer, and he's got some footage Pete thought I ought to see . . . turn left at the light . . . and from what he told me, I think it's something you ought to see, too. It sounds like it might be the kind of thing you're looking for."

"What kind of footage, what are you talking about?"

"Video, some place up near the Zaire border. Gerard shot it last fall. That's all I know. But Pete says it's unbelievable. I've known him a long time, and I know he doesn't get excited easily. He's been all over the place. Beirut, covered the Six Day War, spent a lot of time in your old stomping grounds, too."

"Reuters, you say?"

"Now, yeah. But back then he was Agence France Presse. Did a lot of radio stuff out of Da Nang, but he was all over. He even pulled a few strings and managed to get into Khe Sanh during the height of the siege. In other words, for Pete, it takes more than a cherry bomb to make a bang."

"And what does any of that have to do with my current situation?"

"You think Nkele's getting shafted, don't you?"

"Yeah, I do. But so do you, although you refuse to admit it. All that objectivity you journalists are so damn proud of. Like it's some sort of sin to recognize the . . ."

"Right! Turn right, dammit!"

Ripley spun the wheel without looking, and the Chevy was perilously close to taking the corner on two wheels. "When I was a kid, I used to go to the State Fair. There was a guy named Joey Chitwood..."

"And his Hell Drivers. I know. I've seen them, too."

He shook his head. "You know, if you told me where the hell we were going, maybe I could drive like a normal man instead of like I was in a demolition derby."

"San Marcos? You know it?"

"Never been there, but I know where it is."

"That's where I'm supposed to meet Peter. I don't know any more than I already told you. When we get to San Marcos, we'll both know."

As the city fell away to the south, the character of the area changed considerably. Instead of the mix of shanties and skyscrapers that characterized the capital, the suburban enclave was a patchwork of broad, tree-lined streets and modest houses. Popular with European and American expatriates, it reminded Ripley of Cape Cod. The downtown portion of San Marcos was lined with shops catering to tourists, many of them now closed, their windows full of faded posters advertising everything from artwork to sun block.

"Where to now, Michelle?" Ripley asked, as they rolled through a deserted intersection at the heart of the commerical district.

"Two blocks and then make a left, I think."

Ripley slowed as he approached the second side street, peered up at the road sign, and said, "Avenida Federico."

"That's it. Pete said his place is on the beach at the end of the street. Should be four blocks."

Ripley gunned the engine to give the Chevy a little burst of speed, and tapped the brakes at each cross street. Entering the fourth block, he saw a wooden barricade and, beyond it, sand dunes. "Got to be here," he mumbled. "There's the beach."

He rolled to a stop at the barricade, killed the engine, and got out of the car. Michelle climbed out on her side. A small cottage on the left, just beyond the barricade, badly in need of a paint job, was the most obvious choice. A moment later, a screen door opened, and a tall, ginger-haired man stepped into the sun. "Michelle," he hollered, "that you?" He shielded his eyes with one hand and, when he recognized her, ran to the curb with a loose-limbed gait.

Michelle waved Ripley forward, fanning the air with one hand to make him hurry. "Come on, David."

Ripley stood behind her while the two old friends cooed and chattered for a few moments, then Fletcher said, "Introduce me."

He stuck out a hand without waiting for Michelle to comply, and said, "Pete Fletcher. Nice to meet you."

Ripley took the hand and said, "David Ripley."

Turning toward the cottage, Fletcher said, "Come on in. Gerard is just setting up his gear, and he's brought someone along who can help explain what we'll be seeing."

"What exactly is it we'll be seeing, Pete?" Michelle asked.

"Not sure. Haven't seen it myself, but . . . I'll let Gerard explain."

He led the way inside. The cottage was cool, its windows all open to the sea breeze. In the living room, cluttered with papers, books and stacks of magazines, a small dark-haired man, whom Ripley took to be Gerard de Beauville, was busy connecting cables to an impressive array of video gear. A three-quarter-inch deck was the centerpiece, and as the last connector was snugged home, he looked up.

Fletcher did the introductions. "Gerard de Beauville, this is Michelle Harkness, whom I think you've met before, and her friend, David Ripley."

De Beauville nodded vaguely, his eyes still checking cables to make sure everything was ready. On a sofa in one corner, a short, thin black man sat watching. Ripley nodded to him, and he nodded back.

"What's this all about?" Ripley asked.

"I'd prefer to let the video speak for itself," de Beauville said, with barely a trace of an accent. "Keep in mind that this is edited. There is much more footage where this came from."

He clicked on the monitor, and a tiny bead of white light at the center exploded into a roiling mass of white lines for a moment, then the screen was filled with salt and pepper snow. A soft hiss emanated from the monitor's speaker.

"Ready?" Gerard asked.

"Roll it," Fletcher answered.

De Beauville loaded the thick cassette into the deck and punched the play button. Once more the picture rolled frantically for a few seconds, then the gray returned for a moment, almost immediately replaced by a slide that read "Kumbala, Mawindi. October 2, 1974."

The small man got off the sofa and moved to a point behind Ripley, from which he could see the monitor. Suddenly, the screen was filled with smoke, and as the camera pulled back, the source of the smoke, a ruined hut, came into view. The camera panned left, and another hut, then a third and a fourth appeared. Each time, the camera zoomed in on the ruins. The oddities of destruction seemed to fascinate the camera operator, whom Ripley presumed to be de Beauville himself.

In one hut, a table, its wood charred, but otherwise intact, sat dead center, a bowl on its top. The camera moved in, and the tips of several blackened bananas rose above the bowl's rim. In another a single wall remained standing. A solitary window, its glass gone, its curtains just ashes hanging from a metal rod, held the eye and, as if by design, a puff of smoke welled up as a breeze blew through the ruins, the ashes trembled and, as the smoke cleared, drifted away from the rod, floating the way autumn leaves might in hell.

The camera then shifted its attention from the shattered homes to the more graphic litter of broken bodies. One, just bones under shrunken, blackened skin, leaned against the stub of a wall, its arms curled stiffly in its lap. Another, untouched by fire, lay in the doorway of an undamaged wall, its head and trunk outside, the legs inside. The camera descended a couple of feet to reveal that the rear wall of the building was gone.

Then, scanning the ground with a detachment that could have its equal only in the eye of a scavenger, the camera picked out corpse after corpse, men, women, children, their postures frozen in the agony of flight from sudden terror.

Michelle shook her head and turned away. "Turn it off," she whispered. "Turn it off. David, make him turn it off."

Ripley draped an arm across her shoulders and she turned toward him, burying her face in his shoulder. He stroked her hair, trying to comfort. Her sobbing made his own body tremble, and he was dimly aware of the tears soaking his shirt.

"What happened here?" Ripley asked.

The Frenchman looked at him, his eyes hard as pebbles. "What do you think happened?"

"You tell me."

De Beauville shook his head. "I'll let Senhor Moreira tell you."

He nodded toward the small man and Ripley turned to look at Moreira, who had turned away from the monitor just as Michelle had.

"Senhor Moreira?"

The man nodded, but didn't turn around.

"I'll shut it off, Justin," de Beauville said. Ripley heard a click, and the hiss from the speaker died. The room was filled with light as Pete Fletcher turned on an overhead fixture.

Moreira turned then. "That was my village," he whispered. "Those were my friends and my neighbors."

"But what happened?"

"Soldiers came in the night. They blew up our houses. They killed the people. They . . ." He stopped, looked at Ripley and shook his head as if to say he couldn't talk about it.

"What soldiers? Who were they?"

"They were PAM troops, Jorge Caulfield's men," de Beauville said.

"How do you know that?"

De Beauville smiled. He walked to the table holding the video deck and picked up a thick envelope. He handed it to Ripley. "Look for yourself," he said.

Ripley sat on the floor and opened the envelope. He could feel the heavy paper of photographs and slid them out reluctantly. They were black and white, but there was no mistaking the fury of the flames consuming the buildings. Print after print showed the same thing—Kumbala in its death throes. The camera must have been rather primitive, and the only illumination for the photos was the holocaust consuming the village.

The figures were starkly etched—men in uniform, automatic rifles in their hands, women, their skirts fluttering away from pumping legs, a father with a child in each arm, already falling to the ground, his face a mask of terror—a Bosch tableau.

And the last photograph was the most graphic. It showed a man in uniform, his face in profile, pointing a pistol at a woman lying on her back, one hand upraised as if to ward off a bullet. The man in the uniform was unmistakably Reynaldo Carvalho.

Ripley looked at de Beauville. "Where did you get these pictures?"

"I found the camera in the village. Someone, Justin doesn't know who, must have snapped them during the height of the attack. The camera was singed, but the film was undamaged. Those are contact sheets."

"The negatives?"

"Safe. You may keep those prints." He walked over to the video deck, pushed the ejection button, and yanked the cassette free of the machine. "I understand you want to help Oscar Nkele," he said.

Ripley nodded. "I'm going to try."

De Beauville flipped the cassette to him. "That's a copy," he said. "Do what you want with it. If that can't help him, nothing can."

TWENTY-NINE

❖

A cathedral silence filled the room. Ripley glanced at the monitor over his shoulder, as if fearful that the horrible images would still be there, the slow crawl of the camera from body to body like some terrible insect looking for the perfect meal. Michelle was still crying, her face buried in his shoulder, and he realized that his own cheeks were wet. Pete Fletcher had collapsed onto the sofa, his head shaking in some slow motion spasm.

Only Justin Moreira seemed unaffected. He looked at the others, his face an impassive mask. De Beauville broke the silence. "I'm sorry," he said. "I'm truly sorry, Senhor Moreira."

Moreira nodded as if he had been thanked for the time. "The film is nothing," he said. "To make the film is nothing to be sorry for. To be sorry, to be truly sorry, is to have been there, to have seen it, to have heard the explosions, and smelled the burning flesh. Politics," he said, spitting without apology onto the scarred floor of the cottage.

"Will you come with me, Senhor Moreira?" Ripley asked, his voice almost unrecognizable to his own ears, raspy and rough-edged, like some clawed creature scratching its way to the surface from someplace deep inside him, someplace where words were alien things.

"For what?" Moreira asked.

"To show the film and the pictures to someone."

"For what?" Moreira asked again. And Ripley wondered whether he had heard the first answer, or if it were a second iteration requiring another answer.

"I can see to it that Colonel Carvalho is punished."

"Can you bring back my friends? Is there some bazaar for politicians where you can trade him for my friend Augustinho, or his wife Rosanna? Can you sell him in pieces to buy new homes for those few who survived? Because if you can't, then what is the point. My friends are dead and they will not come back."

"But the man who is responsible for their deaths ought to be punished."

Moreira shook his head. "Listen to you. Listen to your words. 'The man responsible for their deaths.' What does that mean? 'The man who slaughtered them.' Those are words I can understand. But . . . what you are saying . . ." He shook his head. "Those words mean nothing."

"But if you don't do something to stop him, he and his Commandante will be running this country. You can't allow that to happen."

"Can't allow it? Since when does anyone care what Justin Moreira thinks? When did anyone ask me who should run my country? Since when was it even my country? When was I consulted about anything? And why should things be different now? I know how these things work, Senhor. I raise my voice and someone cuts my throat. I have an accident, or I disappear in the dark of night, and my wife and children starve. The man responsible for those things could be any man. It could be Colonel Carvalho. It could be any colonel or major or captain. That is the way it has always been in Mawindi. That is the way it always will be. If I thought one man could make a difference, and I don't, I know that man would not be me. Maybe a man like Joshua Bandolo can make a difference, or a man like Oscar Nkele. But men like that, they soon forget about men like me. They use men like me the way a mason uses stones, to build a stairway to someplace where they want to go and where men like me are not welcome."

"But things *can* change. You can help to change them, Senhor Moreira."

"Let someone else change things. All I want is to be left alone. I have suffered enough. Those people in the film? In some ways I envy them, because their suffering is over. It is the survivors I pity. You go, take the film, take the photographs, go from house to house and knock on doors. If you find someone who cares, you come back and see me. Maybe then I will try to change things. And maybe not."

"I understand your resentment, but . . ."

"Resentment? That is such a pretty word. It is a word for poets and politicians, but I am neither, Senhor. I am just a simple man who wants to live out his life as best he can. My back will break someday, but until then I will put food on the table. There will be a roof to keep the rain from the heads of my children. And in that way, I will be a success. It is the most a man like me can hope for, Senhor. But you go, and you try. And see how far you get."

Ripley tapped the cassette against his thigh, then tucked it into the envelope of photographs, closed the metal clip, and nodded. "I *will* try, Senhor Moreira."

He patted Michelle on the cheek. "You better stay here, honey," he said.

"Where are you going?"

"To see Mister Karp. He can't ignore evidence like this. He'll have to listen to me now."

"I'm going with you," she said, wiping at her eyes with the back of one hand.

"No, you can't. Someone took a shot at me last night. For all I know, whoever it is followed me here. The best thing you can do, all of you, is get the hell out of here. Get on the next plane and get out of Salazar. Get out of Mawindi."

"Men like Carvalho want us to run," Gerard said.

Ripley nodded. "Of course they do. And if you have a brain in your head, you'll do just that."

"What about you?" Michelle asked. "Why don't you come with us, then?"

"Because there's one last chance, and I mean to take it. If I can stop this insanity, I'll have to do it quickly. Gerard, you should get that film into as many hands as you can. Find as many people as you can who are willing to air that tape. Michelle can tell you all you need to know about Carvalho. Hell, all you need to know is that he's Jorge Caulfield's right-hand man. And if that doesn't cut any ice in France or England, then Senhor Moreira is right. But I refuse to believe it."

"Why do anything?" Gerard demanded. "Bandolo and the MLF are going to win anyway. Caulfield's troops are falling apart. The MLF is less than twenty-five miles away from Salazar. Why not let them take care of Caulfield, Carvalho, the whole lot of them?"

Ripley didn't say anything for a moment. He wondered whether there was anything he could say, anything the Frenchman would understand. "Do you remember Dien Bien Phu, Gerard?"

De Beauville nodded. "Sure, I remember. I

had an uncle there. What's that got to do with anything?"

"Read your fucking history, dammit! The French lost at Dien Bien Phu, and the United States followed them right into the same goddamned quagmire."

"You read *your* history. You know better than that, now. Or at least you ought to."

"We knew better then, and it didn't make any difference. These things take on lives of their own."

"Don't give me any of that tired garbage about dominos and principles, and standing up for democracy," Fletcher barked. "The U.S. swaggers around the fucking globe like some muscle-bound bully, bashing heads in the name of the almighty dollar, talking all the while about dignity and human rights. Where were your human rights in Laos? Where were they in Vietnam? Where were they in Guatemala? And Cuba and Panama?"

Ripley laughed, and he thought for a moment he was going to lose it. "Listen to you, goddamn you. Both of you. You're representatives of the two biggest colonial empires the world has ever seen. Most of the world's problems in the last century can be laid squarely at your doors, and you have the gall to lecture me about what *my* country has done wrong? Don't you dare. If the Brits knew so much, how do you explain the Mau Mau? If the French were such paragons of enlightenment, what about Algeria?"

"Ancient history, Ripley," Fletcher snapped.

Ripley laughed again. "Ancient history. You mean yesterday's news, don't you. That's all your headlines amount to. That's what becomes of your fucking documentaries and your photo essays and your editorials. But right now, people are dying, and you can prevent it. People who don't have televisions, who can't read newspapers, who . . . ah, what's the use. You don't understand."

Michelle backed away from him a step, her face uncertain whether to reflect scorn or confusion. "David, I . . ."

"No, don't say anything. You don't understand because you *can't* understand. You're all the same, really. You live the agony of others, attach yourselves to bleeding carcasses to feed your egos the way lampreys suck the lives out of their hosts. I'm saying let's put an end to it. Let's make everybody see, really see, what's going on, not to win some damned prize, not so you can tell war stories at university dinners. You think you're above it all, detached, empyrean, but you can't live without it, without the pain and the suffering and the blood and the gore. It's what you live for, and all I'm saying is let's make that agony and that suffering mean something. Let's use it to put an end to agony and to suffering."

"You're a bloody fool, Ripley."

"Maybe. But it beats being a vampire." He turned abruptly and headed for the door. He tensed then, waiting for Michelle to call to him, to urge him to come back. But by the time the door banged closed behind him, she still hadn't said a word.

He jumped into the Chevy and rammed the key in the ignition, cranked up the engine and backed into a tight "C" before laying a patch on the sandy asphalt. In the rearview mirror, he saw Michelle come out into the yard and stand there, arms folded across her chest, watching him drive away. She didn't wave, she didn't run after him, and if he didn't know better, he would have thought she hadn't even noticed him leave. She might just have come out for the morning paper or to wait for the next mail delivery.

Only dimly conscious that he might be followed, Ripley gunned the Chevy's engine. Taking the turn onto the main road without slowing down, he skidded into the oncoming lane, narrowly avoiding a Buick headed the other way. He caught a glimpse of the startled face of the driver, and for a moment thought he had seen him before. In the rearview, he saw the car skid into a turn, and enter Avenida Isabella and disappear.

Wracking his brain, he finally realized why the face had looked so familiar. It was the same one he'd seen at the bazaar. Struggling with the urge to turn back, Ripley floored the accelerator. Had he been followed, he wondered. Followed, or had they simply known where to find him?

He patted the seat beside him, where the cassette and photographs lay in their brown envelope. Without taking his eyes off the road, he grabbed the envelope and slid it under the passenger seat, knowing that even a half-hearted search would turn it up.

The streets were deserted, and since it was nearly ten, Ripley sensed that something must be about to happen. He tore through a stop sign, careened around a curve, then rocked into a side street. Taking a right, then a left, then another right, he headed toward the east side of San Marcos. The trees and neat little houses flew by in a blur, and he noticed the speedometer needle hovering around seventy.

Taking another right, he could see a haze off to the left. Several columns of thick, greasy smoke climbed toward the unclouded blue sky, smearing across the horizon. He could hear the deep resonance of explosions now, each boom distant, a faint clap of thunder, barely audible over the roar of the Chevy. It was like standing beyond the fence at a drive-in to watch a war movie.

The MLF was pushing closer and closer. There was some traffic now, and he slowed a bit. He headed back toward the west, to pick up Avenida Cordeiro. Once on the Avenida, he spotted several trucks up ahead crossing the broad boulevard, men in the Pan-African uniform hanging from the rear, and spilling over the sides. They were headed east toward the smoke, and he counted eleven, followed by a single jeep, as he approached the intersection.

At least Caulfield hadn't thrown in the towel just yet, he thought. As he neared downtown Salazar, he could see people hanging out of windows in the taller buildings, small knots gathered on the roofs of the lower ones, some with binoculars. The rumble of artillery was distinct, but distant.

Ripley was still four blocks from the embassy when he heard the high-pitched whine of incoming. Something, he wasn't sure whether it was HE artillery or a 122mm rocket, landed fifty yards behind him, filling the rearview with black smoke. Two more explosions ripped at the asphalt a block ahead of him, and then the road seemed to buckle as a flurry of incoming walked up the road toward him.

Hitting the brakes, he skidded toward the curb, hung a right, and stomped on the gas. People were spilling out into the street now. Crowds were milling in the road, running in every direction, like ants stirred up with a stick. He tried easing the Chevy along, leaning on the horn and racing the engine while riding the brake, but a white man in a car was the least of their worries.

Ripley pulled over to the curb, killed the engine and reached under the set for the manila envelope. Getting out of the car, he started to push his way through the throng. Without the noise of the engine now, he could hear the explosions of artillery and mortar shells.

Glancing up at the sky, he saw the pall of smoke beginning to thicken, like gathering storm clouds.

THIRTY

❖

Marilyn Cisneros looked up as Ripley charged toward the door. "He's got someone in there," she said.

"I don't give a damn," Ripley snapped. He grasped the knob and gave the door a shove. As it swung open, he could hear Cisneros on the intercom. Her voice behind him gave her words a curious echo.

Karp looked up from his desk, and reached for the security alarm, but Ripley was too quick for him. He leaped across the desk and slammed the heel of his hand into Karp's wrist. "Unh unh, Bob. No way," he snarled.

Ronny Lang sat stock still, his mouth open as if he couldn't believe what he was seeing.

"Give me a hand, Ronny, dammit," Karp yelped as he tried to get out of his chair. Ripley shoved him back and the chair banged against the wall behind it.

"Just sit there, Bob, just stay still." He waved the envelope under Karp's nose. "You wanted a reason, I've got your reason right here." He tapped the envelope against Karp's chest until the COS shoved it away.

"I'll have your ass for this, Ripley."

"I don't think so, Bob. I don't think so at all." Turning to look at Lang, he said, "Ronny, you got video gear in the basement, right?"

Lang nodded. "Yeah, but..."

"Go get it. Three-quarter-inch deck and a monitor."

"But..."

"Get it!"

Lang looked at Karp as if for reassurance, but the COS was as much in the dark as he was.

"What the hell is this all about, Ripley?" Karp asked.

"I have some videotape I want you to see."

"What's on it?"

Ripley shook his head. "You have to see it. Then we'll talk, Bob. Not before." Turning to Lang, he said, "Ronny, go get the gear. And don't even think about alerting security. I can guarantee you it will be a mistake, not just for Mister Karp, but for yourself. I'm not holding him hostage, but I *am* insisting that he do his job. You interfere, and it'll be your career."

"Ripley, what . . . ?"

Ripley turned then. "Bob, just shut up, would you? Tell Ronny to go get the gear. He seems to want to hear it from you."

Karp nodded. "All right, Ronny. Go ahead. And tell Marilyn I don't want to be disturbed."

Lang got up and made for the door as if he'd just been given a reprieve from the gas chamber. When the door closed behind him, the room grew deathly still.

Ripley sat on the corner of Karp's desk, tapping the envelope on his knee. In the silence, the slap of the paper sounded like a ticking clock.

Karp was beginning to sweat, and he brushed a lock of damp hair off his forehead. "You want to give me some idea of what this is about, David? Are you holding the first Salazar International Film Festival? Is that it?"

Ripley glared at him. "You better hold the wisecracks, Bob. When you see what's on this tape, you're not going to think anything is funny. Maybe ever."

"Must be something, huh?" Karp was trying to smile, but his facial muscles seemed to have lost touch with one another. His cheeks wriggled as if they were a thin skin over a bag of worms, and one corner of his mouth kept twitching.

Ripley looked at the vivarium. The mamba

was nowhere to be seen. Getting off the desk, he walked closer to the glass, leaning forward and tilting his head this way and that until he found it, coiled into a ball among some ferns.

"He's just been fed," Karp said, his voice suddenly vibrant, as if overjoyed to talk about something neutral, a subject where he could regain some control. "He'll sleep for a day or so."

Ripley turned back to look at the COS. "I saw a lot of smoke off to the east on the way in. Sounded like shelling, too. Artillery, mortars, couldn't be sure, because it was too far away."

"Bandolo's making a move," Karp said. His voice was flat, as if he were discussing the weather with a stranger.

"You don't seem unduly upset about it."

"Why should I be? I expected it. Everybody did. You seem to be the only white man in Salazar who thinks the war isn't already over."

"Thanks to you . . ."

"No, no thanks to me. There was never any other way it could end, David. I tried to tell you that. Tried to make you understand, but you were too damn bull-headed to listen."

"I refuse to believe that. I refuse to believe that anyone, even Kissinger, would bother to mount an operation that had no chance, and then just sit back and watch, as if the war were some kind of wind-up toy, a top you set spinning and watch until it slows down, wobbles and finally falls over. I just can't believe that."

"You've got a lot to learn, David."

"No, not me. I've learned more than enough the past six or seven weeks. And I'll spend the rest of my life unlearning it."

Karp shook his head. "It's a pity you're not a team player, David. There's so much you could have done."

"I'm not through yet."

"That depends on what you mean by 'through.' Your career is over, that much I can tell you."

"Good riddance to bad rubbish, is that what you're thinking, Bob?"

Karp, reluctant to antagonize Ripley, shrugged his shoulders. "You wouldn't buy in, David. You knew what was happening, and you refused to accept it. I tried to tell you, but you were too damn busy crying in your beer. You wouldn't let go of the past. You were still back in Saigon, David. Still are. Hellfire is about to come down around your ears, and you think it's Charlie. But it's not. This is Africa, David. And the rules have changed."

Ripley shook his head. "No, the rules haven't changed. What you don't realize, and what I didn't understand until very recently, is that there *are* no rules. Only pawns and players. But I'm not going to be a pawn anymore, Bob. I'm—"

The door banged open, and he turned to see Ronny Lang pushing a metal cart through the door. He turned primly, like a room service waiter at a five star hotel, and closed the door, before rolling the cart toward the nearest electrical outlet.

Neither Ripley nor Karp spoke while Lang plugged in the equipment and made sure his cables were in order. Satisfied, Lang turned and looked at Karp, who nodded toward Ripley. "It's his show, Ronny. Ask the maestro what he wants."

Ripley opened the envelope and removed the cassette. He walked to the deck himself and inserted the tape. "What I want," he said, "is for you to watch this tape and tell me I'm wrong."

He glanced at the monitor, found the switch and clicked it on. Pressing the power switch on the deck, he let his thumb rest on the playback button while the monitor screen seemed to expand from a tiny white dot into infinity. The soft hiss of the speaker filled the room.

"The volume control is—" Lang began, but Ripley cut him off.

"There's no sound." He pressed playback, and stepped away from the gear, watching the screen until the slide appeared.

"Kumbala, where's that?" Lang asked.

"Shut up, Ronny," Karp said. His voice was tight, sounded almost a half octave higher than usual.

Then it began, and Ripley kept his eyes on Karp's face. He moved away a little further, so he could see the screen from the corner of his eye. Karp rubbed his chin nervously as the camera zoomed in and out, the endless skein of destruction, buildings, bodies, rolled by.

Karp's face was drawn now, and his tongue kept darting from the corner of his mouth, as if his lips were dry, and his tongue unable to moisten them. From his angle, Ripley could see a faint image of the monitor screen reflected in the vivarium glass. Turning away, he saw another, fainter reflection on the polished wood of Karp's desk. It seemed as if, no matter where he looked, he couldn't get away from the ghastly flicker on the screen.

Lang gasped, and Ripley turned to confront the screen head-on again, just as the camera pulled back to reveal a panorama of the shattered village, its human litter dwarfed by the towering trees of the forest beyond the broken buildings.

Karp was nodding his head when Ripley looked back at him.

"What do you want me to say, David?" he asked. "These things happen. It's war, after all."

"Those were civilians, Bob. Did you notice that? Did you see the women? The children?"

Karp nodded his head slowly, his eyes suddenly wary. "Yes. I saw. But I don't see what it has to do with me."

"Do you know who is responsible for that horror?"

Karp shook his head angrily. "Don't you say me, because I . . ."

"Not you, Bob. At least not directly. That was

the work of one Colonel Reynaldo Carvalho. You know him, don't you, Bob?"

"You can't prove that. You can't prove he did it."

"Not from the tape, I can't, no. But," and Ripley waved the envelope high over his head, "with these, I can do just that."

"What? Let me see." Karp took a step forward, one hand clutching almost spasmodically for the envelope. Ripley lowered it, stepped closer to Karp's desk, and showered the prints across its gleaming surface.

"Go ahead, Bob. Check it out."

The COS snatched at one of the photos, but it slid away from his fingers, and he slapped a hand on it. The report of palm on walnut was like a gunshot. Ripley heard the scrape of paper on wood as Karp wrestled the print to the edge of the desk and grabbed it. One after another, he glanced at them, his hands moving faster and faster. As he was done with each, he tossed it away, and Ripley saw Lang bend to retrieve several of the photos from the carpet. "I don't see any . . ."

"Keep looking, Bob. You'll find it."

"Oh my God," Lang muttered. "David, these—"

"Ronny," Karp interrupted, "just sit down and shut up. This doesn't concern you."

And then he found it. The profile shot of Carvalho and the woman, her extended hand far too fragile a thing to stop the bullet the Colonel was about to fire.

"Well?" Ripley said. "It's him, isn't it, Bob?"

Karp didn't answer.

"Bob? It's him, isn't it?"

Karp nodded. "Yeah. It's him. It's Carvalho."

He turned then, his eyes darting nervously from Ripley's chin to a point just beside his left ear, then toward the ceiling. "It's him. But it doesn't mean that Caulfield knew."

"No, it doesn't prove that Caulfield knew. But you know what, Bob? I don't think the press is going to care whether he knew or not. They'll say he *should* have known. And they'll be right. He should have."

"I can fix this. I can fix this. I'll talk to Jorge. *We'll* talk to Jorge. I can fix it."

"Bob, be realistic. This is not something you fix. Those are innocent people, and they're dead. And your boy is responsible. You can't fix it. You can't bring those people back."

"I can fix it. We're going to see Caulfield, tonight. You and me, David. We'll get to the bottom of this, and we'll put it right. We'll fix it."

THIRTY-ONE

✦

Karp drummed his fingers on the wheel as he drove. Ripley didn't mind the noise. It was better than silence, and he didn't feel like making small talk. Karp seemed to have recovered his equilibrium, and Ripley wondered about it. How, he asked himself, could a man see what he had seen, and just brush it off, as if it were no more than sand from a day at the beach?

In the distance, bright flashes split the night, and a deep rumble followed every flash. But the sky was clear and Ripley knew the lightning and thunder were man made. The war was creeping closer and closer, like something incomprehensible in a Yeats poem, something that had no name, and that no man could describe, because no man looked on it and lived.

Staring at the blacktop, the high beams fanning out in broad cones to brush against the undergrowth creeping toward the road on either side, he had the sensation of being in a pneumatic tube. It was almost as if he and Karp were shuttling in Karp's Oldsmobile from one corner of the earth to another. The steady hum of the big engine made the floor of the car vibrate, and Ripley could feel the trembling all the way to his knees.

They were heading south, and there was no moon. The ocean was black and limitless, marked with small curls of phosphorescence where the waves rose and fell. Ripley had his window down, and from time to time the rumble of a particularly big breaker would override the car's engine, then fall away with a mutter and one last whispering hiss.

Karp handled the car easily, and the twists and turns of the shore road were gentle enough that motion was all but unnoticed. The envelope with the videotape and contact prints of Kumbala sat across his knees, and he had his hands folded across the package, almost in an attitude of circumspect prayer.

Karp braked, and Ripley, from the corner of his eye, noticed the red glow of the brake lights washing through the rear window. The car turned toward the sea, heading at an oblique angle through a pair of stone pillars, their mortar-work studded with large seashells. It looked for all the world like the entrance to a place at the Hamptons. All that was missing was a cutesy sign reading, "Foam Crest" or "Enchanted Cove."

They were on an asphalt driveway that squirmed like a sidewinder among dense shrubs, most of them full of heavy blossoms.

"What's this place?" Ripley asked.

Karp didn't answer. A large stone house loomed up suddenly through a gap in the foliage, its second story framed with large pink flowers and rubbery green leaves. Ripley could hear the tires of the Olds hissing on the windblown sand coating the asphalt, then the house was right in front of him, its trim an iridescent white in the glare of the headlights.

Karp braked, threw the automatic transmission into park and shut off the engine. The lights died with a click, and Ripley wondered if the House of Usher could have looked more foreboding. Without a word, Karp got out of the car, walked a few paces, then waved impatiently for Ripley to follow him.

Two men in PAM uniform appeared in the doorway, AK-47's slung over their shoulders. Karp walked up the broad stairs to the wide porch, Ripley right behind him. Karp nodded to the two guards and entered the house. Without slowing down, as if he knew the place from basement to attic, he walked down a long, broad hall, his leather heels rapping on the polished wood.

A dim glow shone through thick drapery at the far end of the hall, where a pair of doors, also draped, towered toward the high ceiling. Karp stopped just long enough to grasp the knob, then yanked one of the doors open and stepped outside through the sudden rush of light. Ripley could see a broad patio now, and the sound of the surf was loud and steady.

Following Karp outside, he found himself staring through the flood of light out toward the restless waves where the ocean stretched away almost as black as the sky overhead. Off to one side, under a large flowered umbrella that shaded a round table, sat Jorge Caulfield. Next to him, Reynaldo Carvalho glanced up for a moment, then turned his attention back to his drink.

"Karp, wait a minute. What . . . ?"

Karp turned then. "You wanted to get things straightened out. So do I. Now's the time, David. Now's the time." Karp was almost expansive, and Ripley looked at Carvalho, who seemed uninterested in the newcomers.

Caulfield got up and walked toward Karp, his hand out. Karp shook it. "Jorge, I'm glad we could get together so soon. As I told you, this really can't wait."

"What is so urgent?"

Karp held up a hand. "I'm forgetting my manners," he said. "You know David Ripley, of course."

Caulfield nodded. He adjusted his shades, then shook Ripley's hand.

Moving toward the table, Karp took a seat, gestured for Ripley to sit across from him, and waited for Caulfield to resume his own chair. "We have a bit of a problem, Jorge," Karp said.

"What sort of problem?"

"How can I put this delicately? Let's say, ummm, a public relations problem."

Caulfield seemed confused. "I don't understand. What sort of public relations problem?"

"Have you ever heard of a place called Kumbala, Jorge?"

Ripley glanced at Carvalho, who set his drink down on the metal table with a sharp crack. Caulfield shrugged. "A little village up north. There are hundreds like it. I don't really know any more about it than that."

"Well, it might interest you to know that there is no such place any longer."

"What do you mean, Mister Karp? Please stop talking in riddles."

Karp stroked his chin and nodded. "All right. Maybe I should let David handle it from here."

Ripley sucked on a tooth for a moment, then patted the envelope before opening it. Removing the cassette, he set it to one side.

"What is that?" Caulfield asked.

"It's what's left of Kumbala," Ripley said.

"I don't understand."

"It's a videotape that was made the morning

after the village was attacked and detroyed. You can watch it at your leisure . . . if you have the stomach for it. Nearly a hundred people were killed. It was indiscriminate slaughter—men, women, children. From what I understand, not even livestock were spared."

"I don't see what this has to do with me, Mister Ripley."

"I'll show you, Commandante. I'll show you."

One by one, he removed the photographs. He passed each to Caulfield and watched the man's face as he scrutinized the pictures, sometimes leaning away from the umbrella to see them more clearly. After the fourth, Caulfield reached up and removed his sunglasses, blinked a moment, and reached out for the fifth print.

Caulfield's jaw went slack. He kept looking at Ripley, then at Karp and finally at the photograph. "These are MLF soldiers. I recognize the uniform. Surely you must also see that. I don't see what—"

"Wait, Commandante. Just wait," Ripley said. He escalated the removal of the prints now, and Caulfield glanced at one after another, stacking them neatly as he reached out for the next and the one after it.

Carvalho was restless. His hands were busy twirling the glass in a pool of condensation. The movement made the ice tinkle against the side of the tumbler. Out in front of the house, another car arrived, and Ripley looked at Karp, who just shook his head, his face expressionless.

Finally, Ripley had the last print in his hands. He looked at it once more, as if wanting to be certain it had not changed since the last time he'd examined it, then handed it across the table to Caulfield.

Once more, he bent over a photo, and his face seemed to crumble as he realized just what it was he was seeing. "Reynaldo! You?"

Carvalho tossed off the rest of his drink. Then he nodded.

"But why?"

"They wanted Bandolo to—"

"Innocent people? You did this? To innocent people?"

"They were—"

"No, I don't want to hear. Get away from me."

Caulfield got up from his chair and backed away as if Carvalho were the devil himself. "War is one thing, but this . . . this is infamy . . . get away. Go! Now!"

Karp rapped on the table. "That, I'm afraid, just won't be good enough, Jorge. Thanks to Mister Ripley, here, we have the evidence. But Colonel Carvalho is a genuine liability."

His hand moved again, and Ripley thought he was going to pound the table again. The loud report caught him by surprise. Carvalho started to rise, but the sudden appearance of the bullet hole in his forehead seemed to arrest him in mid-ascent. He teetered for a moment, and Ripley watched in astonishment as the colonel crumpled to the flagstones.

Blood and sticky clumps of brain tissue dripped from the underside of the umbrella, splashing on the table and making flowers of another kind on the shiny white metal.

"That, I think, takes care of that," Karp said.

"The hell it does," Ripley whispered. "There's still the matter of the press. You can't just sweep this under the carpet. No way. If you think . . ." He stopped when he realized that Karp was smiling. And when he realized the smile was directed at someone behind him, he turned to see Michelle crossing the patio. Behind her, Pete Fletcher and Gerard De Beauville staggered through the door and out onto the flagstones. Behind them came a man he knew he had seen before, and now he knew where. It was the man he'd seen in the bazaar. And at the wheel of the Buick at Avenida Isabella.

Ripley jumped up and ran to Michelle. "Are you all right?"

"I'm fine, David. I'm fine." Her voice was distant, and she kept looking past his shoulder so persistently that he turned to see what had captured her attention. But there was nothing there to see.

"We are almost all here," Karp said, getting to his feet.

"What do you mean, almost?" Ripley asked.

"We can't resolve this without Doctor Nkele,

can we?" And when Ripley didn't answer, he added, "Of course we can't."

Karp went to the door, saying, "I'll be right back."

Ripley reached out for Michelle, but she shook her head. "Not now, David," she whispered. "Not now."

Something was wrong, but before he could put his finger on it, Karp reappeared. Behind him, Oscar Nkele loomed in the doorway for a moment, then stepped onto the patio. James followed him out.

"Now we can tidy things up," Karp announced, sounding proud of himself. He seemed curiously unruffled, and Ripley was getting edgy.

Nkele nodded to Ripley, then his eye fastened on Carvalho slumped on the floor. "What happened here?" he asked, moving to the colonel's side and kneeling on the flagstones.

"Never mind that, Doctor," Karp said. "Colonel Carvalho is beyond the reach of medicine." Karp sat at the table again, folded his hands neatly on the table and cleared his throat. "We have a serious problem here," he said, "but I think I know how to handle it."

"You bet your ass, you have a problem, Karp," Ripley said. "And there's no way to handle it. None."

"I wouldn't be too sure, David. Let me try to sort things out, all right?" He jabbed a finger at

Carvalho's crumpled body, a pool of blood slowly spreading away from the shattered skull, sending long, dark, glistening fingers probing along the mortared grooves between the flagstones. "The colonel there was one part of the problem. That part has been solved.

"Doctor Nkele is another part of the problem. You understand that, don't you, David?"

"No, I don't."

"Then let me make it clear to you." He was using the strained patience of an irritated schoolteacher. "If you had let well enough alone, as you were instructed . . . if you had done your job as it was laid out for you, instead of as you saw fit to define it, things would have been so much neater, so much more efficient. But you didn't do your job, David. That means that Doctor Nkele is a liability." He nodded his head in Nkele's direction, and Ripley turned to look at the big man, who was still bent over Carvalho's lifeless body.

"Look out!" Ripley shouted, and started to move, but James was quicker. As if in slow motion, he saw the driver's hand come up, the squat, ugly mouth of the automatic in his hand just below Nkele's ear. The report of the pistol shot exploded, and its echoes bounced off the walls of the house and drifted out over the ocean, where they were swallowed by the sound of the surf.

Ripley went for the Browning, but someone grabbed him from behind, pinning his arms to his sides. He heard the Browning being lifted from its holster as he tried to break free. The cold steel muzzle against the back of his head brought him to a standstill.

Nkele dropped like a felled tree. Caulfield ran to the fallen giant. "Oscar, I didn't know," he said, dropping to his knees and cradling Nkele's blasted skull in his hands. "I didn't know. I didn't know." He looked at Karp then at Ripley, tears streaming down his face.

"Of course you didn't, Jorge. Of course you didn't," Karp said. "But you're a good soldier. You'll get along just fine, now."

Ripley looked at Michelle, who seemed unmoved, almost absent, her head tilted to one side. And the only thing Ripley kept thinking was Michelle didn't jump, she didn't wince, she knew it was coming. She knew it!

"That," Karp said, "takes care of part two."

Ripley exploded then. "You murdering sonofabitch, Karp. You think you can just walk away from this, do you? Are you crazy?"

Karp smiled. "Remember what I told you, David? About how you can just be walking along, when *bam!*, out of the blue it comes? I did tell you that, didn't I?"

Karp shook his head, arranged his features into a somber mask, and said, "But you didn't listen."

Ripley looked at Michelle. "Honey, you . . ." he said. But she wasn't listening. She turned her back, folded her arms, and walked toward the edge of the patio to stare at the sea.

"And that," Karp continued, "brings me to the third, and last, part of the problem. I'm afraid, David, that you and our gentlemen friends from the fourth estate represent somewhat of a nuisance. But fortunately, I know how to handle it. James, take care of them, would you, please? Down on the shore, so there's no more mess."

James leaned close to Ripley's ear, and whispered, "I told you you was one sorry assed white boy, didn't I?" He shoved Ripley toward the back of the patio and on down the steps leading to the sloping lawn and, beyond it, the sea. Fletcher and De Beauville stumbled in his wake, prodded by the muzzles of a pair of AK's.

Ripley kept looking back over his shoulder at Michelle, but she was looking past him, out over the Atlantic. He called once, "Michelle?"

The echo mocked him before it died away. By then, he was halfway to the shoreline. If she answered, the pounding surf drowned out her reply.

EPILOGUE

❖

November 1, 1975

The war, as wars will, ground on. The noose around Salazar slowly tightened as Joshua Bandolo and the well-armed soldiers of the Mawindi Liberation Front pushed inexorably closer. With the disappearance and widely rumored death of Oscar Nkele, the small pockets of resistance holding the Cardozo Railroad open slowly collapsed as, one by one, the resistance fighters of the African People's Party left for home. With no one to lead them, and no sense of what they were fighting for, it was only natural.

Jorge Caulfield, good soldier that he was, continued to toe the mark until, on September seventeenth, Bob Karp left for Kinshasa, Zaire with the last few bones of the skeletal embassy staff. As the two C130's lifted off from Runway 170, the message of that departure was not lost on Caulfield's men and, effectively, the Pan-African Movement ceased to be a viable force and, within days, altogether ceased to be. Its members squeezed out of Salazar like toothpaste from a tube as the MLF circle drew closer and closer, shrinking like a garotte and choking the life out of all opposition.

Late in the evening on September eighteenth, Joshua Bandolo led a triumphal procession into the heart of Salazar and the war was, for all intents and purposes, over, ending exactly as David Ripley feared it would.

On November first, in a ceremony on the ornate balcony of the Mawindi People's Parliament building, its two hundred year old stones trembling with every huzzah from the huge throng gathered in the newly renamed Nkele Square, Joshua Bandolo was sworn in as the first president of the People's Republic of Mawindi.

At the post inaugural press conference, the honor of asking the first question of the new poet-president fell to Michelle Harkness.

CHARLIE MCDADE is a full-time writer and freelance editor. He is the author of numerous westerns for HarperPaperbacks and several previous novels. He lives with his family in Monroe, New York.

HarperPaperbacks *By Mail*

EXPLOSIVE THRILLERS FROM THREE BESTSELLING AUTHORS

LEN DEIGHTON

Spy Sinker
British agent Bernard Samson, the hero of *Spy Hook* and *Spy Line*, returns for a final bow in this thrilling novel. Through terrible treachery, Samson is betrayed by the one person he least suspects—his lovely wife, Fiona.

Spy Story
Pat Armstrong is an expert at computer generated tactical war games. But when he returns to his old apartment to find that someone who looks just like him has taken over his identity, he is thrust into an international conspiracy that is all too real.

Catch a Falling Spy
On the parched sands of the Sahara desert, Andrei Bekuv, a leading Russian scientist, defects, setting off a shadow war between the KGB and the CIA. Yet, nothing is what it seems—least of all, Bekuv's defection.

BERNARD CORNWELL

Crackdown
Drug pirates stalk their victims in the treacherous waters of the Bahamas, then return to their fortress island of Murder Cay. Then comes skipper Nicholas Breakspear with the son and daughter of a U.S. Senator. What should have been a simple de-tox cruise soon lurches into a voyage of terror and death as Breakspear is lured into a horrifying plot of cocaine, cash, and killings.

Killer's Wake
Suspected of sailing off with a valuable family treasure, sea gypsy John Rossendale must return to England to face his accusing relatives. But in the fog-shrouded waters of the Channel Islands, Rossendale, alone and unarmed, is plunged into someone's violent game of cat-and-mouse where a lot more is at stake than family relations.

CAMPBELL ARMSTRONG

Agents of Darkness
Suspended from the LAPD, Charlie Galloway decides his life has no meaning. But when his Filipino housekeeper is murdered, Charlie finds a new purpose in tracking the killer. He never expects, though, to be drawn into a conspiracy that reaches from the Filipino jungles to the White House.

Mazurka
For Frank Pagan of Scotland Yard, it begins with the murder of a Russian at crowded Waverly Station, Edinburgh. From that moment on, Pagan's life becomes an ever-darkening nightmare as he finds himself trapped in a complex web of intrigue, treachery, and murder.

Mambo
Super-terrorist Gunther Ruhr has been captured. Scotland Yard's Frank Pagan must escort him to a maximum security prison, but with blinding swiftness and brutality, Ruhr escapes. Once again, Pagan must stalk Ruhr, this time into an earth-shattering secret conspiracy.

Brainfire
American John Rayner is a man on fire with grief and anger over the death of his powerful brother. Some say it was suicide, but Rayner suspects something more sinister. His suspicions prove correct as he becomes trapped in a Soviet-made maze of betrayal and terror.

Asterisk Destiny
Asterisk is America's most fragile and chilling secret. It waits somewhere in the Arizona desert to pave the way to world domination...or damnation. Two men, White House aide John Thorne and CIA agent Ted Hollander, race to crack the wall of silence surrounding Asterisk and tell the world of their terrifying discovery.

MAIL TO: **Harper Collins Publishers**
P. O. Box 588 Dunmore, PA 18512-0588
OR CALL: **(800) 331-3761 (Visa/MasterCard)**

Yes, please send me the books I have checked:

- ☐ SPY SINKER (0-06-109928-7) $5.95
- ☐ SPY STORY (0-06-100265-8) $4.99
- ☐ CATCH A FALLING SPY (0-06-100207-0) $4.95
- ☐ CRACKDOWN (0-06-109924-4) $5.95
- ☐ KILLER'S WAKE (0-06-100046-9) $4.95
- ☐ AGENTS OF DARKNESS (0-06-109944-9) $5.99
- ☐ MAZURKA (0-06-100010-8) $4.95
- ☐ MAMBO (0-06-109902-3) $5.95
- ☐ BRAINFIRE (0-06-100086-8) $4.95
- ☐ ASTERISK DESTINY (0-06-100160-0) $4.95

SUBTOTAL	$ _____
POSTAGE AND HANDLING	$ 2.00*
SALES TAX (Add applicable sales tax)	$ _____
TOTAL:	$ _____

*(ORDER 4 OR MORE TITLES AND POSTAGE & HANDLING IS FREE!
Orders of less than 4 books, please include $2.00 p/h. Remit in US funds, do not send cash.)

Name _____

Address _____

City _____

State _____ Zip _____

Allow up to 6 weeks delivery.
Prices subject to change.

(Valid only in US & Canada)

HO271